LIAR

C.L. Sutton

For my children

— my absolute everything.

Chapter I

The bushes sway in the garden, the rustling sound cutting through the silence of the empty house. My pulse skitters, imagination instantly conjuring shadowy figures lurking beyond the window.

I slam it shut and step back from the breath-steamed glass, wrapping my arms around my waist. I'm just being silly. It was just a fox. Or the wind. Nothing dangerous, nothing sinister. Right?

I hate being alone. *Hate it.* There's something fundamentally wrong about solitude – it's barbaric. What if something happens to me? Like a heart attack? What if an axe murderer decides tonight is the perfect night to break in? What if the electrics go wild, sparking a fire and trapping me in here to die a slow, painful death? If anything bad happened to me now, hours would pass before anyone would know.

I clutch my phone tighter. Just in case.

21:02.

Caleb's only been gone for just over an hour, and I miss him terribly. The house feels unbearably empty without him here. I miss the familiar soundtrack of his computer game – the gunfire and explosions. The splatter of blood. I miss the aroma of his cafetière brewing on the countertop. I even miss bringing him little snacks when he gets that adorable grumpy look.

21:03.

I flick the kettle on for my nightly hot chocolate, leaning against the counter as I watch the steam begin to rise.

It's good that Caleb has a tight-knit group of friends to go out with. He deserves it – he's a genuinely friendly and sweet guy. The thought of him warms my cheeks and I stand on my toes, my love sweeping me away. I'm the luckiest girl.

I picture him standing in the Stag and Pheasant, nursing his third pint of Guinness. A proper drink for a true man. He's probably talking football with the boys or debating which game console is superior, totally oblivious to the women who inevitably notice him, and that flirtatious older barmaid with her desperate cleavage.

When he drinks, his face flushes that adorable shade of pink. I just hope he remembers to pace himself like he promised. Drunk Caleb is entertaining – all sloppy affection, clumsy movements, and singing far too loudly.

It *is* funny. Sometimes.

The kettle whistles, building into a crescendo before climaxing with a pop. I pour the hot water over the chocolate powder, stirring until it forms dark brown sludge. It smells divine as I pour warm milk over the top to smooth it out.

My phone dings and I snatch it up eagerly, only to learn it's just a calendar notification about someone's birthday tomorrow.

Wait – Dierdre. That's Caleb's aunt. Surely he'd want to know? Actually, he *needs* to know. He might want to grab a card or something before the shops close.

I send him a message: *Hey gorgeous. Only me. I hope you're having an amazing time. Just to let you know, it's Dierdre's birthday tomorrow. Miss you... xxx*

Caleb:

I watch for a solid five minutes, waiting for the tell-tale dots that signal he's typing out a reply. Nothing. The blank screen mocks me. With a frustrated huff, I slam my phone down and take a sip of my hot chocolate.

I just want to be helpful. To make Caleb's life easier. That's what good girlfriends do.

Resisting the urge to look at the screen again, I scoop up my phone and head into the living room where I sink into the sofa.

Outside, life continues. Lights illuminate the neighbours' windows and they look like television screens against the darkness. I wonder what they're all doing. The Jennisons are probably having another argument – that seems to be their Friday night ritual. That old cow down the road is probably curtain twitching. Nosy bitch. The young couple across the street might be singing their new baby to sleep.

Something about that last image makes my chest tighten with yearning. One day that will be us – Caleb cradling our baby while I watch them both with overwhelming love.

I should close the curtains. I feel horribly exposed with the darkness pressing against the glass. Some pervert could be eyeing me up this very second.

As I raise my mug for another sip, my phone beeps. The noise makes me jump and I splash brown all down my crisp white nightdress.

Ignoring the stain, I grab for the message.

Alright. Thanks for letting me know. xxx

That's it? Nothing about his night, no questions about mine? Doesn't he want me to run out and get her something? Maybe he's just trying to be considerate, not wanting to burden me with errands.

Want me to run out and get her something? I can get chocolates from the supermarket? xxx

This time the dots are immediate, making me smile.

No. Mum will do it. I've never bothered. Speak later.

I stare at the screen, stunned. The dismissive tone, the missing kisses – both equally wounding. Since when has Caleb 'never bothered' with his aunt's birthday? And since when does he sign off without his usual three kisses?

A knot of hurt grows inside me as I carry my cup into the kitchen where I dump the remaining drink into the sink. My craving for sweetness has evaporated, replaced by the bitterness of my outrage.

Headlights flash across the kitchen wall as a car speeds past, momentarily blinding me. As the car disappears around the bend, a movement outside catches my eye. A figure is standing beneath the streetlamp, perfectly centred in the rectangle of my kitchen window.

I can make out the glint of eyes in the gloom. I think they're watching me, unblinking and intense. Panic sparks through me as I lunge for the blinds, yanking them down to shut out that predatory stare.

My breath comes in shallow bursts. An unsteady dizziness washes over me. God, I wish Caleb were here. We'd be curled up together rewatching *Breaking Bad*, blissfully ignorant of the weirdo lurking outside. Caleb makes me feel safe; protected. When he's not here, I'm stripped bare, my safety blanket gone.

I force several deep, calming breaths and return to the living room. I draw the curtains in here too, not daring to look outside in case I see those same eyes peering at me through the bushes in the front garden. Or pressed against the glass.

I shiver.

But there it is again, that rustling noise. Only louder this time. I step back from the now-covered window and bite my lip. Was that the sound of footsteps outside the front door? No, surely not. My mouth goes dry.

What do I do now? Where's the line between rea-sonable caution and paranoid overreaction? Calling the police feels a little drastic. *Sorry, officer, the bushes moved. Can you come and help me?*

I'm frozen in place, torn between wanting Caleb's protection and not wanting to be clingy and ruin his night out. I'm not *that* kind of girlfriend.

What I need is more information. I creep toward the front door, checking twice that the deadbolt is slid across before pressing my eye to the peephole.

I have to remind myself, I'm just being silly. I'm safe. I'm okay.

The doorstep remains empty. Beyond it sits my car in the driveway, Caleb's gleaming motorcycle nestled beside it like a faithful companion.

Even my car has better company than me tonight, I think, with a bitter twist of my lips.

I'm about to pull away when I notice movement again – the same figure from before, now moving towards the house with unsettling slowness along the pavement. The streetlights illuminate a bulky frame in a sweatshirt, hood pulled up so far I can't make out a face. But the size of him, the deliberate way he moves – powerful, bullish – sends my thoughts into turmoil.

He pauses, looking around furtively. Checking for witnesses, I realise with a sick jolt. Then he stops at the end of our garden path and shoves his hands deep into his pockets.

No more watching. This requires action.

I grab my phone, fingers trembling as I hit Caleb's number. It rings through to voicemail. So much for being my emergency contact. I hang up without leaving a message.

Pacing the living room, I stare at my phone, willing it to ring. Nothing.

I try again.

"Maisie." His voice sounds clipped, impatient. Maybe I've caught him at a bad time. Maybe he needs to go to the loo or something.

"Caleb. There's someone outside." My words come out in a panicked rush.

"What?" The background noise at the pub nearly drowns him out.

"Can you go somewhere quieter?"

"Hang on, I'll go somewhere more quiet. It's noisy in here." He sounds tipsy already.

I tap my foot anxiously, listening to the muffled sounds of him making his way through the crowd, the bar noise fading into the distant murmur of voices outside.

"Maisie. What is it?" His tone has that edge I've come to recognise – half concern, half annoyance at being interrupted.

"There's someone outside," I whisper, though there's no logical reason to lower my voice. "Standing there, watching the house. It's really creepy, Caleb."

A beat of silence. "Look, I …"

"He looks big, like he could snap me in half."

He sighs. "Just ignore him. It's probably just a delivery guy looking for the Jennisons' house again. They really need to get a new number for their door …"

"*Please*, Caleb." My voice catches.

He sighs, the sound crackling through the connection. "Lock the door. You'll be fine. Maybe put some *Desperate Housewives* on or something. You like that."

"No, I—"

"Look, I won't be late. You'll be okay." His voice grows fainter, like he's already pulling the phone away.

"Caleb, wait!" The line remains open, but he doesn't respond. I spin around, eyes darting to each window, suddenly certain I'm being watched from all sides. "They're at the door. I can hear them."

"So? See what they want?" He sounds downright pissed off now.

A woman's voice calls something in the background, her tone light and teasing. Something snaps inside me. I scream.

"Maisie, honey! What is it?" His voice is sharper now. I've got his attention.

"They're banging. Caleb, I think they might be about to knock the door down!" I let my tears flow freely, my breath hitching dramatically.

Caleb stutters. "Okay, okay. I'm getting a cab right now. Honey, I'm going to hang up so you can call the police. Okay? Call them right now!"

The line goes dead.

I lower my phone and wipe away the tears that have served their purpose. I'm not frightened; I'm excited, satisfied. I've always loved when Caleb rushes to my rescue, the way his eyes darken with concern, how his arms feel when he pulls me against his chest.

There's no point in overdoing the dramatics now. I have about twenty minutes until he arrives home. Plenty of time to perfect my performance.

With a small, secret smile playing at my lips, I head to the kitchen to prepare another hot chocolate. This time, I'll add marshmallows. A little celebration is in order.

Chapter 2

I watch as the clock ticks over to 9.00 am before taking the black coffee and toast upstairs. Morning sunlight filters through the hallway windows as I balance the tray carefully. The bedroom is still dark, so I place the tray down on the chest of drawers and throw the curtains open with a flourish.

Caleb groans and buries his face under his pillow, pulling himself into a tiny ball. "Maisie, what are you doing?" His voice is muffled against the pillow, thick with sleep.

"Bringing you breakfast in bed!" I reply cheerfully. "I thought you deserved it after saving me last night." The memory of his rushed entrance, breathless and worried, sends a flutter through me.

He huffs and flops around in bed before admitting defeat and sitting up to see what I've brought him. His face lights up when he sees the bonus doughnut I've slipped onto the side of the plate, sugar glistening. "Ah, Maisie, you're a legend."

And there it is, the gratitude I was waiting for. That little spark of appreciation. I chuckle and place the tray down on his lap, watching as he eagerly tucks in. "What time is it?"

"Nine. I thought we could do something nice today." I perch on the edge of the bed, close enough to feel his warmth.

"Yeah? Like what?"

"Oh, I don't know, you decide." I keep my tone casual, but I've already mentally planned three different options depending on his mood.

He nods, though doesn't look very committed. He tears off a chunk of doughnut with his teeth, his eyes drifting towards the motorcycle magazine on his nightstand – the one with the custom shop feature he's been obsessing over lately. Maybe he's not ready to make plans; the poor guy still looks half asleep.

I change the subject. "Thank you for coming home early last night. I don't know what I would've done without you." I soften my voice, a damsel in distress.

He gives me that sideways smile that made me fall in love with him in the first place – the one that makes his eyes crinkle at the corners. "Probably watched shit

TV and ate some ice cream? A whole lot of drama over nothing, as usual."

He's right of course. The man outside was long gone by the time Caleb arrived home. Not surprising really, considering he'd found the Jennisons' house and left a takeaway on their doorstep. The delivery logo on his jacket gave the game away.

"But it could've been bad. Caleb! He could have raped me and left me for dead." My voice rises slightly, indignation flaring at his dismissal.

Caleb laughs. It's a low, thoughtless sound that twists my stomach. Is this funny to him? No. He's just clueless. A clueless man. He doesn't understand what it's like to be a woman. How even the most banal-seeming things can actually be threats.

But when he leans forward for a kiss I completely forgive him, the familiar scent of sleep and coffee enveloping me. "Honey, you were fine. Just don't answer the door to strangers. Didn't your mum ever tell you that?"

I scoff. I don't think Mum ever taught me anything useful, her attention was always elsewhere. Still is. Always focused on my sisters, those perfect twins who can do no wrong.

"So, how was last night? Who went?" I watch him carefully, looking for any hint of a lie – the slight eye shift, the unnecessary detail, the tells I've learned to disguise in myself.

"Well, I wasn't there for long. George was there, poor guy was knackered, he'd just finished a thirteen-hour shift. Luke had only just arrived as I was leaving. The Craw cousins were there, but they were too busy chatting up some bird at the bar." He takes a sip of coffee. "Troy was there too – poor sod." He snaps his mouth shut like he's said too much.

I cock my head to the side. "What's wrong with Troy?"

He shoves more food in his mouth and chews theatrically, stalling. "Ah, just woman troubles. It's nothing really." His hand reaches for the motorcycle magazine, flipping it open to a page he's marked with a Post-it. His attempt at ending the conversation is comical and transparent.

"What happened with Evelyn? I thought they were all loved up?" I haven't met Troy and Evelyn many times, but I always thought they were so sweet together. High school sweethearts with matching tattoos and easy laughter. Troy clearly dotes on Evelyn and I always considered him a good role model for Caleb. So to hear they're struggling is truly upsetting.

He groans. "They *are* loved up. Just going through a hard patch." He looks away shiftily, like he's keeping something from me. I hate being kept in the dark. He knows he can trust me.

I pout and snuggle up next to him on the bed. "Tell me the truth, Caleb. You know I don't like it when you keep things from me."

He shoves the last bite of doughnut into his mouth and chews thoughtfully, mulling over his next words. I realise he's trying to decide whether to tell me or not and I give him a playful/not-so-playful tap on the arm.

"Come on, Caleb, don't be mean." I brush the sugar off his lips, my fingers lingering perhaps a moment too long.

He sighs. "Okay, but you can't tell anyone this." He pauses, his eyes serious. "Okay?"

"Okay!" I say, hands raised in a gesture of innocence. I motion zipping my lips closed.

"He's been cheating on her."

I jolt so violently that I knock the tray onto Caleb, pushing the coffee he was sipping into his face. Hot liquid splashes across his bare chest, and he yelps in pain. "Jesus Christ, Maisie! What was that for?"

But I've already left the room to retrieve a towel from the cupboard. I'm so stunned it takes me far too long to find what I am looking for, my mind racing with implications. When I return, Caleb is wiping the stain with my pillow, making everything a hundred times worse. "Here, let me," I tell him, nudging him out of the way.

Caleb stands up and watches me from the window, completely unconcerned about his nakedness. The whole world is able to see his bare arse through the second-storey window. "Caleb, you're naked!" I say, motioning between his manhood and the window. He doesn't move. He doesn't give the slightest damn.

I'm unsure whether to feel embarrassed or thrilled that everyone can see what a lucky girl I am.

"Who's he having an affair with?" I eventually ask, admitting defeat and tossing the soggy towel into the washing basket. I might just throw the browned bedsheets away and be done with it.

"Who?"

"Troy!"

"Oh, Maisie. Just leave it, will you? It's just some birds he hooks up with on nights out. There's nothing to tell." He shrugs as if infidelity is as casual as choosing what to have for lunch.

"As in, one-night stands?" I crinkle my nose in disgust.

"I guess so."

"And have *you* ever seen him chatting up other girls?" I watch his face carefully, looking for any flicker of guilt that might mirror his friend's behaviour.

He shrugs but keeps his mouth tightly shut. He looks out the window, feigning interest at a bird flying overhead. The evasion is answer enough.

"So why 'poor Troy'?"

Shrugging again, he says, "It's just been weighing on his mind, I suppose. The guilt. He needed someone to talk to." He scratches his balls – not the most sophisticated look – and avoids my eyes.

"Well, he *should* be feeling guilty. What did he expect? You can't act like that and not feel anything. That's psycho behaviour."

Caleb scowls, but when his eyes meet mine, his expression softens. "Honey, why so worried? You know you don't have to worry about that, don't you? I'd never do that to you."

His words make me feel a little better, but the vicarious betrayal still hurts. I have always thought Caleb was loyal. But then, Troy gave that impression, too. Maybe my judgement of character isn't as good as I thought.

Truth be told, I'm frightened. I remember hearing the woman's voice in the background while I was speaking to Caleb last night. Who was that? Was she talking to him?

And I remember the rumours of him at his Christmas party last year, him and the receptionist with the sleek bob and perfect makeup. He denied it, of course, and she was soon fired, thus removing the threat. But still, it injected me with an awful sense of jealousy that I haven't yet managed to shake off.

Without waiting for a response, Caleb makes his way to the ensuite where he turns on the shower. I follow him, unwilling to let the conversation drop. "So what did you say to him?"

Caleb inspects his teeth in the mirror. "Nothing. I just listened, you know? He'll figure it out."

"Caleb!"

"What?!"

"You need to tell him it's wrong. It's gross! Honestly, what's wrong with you men?"

But he ignores me and just steps into the shower, the door slamming shut behind him. The glass immediately begins to fog, obscuring my view of him.

Is this really what Caleb thinks of affairs? Does he really think it's no big deal? Does he really think so little of love?

I yank the door open and a soaped-up Caleb turns to me with a scowl. "What, Maisie? Can't a guy shower in peace?"

"Not until we've sorted this out, no."

"What's to sort? This has nothing to do with us."

"I think we should tell her."

"Who?"

"Evelyn!"

"You've got to be fucking kidding me. No! Troy is my mate. There's no way in hell I'll betray his trust."

"Anonymously, then."

"Maisie, listen to me – you've got to keep out of this. They'll sort it. Keep your nose out of it."

Maybe he's right. Maybe I should just turn my back and let them live their lives. I don't even know them all that well. Troy is Caleb's friend, not mine, and I barely know Evelyn. Poor woman. She'll be so heartbroken.

"Maisie, please. Don't say anything. For me?"

He looks so damn cute with his soap beard and flattened hair. Maybe Caleb needs to be taught a lesson about staying faithful. I allow my eyes to trace down his

body, my eyes drawn to that spot that gives me butterflies.

He's hard.

Yes, he needs to know exactly what he'd be giving up
should he ever cheat on me.

I strip off slowly, step into the shower, then get on my
knees.

Chapter 3

Imarah always looks so well put-together. She breezes into the coffee shop, glistening chocolate-brown hair down to her waist, not a strand out of place. Her cashmere top is bobble-free and the perfect jade green to complement her dark skin. Her jeans hug curves that speak of dedicated gym sessions, showing off thick, toned thighs. And she bounces in wearing casual Converse pumps that somehow make her look tall and elegant – the same shoes that would make me look short and dumpy.

She flashes me a smile that lights up her entire face, drawing admiring glances from nearby tables. She has that kind of natural radiance people are drawn to. I know if she wasn't so shy and unsure of herself, she'd have a thousand more friends she'd prefer to see over me.

"Maisie. Hi!" she says brightly, her voice carrying that hint of warmth she reserves for me. I greet her with a tight hug. "How are you doing?"

Imarah and I met over twenty years ago. We both had the hard task of starting school part way through the year, me three weeks before Imarah. I spent those excruciatingly long weeks feeling utterly alone and miserable, laughed at by my peers for not having the friendships they refused to grant me. Friendship groups were already tight and there was no room left for me. I'd walk home from school crying into the sleeve of my blazer, tears I was careful to wipe away before reaching my doorstep. I stopped eating and hid in my bedroom, certain no one in my family even noticed. My sisters were too busy with their own dramas, and Mum was always stretched too thin to notice one child's misery.

Then, Imarah came along and everything changed. I walked into the form room one day with my head hanging low, in my usual state of anxiety, and Imarah was sitting at her desk writing in a journal, her tongue poking out of the corner of her mouth.

I'd never seen her before and assumed she'd just been on holiday. I watched her all morning, waiting for her friends to join her. But they didn't. She was as alone as I was.

Finally, during afternoon registration, Mr. Smith, the charismatic science teacher, finally thought of introducing Imarah to the class and all eyes turned towards her. Imarah's cheeks burned red and her eyes grew wet. I saw so much of myself in her, and I wanted to reach out to her and take her hand.

I didn't though. I didn't have the courage.

Then, to my surprise, as I was walking home a few days later, someone called out to me. "Maisie, isn't it?"

I spun around to find Imarah rushing to catch up with me, her school bag weighing her down. Back then she was spotty and awkward. A far cry from the beauty she is today, and an image of herself she's never managed to shrug off.

I didn't know what to say, I just stared at her. Surely she'd got me confused with someone else?

Finally catching up, she looked me dead in the eye and said, "Mind if I walk with you? I could use a friend. Those bitches at school are so cliquey."

And that was that. We've been stuck together like glue ever since.

We'd built our friendship on shared vulnerability – both outsiders, both desperate for connection. Maybe that's why we overlooked things that others might have questioned in each other. Why Imarah forgives my occasional lies, my tendency to embellish stories. Why I pretended not to notice when she faded away during our university years, too busy with new friends until she needed me again. Our friendship has always been a strange dance of dependence and distance. But it had survived twenty years. That had to count for something.

"I'm okay," I tell her now, pulling out of the hug.

"I smell bullshit," she says a little too loudly. The people sitting at nearby tables turn to look at us. I notice they give *me* a dirty look, like I was the one to cuss and not the pretty girl who actually committed the crime. "What's up?"

A teenage boy brings over our drinks, a welcome distraction. I wasn't going to tell Imarah about Troy and Evelyn – I promised Caleb on our lives that I'd keep quiet. But then, Imarah doesn't even know them. Who's she going to tell?

Imarah is fantastic at giving advice; she's compassionate, caring, and yet always objective. No, I can trust her with this. Besides, I need to talk to someone who might understand the twist of anxiety in my gut every time I think about anyone cheating.

"You know Caleb's best friend, Troy?"

"That guy who looks like an ape?"

I laugh. Trust Imarah to lighten the mood. "That's the one. Well, it turns out he's been cheating on his girlfriend."

Imarah, to her credit, tries to look shocked, but it immediately dies a quick death. "And?" she breathes. "Why do we care?"

"Imarah, he's been with his girlfriend for like, forever. Don't you think that's a pretty big deal?"

"Well, if I knew them, then yeah. But Maisie, I've met them maybe twice and I didn't even engage in conversation. I thought they looked pretty stuck-up, actually."

Shaking my head, I tut. "Does it matter? He's cheating on her, that's pretty fucked up."

"I just don't see the big deal," Imarah says, blowing on her latte. She scrutinises me over the rim of her mug, seeing right through me in that way she's always been able to.

"You wouldn't care if your boyfriend cheated?" I press.

Imarah lifts a shoulder. "Wouldn't happen. You know I can't hold down a relationship longer than it takes to suck a mint."

"But if it did?"

"Then I'd be done. Instantly." Her voice is sharp.

I frown. "That easy?"

She sets her cup down a little too hard. "I can't stand liars, Maisie. You know that." She leans back in her chair and eyes me carefully. "Maisie, what's this really about? Is this about Troy and Evelyn? Or you and Caleb?"

My chest tightens. I hate that she's right. This isn't about Troy. It's about the sick feeling that won't go away, the one I've been shoving down since last Christmas when the rumours first started.

I can still see the receptionist's smug little smile, the way she tilted her head as if she pitied me. *Nothing happened, sweetie. I swear.* I'd wanted to believe her, but the way Caleb avoided my eyes afterward? That's what's haunted me.

So now Imarah's words are like a punch to the stomach. I sigh and drop my shoulders. "It's just given me a shock, that's all. I thought Troy and Evelyn were tight, you know?"

She reaches over and grips my hand in her manicured fingers. "That's understandable. Last Christmas was tough on you."

I wince. I *hate* talking about last Christmas. It was so humiliating. I thrust my fingernails into my mouth and start chewing.

It wasn't always this hard between Caleb and me. On our third date, I'd gotten food poisoning, and instead of bailing, he'd come over with ginger ale and crackers. "I like taking care of people," he'd shrugged when I thanked him, embarrassed. "And you're different – you say what you're actually thinking." The irony isn't lost on me now.

Imarah thoughtfully stirs her drink before continuing, "Maisie, Caleb worships the ground you walk on. You've been together forever."

I search her face, waiting for her to meet my eyes, but she doesn't. "You really think so?" My voice is too small.

"Of course." A little too quick.

Forever? Five years is hardly forever, but given the speed of its development, it could be. Six months after meeting, I moved into Caleb's cute two-bedroom house, where I have eagerly awaited a proposal ever since.

"Besides," Imarah says, releasing my hand. "I thought that receptionist woman was fired? She clearly had a screw loose."

Yes and no. She did indeed get fired, but her head was tightly screwed on. She may have been accused of losing her mind with her customers but, truth is, that was my doing. I wrapped it up in a neat little bow and got her swiftly removed from our lives. It's amazing how far a few complaints can go.

But I never discovered the truth about the kiss. I daren't keep pressing Caleb, in case he confirms it was true. It's far easier to live amongst your lies than to admit your life is falling apart.

"The way I see it, Maisie, if that guy is cheating, he'll get caught out. There's only so long you can live a second life before the truth comes tumbling out. Then the shit really hits the fan. And, trust me, you don't want to be standing in the middle of it all."

I shift uncomfortably. Maybe Imarah is right. Maybe I should just keep my nose out and let everything play out by itself. But I'm just not that kind of woman. What happened to *girl power*? If we don't have that, we don't have anything.

I need time to mull this over.

"How's work?" I ask Imarah. She's just been given a massive promotion, and I can see she's practically vibrating with excitement to talk about it.

She immediately jumps into tales of her new responsibilities as Lead Costume Designer at the local theatre. She gives me all the gossip on who's a bitch and who's put on so much weight that she's had to order more material. She tells me about the hot guy she *still* hasn't said hello to, despite working in the same building for over a year.

I'm enthralled. Imarah's job sure beats mine as an admin assistant at a stationery manufacturer. There's not much to say about handling orders for white six-by-nine windowed envelopes, so I really enjoy Imarah's recounts.

Every time I meet with Imarah, I'm reminded of how lucky I am. In a world that doesn't realise I even exist, it's so nice to feel seen. It was Imarah who brought me out of my shell; she'd even backhandedly introduced me to Caleb in the bar that night.

"Hey, Maisie. He is totally your type," she'd said, poking me in the ribs.

I'd seen Caleb standing at the bar, alone, waiting patiently for the bartender to notice him. "Me? God, no. Someone like that would never be interested in someone like me?"

"You're kidding me, right? You look incredible tonight. Your arse is banging in those jeans."

I remember I'd blushed, loving the compliment.

Then she'd jabbed me again. "Go on. I *dare* you."

I'd downed my drink, and the rest is history.

Now, I cling to everything I've got with all my might. When you've got so little, it's so easy to lose everything. That's not something I can risk.

Chapter 4

I can hear the babble of chatter from down the street – the squeals of excitement and gasps of joy. I pause on the rain-soaked path, considering retreat, but duty propels me forward.

Of course, I've had to park my car on the next street over. The spare spaces in Mum's drive are always reserved for my sisters: Rainy, because she's pregnant (again); and one for Faith, because being born six minutes earlier than her twin somehow grants her permanent parking privileges.

By the time I reach the door, I'm drenched. The rain has worked its way through my jacket, my blouse sticks uncomfortably to my skin, and my styled hair now hangs in rat-tails around my face, dripping icy rivulets down my neck.

I take a deep breath before entering. These Sunday 'family gatherings' are exercises in emotional endurance. My sisters perform their choreographed dance of one-upmanship while I fade into the wallpaper, only noticed when someone needs tea made.

"Maisie! You're dripping all over my carpet!" Mum's voice cuts through the hallway as she emerges from the kitchen balancing a tray. Gingernuts fan out across the plate like a wheel of disappointment. I hate gingernuts.

I shrug and give her a look that says, *What exactly am I supposed to do about the rain?* But she's already tutting her way back to the living room, where my sisters await.

For a second, I consider slipping back out the door. Would anyone even notice? Perhaps Mum might glance at my empty corner an hour from now, furrow her brow momentarily, then immediately return to marveling at the miracle of Rainy's sixth pregnancy.

"Nice to see you, too," I mumble under my breath. My gaze falls on Rainy's new beige coat – expensive-looking and perfectly dry – hanging on the rack. I use it to blot my dripping face. Foundation smears across the pristine fabric, and I feel a flicker of satisfaction as I push it deeper into the rack, hiding the evidence.

When I enter the living room, no one bothers to look up. Faith's hand makes a half-hearted movement in my direction, before Rainy makes a theatrical groan, clutching her stomach. Faith instantly pivots toward her, rapt with attention as though witnessing a miracle and not the same performance Rainy's given five times before.

I sink into the lumpy armchair in the corner, my damp clothes making an embarrassing squelching sound. I sit there, invisible.

Eventually the baby drama subsides. Mum, noticing me with what seems like genuine surprise, gestures to the teapot. "Tea?"

"I'd love one. I'm freezing."

"Well, the pot's empty. Would you mind putting the kettle on, love?"

Before I can even rise, Rainy chimes in, "And grab more gingernuts while you're at it! The baby's mad for them."

And there it is. My entire role in the family dynamic distilled into a single exchange: tea-maker, biscuit-fetcher, forever on the periphery.

It's been this way for as long as I can remember. Five years younger than the twins, I was an oblivious toddler when their world was completely shattering. While they processed Dad's abandonment with tear-stained faces and broken hearts, I was barely forming memories.

It has always been clear that Mum loves them more than me. My sisters doted on our father, though I was too young to know any different, and Mum has spent every day since trying to make it up to them. While I faded into the background.

I head to the kitchen but don't step towards the kettle. They can wait for their precious tea and biscuits. Instead, I settle at the breakfast bar, examining the gallery of family achievements that plasters the corkboard.

There's Rainy, resplendent in graduation robes, brandishing her shitty second-class Honours degree in History of Art like it's a Nobel Prize. And Faith with that damned dalmatian puppy she neglected for months before dramatically 'rescuing' it by giving it away to the neighbours. My eyes are drawn to the photo of Rainy and Steven – the bricklayer with apparently superhuman fertility – surrounded by their ever-expanding brood. Baby number six is due any week now, and judging by Steven's perpetually smug expression, number seven is probably already on the production line. Then there's Faith again on some Greek beach, fluorescent cocktail in one hand, tanned muscled arm of her latest holiday romance in the other, looking like she's won at life.

And where am I in this carefully curated family display? There – almost hidden – tucked behind an old receipt, for jeans that Mum has probably grown out of by now. It's a photo of Caleb and me, his arm draped protectively over my shoulders. He towers over me, all perfect teeth and chiseled jawline, while I gaze up at him adoringly. We look happy. We look in love.

We still are. At least that's something to hold on to when everything else feels like quicksand.

"You look beautiful there," Mum's voice startles me as she appears behind me. "Absolutely radiant."

The compliment catches me off guard – a rare gem I want to pocket before she can take it back. But almost immediately, her expression shifts, and the moment is gone. "What happened to that tea? I thought you were putting the kettle on?"

And the bubble bursts.

I watch Mum as she moves about the kitchen with the casual routine that can only come from living in the same house for the last four decades. She arranges more of those wretched ginger biscuits on the plate, fills the kettle, and waits. Having momentarily run out of tasks, she turns to me with manufactured interest. "How are things with you, then? Caleb alright?"

"Oh, he's fine," I reply, suddenly fascinated by the arrangement of apples and bananas in the fruit bowl. I know she's only asking because she's temporarily out of twin-related topics. Her interest is performative, a box to be ticked before returning to what really matters: Faith and Rainy.

According to my sisters – and this is recited religiously every Christmas after a few glasses of wine – everything was perfect before I arrived. They'd tell me how Dad took them to the shabby theme park two towns over. He read them stories every night until their sides ached from giggling. The house rang with laughter and love.

And then I was born.

My unplanned arrival supposedly plunged Dad into depression. The difficult pregnancy, the financial strain, the crying in the night – it was all too much. He walked out when I was twenty-one months old, and apparently, it was all my fault.

To my surprise, Mum slides onto the stool opposite me. "Everything okay at work?" Her tone is gentler than usual, almost concerned. She almost looks like she cares.

I scramble to recall our last conversation. "You mean with Kylie? Oh, it's … manageable."

"You sure? Your face suggests otherwise."

I meet her eyes and feel a strange pull at having her undivided attention. It's intoxicating. "It's getting worse, actually. She's just so ... *nasty*, Mum. I can't even eat lunch in the lunchroom anymore because she starts with the comments. I have to sit in my car with my tuna sandwich."

The lie materialises before I even realise I'm crafting it. There is no Kylie – never has been – but the story's been building over weeks, and now I'm trapped in its expanding architecture.

Mum's face twists with horror. I should backpedal, laugh it off as exaggeration. But, when she leans forward, eyes wide with genuine interest, something inside me responds hungrily. I nod, adding weight to the fabrication. I should feel shame. Instead, I feel seen.

"Have you spoken to your manager? Surely that's workplace bullying?"

I shake my head. "They adore her. If I complained, they'd probably find a reason to let me go."

"Would that be so terrible? You could find another admin position. It's not exactly highly skilled work."

The comment stings. "I'm not letting that cow drive me out," I say, biting my lip. "I love my job, Mum. Even if it *is* unskilled work."

"Oh, darling, I didn't mean any offence—"

"Yeah, sure."

She turns away, pouring hot water into the teapot and already humming to herself, my fictional crisis already fading from her thoughts.

"She did something really awful last week," I blurt, desperate to recapture her attention.

"Who did?"

"Kylie! God, Mum, try to keep up."

With a sigh that's equal parts exasperation and resignation, she turns back. "What did she do?" I can't tell if she's asking out of concern or gossipy curiosity.

My eyes dart around for inspiration and land on her prescription bottle. "She spiked my drink."

Her hand flies to her chest. "She did WHAT?"

"Laxatives," I explain, warming to my theme. "I had to leave work early. Spent the whole afternoon on the toilet." The part about leaving early isn't entirely false – I did take a half-day last Tuesday, though it was for a hair appointment, not intestinal distress.

"What a b-i-t-c-h," Mum whispers, spelling out the word like we're in Sunday school. "Does Caleb know about this?"

"No, and you can't tell him," I insist. "You know how protective he gets. He'd storm into the office and do something silly. Make everything a thousand times worse."

"Maisie, this is serious. No job is worth this kind of treatment, especially one that barely pays over minimum wage."

"I got a raise," I counter. Technically true, though only because payroll messed up my hours (and I'll have to repay it next month). Still, it shuts her down. She's got an obsession with how little I earn.

"Mum! Where's that tea?" Faith's voice cuts through from the living room. Like a switch has been flipped, Mum jumps to attention, my plight instantly forgotten as she hurries to attend to her favoured offspring.

I remain at the breakfast bar, the sounds of my sisters' laughter a distant backdrop to my thoughts. Rainy's due date looms, which means Mum will soon be even more distracted, lost in the excitement of a new grandchild.

The Kylie story served its purpose today, but it's losing its impact. I've squeezed all the attention I can from that particular fiction. I'll need to escalate.

The lengths I must go to for a scrap of recognition from my own family are absurd. But necessary.

After all, if you're invisible, what choice do you have but to paint yourself in colours they can't ignore?

CHAPTER 5

I sit in Mum's living room in a foul mood. They're all chattering away about nothing that matters while I'm perfectly content to ignore them, picking at my cuticles until a tiny bead of blood appears. The mindless drone of their voices becomes white noise as I retreat into my own thoughts.

Then, like a spotlight suddenly swinging my way, Faith sets her sights on me. All eyes turn in my direction, and I feel stripped bare beneath their collective gaze.

"So, what have you been up to lately?" Faith asks, pointing her finger at me like some self-appointed interrogator.

I merely shrug, keeping my response deliberately flat. "Not much."

"Caleb proposed yet?"

My entire body goes rigid. Why must she do this every single time? She doesn't even have a boyfriend, just a rotating carousel of men she strings along for her own sense of validation. What gives her the right to highlight that Caleb and I have stalled since moving in together?

It's jealousy, plain and simple. Faith might pretend to love her jet-setting lifestyle as an air hostess, flitting from one meaningless encounter to the next. But that existence must be hollow at its core. Empty. Pathetic, really.

I must have let my contempt show because all three of them burst into laughter, their amusement at my expense cutting through me like glass.

"Oh darling, don't worry, it'll happen when it's meant to. Divine timing and all that," Mum says with practiced sympathy. She reaches to pat my hand in what she thinks is consolation, but I pull back just in time, leaving her fingers hovering awkwardly over the arm of the chair.

Mum's face falls into that sad little smile I've come to hate. Her hand lingers in the air for a few seconds before retreating in defeat. Faith's gaze darts immediately to my bare ring finger, her smirk curving upward with quiet triumph. Heat floods my cheeks.

"Actually, if you must know, I found a ring." I say it so softly that even I strain to hear the words leave my lips.

"An engagement ring. In Caleb's coat pocket." I don't know why I say that – it's not true – but excitement flutters in my belly all the same.

Mum squeals, her unbridled enthusiasm a balm to my desperate need for attention. My sisters visibly deflate in their seats. Rainy bites the inside of her cheek, working to mask her surprise. Faith crosses her arms, her skepticism obvious.

They bombard me with questions about the diamond, where I found it, what I plan to do now that I know. I answer as truthfully as I can, given that the entire scenario exists only in my head. By the time I leave, I'm practically floating on the giddy anticipation of the proposal I'm convinced I'll receive one day.

It feels intoxicating to be the centre of attention for once, even with my sisters' lingering doubt hanging in the air. I cling to that feeling as I leave Mum's and head to the supermarket to navigate the fluorescent-lit aisles.

I'll prepare something special for Caleb tonight. Perhaps I can coax that proposal out of him if I create the perfect moment.

But the farther I drive from Mum's house, the heavier the weight of dread in my stomach. What if my family accidentally – or purposely – let slip to Caleb about me finding a ring?

I'll simply play dumb. *I don't know what they're talking about. Must be their wishful thinking.*

Then again, maybe it would work in my favour. Plant the seed in his mind. Unless he's already purchased a ring, in which case none of this matters anyway. I wrap myself in that comforting thought, letting it spark hope that warms me from within.

In the supermarket, I round the corner into the bakery section, intent on scoring the freshest tiger loaf on the shelf, when I spot that unmistakable platinum blonde hair. She's bent over the breadsticks, her yoga-sculpted body folding in half with effortless grace.

Evelyn. Troy's girlfriend.

I watch as she selects her baked goods, then follow at a careful distance as she glides into the dairy aisle, where she parks her trolley to browse the refrigerated shelves.

She's undeniably beautiful. Somewhat artificial with those plumped lips and eyelashes so long their fluttering could create a breeze, but you can't deny her appeal. She belongs on billboards, not wasting away in whatever mundane career she's chosen.

Troy is a complete idiot to cheat on her. How could he possibly think he'd find better than this grade-A woman who absolutely dotes on him? Though he likely wasn't thinking with his brain at the time. Not the one on his shoulders, anyway.

She places an expensive-looking goat cheese and a pot of natural yoghurt into her trolley before moving on. My feet follow of their own accord, my dinner plans for Caleb temporarily forgotten.

She deserves to know about Troy. Look at her, floating through life with that content little smile playing on her lips. If she's anything like me, she's probably thinking about him right now. About how fortunate she is to have found such a wonderful man.

When the reality is he's a lying, cheating arsehole.

"Don't I know you?" Her voice snaps me from my daze. Those full lips pull into a dazzling smile. I wish I could do makeup like that – it looks professionally applied. "Maisie, isn't it?"

Shit. Focus.

"That's right!" I respond with false brightness. "You're Evelyn. Troy's girlfriend?"

I swear she simpers at the mention of his name. My heart fractures a little for her. "That's right. How lovely to see you again."

I blink at her, momentarily thrown. Is it lovely? She's so nice. Friendly. I hate that I'm about to detonate her world. But then, Troy is the one trampling all over it without a second thought. So, fuck that.

"It's so strange, Caleb was just talking about you the other night," I say, testing the waters, watching her reaction.

"Yeah? All good news, I hope." She grins as if she's made some clever joke.

My face contorts involuntarily.

"What is it?" she asks, her voice wavering slightly. She tilts her head like a concerned puppy. "You look like you've got something to say." She shuffles aside as an elderly woman determinedly shoves her trolley through the narrow space between us.

I press my lips together, caught in indecision. Do I honour Evelyn's right to the truth? Or keep the promise I made to the man I love?

Evelyn stares at me, her eyes widening with growing alarm.

"Oh, it's not bad," I laugh awkwardly. "Don't look so worried."

She exhales visibly. "Oh, thank God for that. For a second there I thought you were going to say something terrible, you looked so serious! You really need to have a word with your face." She laughs.

"My face is fine, thank you," I snap. I hadn't intended to sound so harsh, but the way her laughter abruptly cuts off suggests I've overshot the mark.

"Well, it was nice to see you again. Give my love to Caleb." She turns towards the checkouts and pushes her trolley away with renewed urgency.

Even from behind, she's the perfect blend of femininity and strength. She radiates good energy. I'm filled with jealousy, but I force it aside. I'm better than that.

"Evelyn!" I call out, before sensible thoughts can intervene. She continues walking. "Evelyn!" This time she halts, her shoulders visibly slumping before she turns to face me.

"What is it, Maisie? I really need to get going."

I hesitate. I don't know what I'm doing. I just know I can't let her walk away, back to that piece of shit, without knowing the truth. That would be cruel. But I pause too long, and with a huff of impatience she turns away and continues to the checkouts.

If I'm being honest with myself, there's a part of me that would love to knock her off that pedestal. Drag her down to the real world. The one that isn't all beauty and grace.

"Troy has been sleeping around," I announce, loud enough to ensure she hears me. She freezes mid-step, her spine going ramrod straight.

I'm about to repeat myself, thinking she may not have understood, when she whirls around. "What did you just say?" Her eyes are wide, her mouth opening and closing in shock.

"Troy has been sleeping with other women," I repeat more deliberately. Is it really that difficult to comprehend? "Caleb told me."

She gives a nervous laugh. "No, no. Troy wouldn't do that. He wouldn't dare."

I offer a noncommittal shrug. "Caleb wouldn't lie to me. Our relationship is built on trust." Did that sound boastful? Given the circumstances, I wish I hadn't said that, even if it's true. "I'm sorry, Evelyn. But it's the truth. Nothing serious. Just one-night stands."

She looks like she might vomit, and I take a precautionary step backwards to avoid potential splatter.

"No," she whispers to herself, her face crimson. Then she raises her voice and looks directly at me. "No, you're lying!" And with that, she spins on her heel and storms away.

I watch her retreating figure. As difficult as that was, I know deep down I did the right thing. The poor girl deserves to build her life on truth. Lies are no foundation for a solid relationship.

Chapter 6

"You did WHAT?!"

"Caleb, there's no need to raise your voice. Please, calm down."

He looks like he's aged ten years in an afternoon – exhausted and frayed at the edges. He must have had an especially gruelling day at the garage. I hurry over, encouraging him to sit at the kitchen table while I prepare coffee.

To my horror, he actually shoves me aside and dodges my attempted kiss.

I've been home all of three minutes, and already Troy has called Caleb to tattle on me. Apparently, Evelyn went straight home and confronted him, and instead of dealing with his own relationship mess, Troy decided to drag mine into it.

It's hardly my fault he cheated on her. How am I suddenly the villain in this scenario?

"I told you to keep out of it!" Caleb shouts, his voice bouncing off the walls. "You promised!"

I flinch at his tone. "She had a right to know the truth, Caleb! Surely you understand that relationships can't be built on cheating and lies?"

If he can't grasp that basic concept, we're in deeper trouble than I thought. Does he genuinely believe it's acceptable for Troy to sleep around with impunity?

"But not from some random woman in the supermarket!" He drags his hands through his hair, smearing what looks like engine grease down his cheek. I resist the urge to wipe it off – something tells me he wouldn't welcome the gesture right now.

"I'm hardly some random woman," I counter. "Evelyn and I have met before."

"Maisie, you've barely said two words to her. You said she looks like a stuck-up cow."

"I did not!"

He makes a sound of pure frustration, slamming his palms against the back of his head before stalking into the living room.

I follow at his heels, wincing when he drops onto our sofa in his filthy work clothes. "Caleb, it doesn't matter who delivers the message. Any woman deserves to know when she's being cheated on. It's girl code. Keeping that kind of information from her is barbaric."

"No, what's barbaric is shattering a woman's life in the middle of her weekly shop!"

He has me there. Perhaps my approach lacked tact. But I could hardly control the location, could I? I could have been more subtle, I'll admit. But once I started speaking, the words flowed like water through a broken dam. I didn't even register the audience of curious shoppers until I resumed my shopping.

"I told you to leave it alone," Caleb says, his voice now weary rather than angry. "You should have just let it go. Let Troy handle it in his own way."

"And you should grow a backbone and do what's right."

He drops his head into his hands. "Oh, Maisie," he whispers. He stands, shoulders slumped in defeat. "I just feel so ... betrayed. I thought I could trust you."

"You can trust me, Caleb! Doesn't this prove how important honesty is to me?"

"Oh, bollocks. This isn't about the truth. It's about you dishing out juicy gossip."

"How dare you! You know me better than that. I'm no gossip."

He shakes his head. "There's no talking to you sometimes. This is pointless."

I open my mouth to respond, but he silences me with a raised hand. I press my lips together, fighting the sting of tears behind my eyes.

I wait for him to speak, but he just sighs deeply and walks away. I brace for the familiar creak of the stairs, but it doesn't come. Instead, the front door slams and moments later the growl of his motorcycle engine vibrates through the house.

And then he's gone.

I'm shell-shocked. Caleb and I never fight like this. And he's never walked out on me before. I remain frozen in place, wringing my hands, unsure what to do with myself or this unfamiliar tension.

Does Caleb honestly believe this is my fault? Why is he so defensive, anyway?

The truth is, I couldn't care less about Troy and Evelyn. Troy created this mess, and now he has to face the consequences. And Evelyn, while caught in an awful situation, can at least move forward now. Find someone deserving of her.

What truly disturbs me is Caleb's apparent belief that keeping infidelity secret is acceptable. He's making such an outsized deal of this, it's almost as if he's projecting his own guilt.

Nausea wells up in me as my thoughts race at dizzying speed. I need to know where Caleb is. What he's doing. Who he's with.

The uncertainty is unbearable. Is this the end for us? Have I finally pushed him away for good?

My thoughts spiral out of control, my breathing becoming shallow and painful. I can't stay here, suffocating on my doubts about our relationship.

I grab my car keys.

***

Initially, the drive calms me. I navigate aimlessly, turning down unfamiliar roads, seeking the peculiar safety that anonymity provides.

The argument with Caleb replays on an endless loop in my mind: what was said, what I should have said, his reactions, my feelings. Everything blurs together until I finally take notice of my surroundings.

I've somehow ended up on a narrow dirt track, likely formed by farm machinery rather than regular traffic. The daylight is fading, and when I glance in my rearview mirror, it seems as if the woods have sealed shut the path behind me. I manage to turn my car around in a small clearing, but now nothing looks familiar. The track I followed has vanished.

With fumbling hands, I retrieve my phone from the passenger seat and call Caleb. No answer. I throw my phone down in frustration and grip the steering wheel so hard that my knuckles turn white. He's deliberately ignoring me. He doesn't care that I'm lost, that I need him. No one ever truly cares.

My self-pity erupts into theatrical sobs. I'm at a complete loss. I don't know how to fix this.

Maybe if I disappeared – if something terrible happened – then he'd realise what he has. Then he'd drop everything for me. He'd love me like he used to.

His extreme reaction to me telling Evelyn the truth is deeply unsettling. It screams of guilt. He's pulling away from me; I can feel the distance growing between us. And I can't lose him. I just can't. Without Caleb, I'm nothing.

My mind sifts through treasured memories of him: how he nursed me when I broke my wrist, how he brought flowers when my hamster died.

He's so thoughtful. So sweet.

So *mine*.

A thought slips into my mind like an unwelcome guest. He'll come if I need rescuing. He always has.

I try calling again, but when he still doesn't answer, something hardens inside me. My voice quavers, but now it's deliberate, a breathless sob, a catch in my throat. His voicemail invites me to leave a message, and the words pour out before I can stop them, feeling so real that I begin to believe them myself.

"Caleb, please help me!" I cry. "Something bad just happened. Caleb, please." I pause, summoning an additional layer of despair. I draw my sobs from deep within my core, pouring raw anguish down the phone.

"There was a man!" I wail. "Caleb, he did things to me … And I don't know where I am."

One final pause.

"Caleb, I was raped!"

Chapter 7

I sit motionless in the car, waiting for Caleb to return my call. I'm shocked at the extreme measures I have taken. The magnitude of my lie. But I had no choice. I need Caleb to see reason before he throws away what we have – before he abandons the love of his life.

My stomach knots itself into a painful tangle. If I commit to this path, there's no turning back. This isn't just one of my little white lies; this is a monster of a deception. I know I've bent the truth on occasion, but this crosses into territory I've never dared enter before.

The waiting gives me time to reconsider. Rape was too extreme. It could make Caleb reluctant to touch me again, creating more problems.

No, I'll tell him I panicked and exaggerated.

If I say I was assaulted, it could still solidify our bond. When viewed that way, isn't the lie worth it? The deception will last a few days, perhaps a week at most, before we move forward. The lie can draw us closer so we can live our truth. A small price to pay for a future brimming with love and happiness.

As shocked as I am by my declaration, I'm also thrilled by my own ingenuity. This plan is brilliant! I wish I'd thought of it earlier, before Caleb started going on nights out. Before he lost interest in talking to me after exhausting days at the garage.

It could have cemented our relationship ages ago.

Caleb calls back minutes later. I give a tiny clap of glee that he's no longer ignoring my calls.

"Caleb?" I whimper.

He makes a choked sound. "What happened?" he pleads. "Oh my God, Maisie. What the fuck happened?"

I swallow audibly, ensuring Caleb hears my hesitation. I breathe in, letting the air catch in my throat. "I can't talk about it. Not now. Will you come and get me? Please?"

"Where are you? I'm coming right now."

"I don't know!" I've absorbed some of Caleb's panic, and I'm starting to believe my own performance.

The bizarre truth is, I genuinely don't know where I am. In my distress after Caleb stormed out, I've been driving aimlessly, paying no attention to my surroundings. I'm well and truly lost.

Sensing my disorientation, Caleb says, "Check the GPS on your phone."

I feel silly now. Amid all my emotional turmoil, I've overlooked the most basic tool for determining my whereabouts.

Feeling my pride wane, I tell him, "You think I can think that clearly at a time like this?" I savour the concern in his groan. "I panicked, I didn't know what to do. I just knew I needed you."

His breath comes in deep, shuddering gasps, as if he's crying. "We should call the police."

What?! No!

"Caleb, I need to see you first. I need you. I can't face telling the police, not yet."

He's spiraling into panic – I can practically feel it through the phone. He releases a guttural groan of fury. "Who the fuck was he? Who did this to you?" His growls so deep it sends electricity crackling through my veins.

I need to ease his suffering. This isn't fair. "Caleb, he didn't ... rape me."

"Then what the fuck happened?"

"Are you mad at me?" I whimper.

He stutters. "Oh God, no, not you! Just this situation. Him! Tell me what happened."

I've ventured into treacherous territory. One wrong step and everything could blow up before my eyes. But then again, I've just been attacked! Of course I'm disoriented, dazed. Terrified. It'll be fine. I can make this convincing.

"I don't know," I breathe. "It all happened so fast. One minute I was in my car, lost. The next he was dragging me out and … Oh, Caleb, I can't. Please come and get me. I can't do this over the phone."

The silence that follows feels eternal. Have I finally gone too far? Can he see through the façade?

Strange panting sounds come from his end, like he's moving away from the phone. "Caleb? Where are you? Come back."

"Found you on that app you downloaded for us. The one that tracks our phones. Be there as soon as I can."

"Don't go!"

"I'm not going anywhere. Ever again. Are you in your car now?"

I nod reflexively. "Yes."

"Lock the doors. Don't open them to *anyone*. Jesus Christ, Maisie. How did you get all the way out there? You're practically in Buddingbury."

I let out a pathetic whimper. "I was upset. I didn't mean to disappoint you, Caleb. I just needed space to think after our argument."

"For fuck's sake, Maisie. None of that matters anymore. Stay right there. I'm coming. I'm on my way."

True to his word, I hear his work van roar to life.

He stays on the line but doesn't say much during his journey. When he does, he simply asks if I'm okay. Occasionally something rustles in the woods, making me jump. I might slightly amplify my reactions, just to add gravity to the situation.

I catch my reflection in the rearview mirror.

Shit. Apart from puffy eyes from crying, I look perfectly normal. Far from the victim of an assault. I might *sound* like someone who's been attacked, but I certainly don't look the part.

I hang up on Caleb without warning, adding a little more fuel to the fire.

Stepping into the cold, windy evening, I shiver involuntarily. The rain has stopped, but everything feels damp, the moisture seeping into my bones. The trees tower so high I can't see the moon through their dense canopy. It's pitch black. An owl calls overhead, its shrill cry piercing the silence.

I know what needs to be done, but it feels so degrading. I hesitate, searching for an appropriate spot. But each spot looks the damn same anyway, so I just approach the nearest tree and gingerly lie down before fully committing to my lie by rolling in the dirt. I drag my head through the tree roots, ensuring leaves entwine themselves in my disheveled hair. I smear mud up my back.

Better, but it's not enough. This needs to be believable.

I grasp the tiny zipper of my jeans between my fingers and violently yank until the fabric makes a satisfying ripping sound. The zipper snags so it will no longer pull up.

Getting there.

If I were truly attacked, I'd fight back. I wouldn't let someone overpower me just like that. I'd need to be restrained.

I return to the warmth of the car and raise my hands to my neck. Taking a deep breath, I wrap my fingers loosely around my throat. I close my eyes and brace myself. I squeeze. My fingers tighten until I fear I might lose consciousness. Panic surges, and I release my grip, coughing so violently I fog the windshield.

This will not do. Is it even possible?

I pull out my phone and Google my dilemma. I scroll past self-help articles and scan Reddit threads. The information is sparse, but I understand that if I'm going through with this, I must fully commit.

Once more, I press my fingers to my throat and squeeze. Higher up and harder this time. I focus on Caleb, how I'm doing this for him. For *us*.

This isn't madness. It's love.

I persist, fighting through the pain and rising panic. My eyes bulge and the world suddenly feels heavy. My head begins to roll around. *Stop!* my mind screams. But I need visible marks. I need Caleb to believe me.

I need him to understand that he's mine. And I'm his.

This agony is worth it.

***

"Maisie!" Caleb screams through the door, dragging me back to awareness. He pounds on the glass, trying to force his way in.

"Caleb, stop—" I try to say, but my words come out distorted. My throat burns with every attempt to speak. "Stop!" I repeat, louder now. I cough painfully. It's as if I have swallowed barbed wire.

He pulls back, profound relief washing over his face. He presses a hand against the window. "Maisie. Please open the door."

Disoriented, it takes me several attempts to locate the door handle before I pull it, releasing the latch with a deep thunk.

Caleb immediately crouches down and gathers me into his arms. "Oh, Maisie. I'm so sorry. I'm so, so sorry." He's weeping thick, mournful tears that trigger my own. Within moments I'm out of the car and cradled against him, my legs trembling with the relief of his presence.

I'm filled with such profound love and gratitude it threatens to burst out of me.

He draws back to examine me, his eyes widening at my disheveled state. Embarrassment floods me when his gaze travels downward, lingering on my jeans where my yellow underwear peeks through the broken zipper. I want to hide from him.

He sighs heavily. "Come on, in the van," he says gently.

"But what about my car?"

"I'll come back for it tomorrow. Let's just get you home."

Home. Where mere hours ago I feared I was losing Caleb forever. And now, thanks to my creative solution, we're reunited and whole again. Nothing can beat us now. Nothing can come between us.

Nothing.

I climb into his van where the heater blasts warm air. My hand instinctively reaches for the radio. But I stop myself – normal Maisie would turn on music. This Maisie, a sexual assault victim, wouldn't want to listen to music. I need to be very careful here.

Caleb hasn't joined me, and I glance around nervously. The woods are impenetrably dark beyond the reach of the headlights, and I have to strain to make out his silhouette. He's investigating the tree where my 'attack' occurred.

To my horror, there's a flash of light. Then another.

He's taking photos.

I frantically press the window button, cursing its slow speed. "Caleb, what are you doing?!" My voice sounds overly harsh, and he looks back sharply. Shit, is he suspicious?

"I'm so sorry. I didn't mean to upset you!" he calls back. "I just thought it would be good to take some photos. Evidence. That bastard will pay."

"Stop it!" I scream, too loudly. My throat sears in protest. "Please, just stop it."

A pause follows before Caleb joins me in the van. "Sorry. That was a little insensitive of me."

Without another word, he grits his teeth and drives us away.

Eventually, as we re-enter civilisation, I murmur, "Please can we just forget this ever happened? I want to move on. I want to still be me. The me before all this."

His hands grip the steering wheel tighter, but he remains silent.

My heart hammers against my ribs. "Do you understand? I just want to go back to being me. Me and you. I don't want you to see me differently. I'm not a *victim*, Caleb. I'm better than that."

Finally, through gritted teeth, he says, "You need to go to the police, Maisie."

"I can't," I whisper.

"I'll take you there now. I'll be right beside you the whole time."

Panic surges through me, my arms flailing involuntarily. "Caleb, no! I can't go to the police. Please! Don't make me go there. I can't. I just can't!"

He side-eyes me, concern mingling with something else. What is that? Irritation? "Maisie, you've got to. That monster can't do that to you and get away with it."

"Just not tonight, okay? Caleb, I can't go through that tonight. It's too much. It would break me. I can't face it. Can we please just go home?"

"Maisie ..."

"No, Caleb. Don't I get a say in what happens next? After what I've been through, don't you think I deserve to decide what happens to me? What is it with you men walking all over us women like you own us?!"

He recoils as if I've physically hit him. I almost feel remorse. But my point stands. After being sexually assaulted, how *dare* he force me into something I don't want to do?

"Sorry," he mumbles. He stares blankly at the road ahead, tears glistening in his eyes. I turn away and curl into a protective ball.

We're entering our housing estate when he finally speaks again. "So, what did he do to you?" he asks so softly, as if a louder voice might shatter me. "Can you at least talk about it with me?"

I consider carefully. What kind of lie am I creating here? Something nasty enough that Caleb would never dream of leaving me. But nothing so severe that he'd insist on involving authorities. I need him to let go of that idea.

I sigh deeply as our eyes meet. "I called you," I whisper. "But you didn't pick up."

Tears spill down his cheeks. "I'm sorry, Maisie."

Groaning, I rub my hands over my jeans as if grounding myself. I wave away his apology. "When I hung up, he was just standing there," I gesture toward the side window. "Staring at me."

Caleb grips the steering wheel harder. "What did he look like?"

"I don't know. Bald, definitely. Scary eyes. But Caleb, I was so shocked, I couldn't think clearly. I should've locked the doors. I'm so stupid. Such an idiot."

"You're not, Maisie. You're brave, and beautiful, and strong."

I brush off his compliments, though secretly absorbing them, letting them thaw my frozen core. "Before I knew what was happening, he yanked my door open and grabbed my wrist. He dragged me out."

I feel sick. It's almost as if it really happened to me. I can visualise him with disturbing clarity. "He was pulling at my jeans. Trying to get them off. But I lashed out. I think I hurt him." I look at Caleb, expecting a glimmer of pride, but he's fixated on the road, eyebrows furrowed, tears streaming unchecked. "I wouldn't let him. I fought him off. I was screaming."

"So, he didn't …?"

"He didn't have sex with me, no. But he touched me. Down *there*."

Caleb begins hammering on the steering wheel. His rage erupts so violently I fear he might crash.

"When did he strangle you?" His question startles me. I'd forgotten to include that detail.

"I'm not sure," I say cautiously. "How did you know?"

"You're bruised, Maisie!" he shouts. Though I understand his anger isn't directed at me, it still stings. "Look at your fucking neck!"

I pull down the visor and admire my handiwork. Dark red finger marks line the sides of my neck. Deep thumb imprints are already purpling across my throat.

"It's all such a blur," I murmur.

"You don't think he strangled you until you were unconscious, and then …"

"No, Caleb," I snap. "There was no sex involved." I refuse to let him think I'm tainted. Like I've been unfaithful. "I would know."

We finally arrive home, and he pulls up to the kerb. His motorbike sits in the gap on the drive where my car should be, and I'm flooded with rage at the sight of it.

If he hadn't stormed out on that thing earlier, none of this would have happened.

This is entirely Caleb's fault.

And he's going to make it up to me.

Chapter 8

I've spent the last three days luxuriating in bed and relishing every second of it. Caleb has taken sick leave from work to attend to my every need – bringing me endless snacks, making special trips to the deli on the high street for my favorite treats, and constantly refreshing my tea. I've even heard the unfamiliar sound of the hoover running downstairs, something he's never done before.

When he's not scurrying around like my personal butler, he's curled beside me, holding me close, whispering sweet reassurances against my hair. If not for his relentless nagging about going to the police, it would be absolute perfection.

"Maisie, you've got to tell them. This guy cannot get away with this." It's become his mantra, repeated so often I could recite it in my sleep. Each time he says it, guilt coils around my insides like a snake. I press my face into my hands, releasing a choked sob – partly for effect, but also because maintaining this act is utterly exhausting. Yet, Caleb doesn't stop. His persistence should make me feel protected, cherished. Instead, it makes me feel trapped.

The lie is proving a precarious tightrope to tread. I've deliberately kept details of the 'attack' vague and I refuse to discuss it further when he brings it up. I'm too traumatised to speak about it, both from the supposed horror of the assault and because ... well, because it's all a monumental lie.

It's Friday now, and Caleb hovers awkwardly by the bedroom door, shifting his weight from foot to foot like a schoolboy awaiting punishment.

"What's wrong, Caleb?" I ask, momentarily forgetting to put on my distressed voice. He looks at me with a flicker of hope in his eyes. Does he think I'm recovering?

"I just— I need some air, okay?" His eyes dart toward the window as if searching for escape. Then, his voice softens. "I'll bring you back something nice."

I turn away, burying my face in the pillow. "That's okay," I murmur. "You go out. I'll be fine."

He rushes over to my side of the bed and sits down, his weight causing me to roll towards him. He places his large hand on the back of my head, fingers gently tangling in my hair. "I can stay if you want?" he offers, but there's a hollowness to his words. He wants to leave.

"Just lock the door when you go. Just in case ..."

"Maisie," he sighs deeply. "No, it's okay. I'll stay."

I need to be strategic here. No matter how much I crave Caleb's presence, I understand that forcing him to remain cooped up might eventually make him resentful. Resentful of the situation. Resentful of me.

And I cannot have that.

"No, you go out. I'll be fine." I offer a watery smile. "I mean it."

He studies me doubtfully. "You sure?"

I notice he doesn't put up much of a fight. I reach out and stroke his stubbled cheek. "I'm sure. I should get up, anyway. Take a shower. Try to feel normal again."

He chews thoughtfully on the inside of his cheek. "I won't be gone long."

I pucker my lips, and he takes the hint, planting a firm kiss on my mouth. I yearn to pull him back into bed, to feel his body between my legs again. But that might shatter the façade somewhat.

Patience is key here.

He pulls away and strides to the door. "I'll bring you a surprise back with me," he says cheerfully. And then he's gone.

"Caleb!" I call out, catching him before the front door slams shut.

"Yeah?"

"Where are you going?"

I hear him hesitate, then clear his throat. "Meeting Troy for a drink."

I hear the door close and seconds later his motorbike roars to life, the sound fading quickly as he speeds away.

Troy. The very person who caused this entire mess. It's his fault Caleb and I fell out that night. His fault I had to fabricate this lie. And it's his fault I now must live with this for the remainder of my life.

***

Thirty minutes later I'm dancing around my bedroom to Beyoncé, having showered and dressed myself for the first time in days. I feel rejuvenated. Brimming with optimism.

I'm belting out 'Crazy in Love' when I hear her. "Maisie? Hello?"

Imarah.

"Coming down!" I call out, switching off the music and checking my reflection one final time before heading downstairs. My mousy brown hair falls limply to my shoulders, desperately needing a trim. My eyes appear sunken from forced distress. And I seem to have gained a few unwelcome pounds recently.

I head down the stairs slowly, my damp hair clinging uncomfortably to the nape of my neck. The scent of vanilla shampoo lingers around me, but it does little to mask the stale air in the house. Apparently, Caleb hasn't thought to crack open a window or two.

At the bottom of the stairs, Imarah stands with her arms crossed, her brow furrowed in a way that makes my stomach clench with apprehension. She watches me carefully before reaching out to take my hand. "Jesus Christ, Maisie, are you okay?" she asks, her voice heavy with concern.

"Caleb told you then?" Fury rips through me. How dare he share my deepest, most traumatic 'secret', when he swore on his life he'd keep it to himself? It isn't his decision to make. It's mine!

It feels as if a thousand insects are crawling across my skin. Just wait until he gets home. I'll give him a piece of my mind he won't soon forget.

Now I feel exposed. Words fail me.

Imarah gives my hand a gentle squeeze. "Come on, I'll put the kettle on."

We move into the kitchen where she guides me onto a stool and begins bustling around, helping herself to mugs, coffee, and cream as if she lives here. She works silently, occasionally throwing cautious glances in my direction before placing our drinks on the breakfast bar. She takes the seat opposite me and examines every inch of my body as if cataloguing injuries. Her eyes linger on my neck where the bruising has begun fading to a dirty shade of green.

"Tell me everything," she says sternly. "Leave nothing out."

Confused, I shake my head. I'm not doing that.

She reaches across the counter and places both hands over mine, then bends her neck to look directly into my eyes. I dare not break eye contact, in case she truly sees me. Sees my truth.

"Caleb told me you haven't spoken to anyone about this. Maisie, you can't bottle all this up. It'll eat you alive."

"Imarah, I'm okay. I'm dealing with it."

"Are you, though? Maisie, you haven't left your bed in days and you haven't called the police. I'd say you're *far* from okay."

I close my eyes, exasperated, but also touched by Imarah's genuine concern. It's nice having her here, doting on me. "I'm not going to the police," I state with conviction. "Nag me all you want. I'm not doing it."

She frowns, but to my relief, releases my hands to take a sip of her coffee. "If you won't talk to the police, you have to at least talk to me."

"I have Caleb to talk to."

"He can't carry the weight of all this alone, Maisie. It isn't fair to either of you. This is *huge*."

It isn't huge. It's literally nothing. I frantically search for ways to shrink this situation back to manageable proportions. But I need the full picture before I risk saying something incriminating.

"What exactly did Caleb tell you?" I ask carefully.

Imarah's eyebrows knit together and her voice drops to a softer register. "He told me he found you in the woods, your clothes torn, and you were injured. He said you'd been assaulted."

"But not raped," I clarify emphatically. I need her to understand this isn't as serious as she's making it out to be so that she can let this go.

"No, not raped. But, Maisie, this is a big fucking deal. What he did to you was predatory. It's horrifying! How are you coping?"

"I'm managing," I say truthfully. This situation hasn't exactly been easy on me, but I've been handling it reasonably well. "I'm just trying to distract myself, you know?"

She nods knowingly, as if she understands. She doesn't, of course. What could she possibly know about what I've been through? Real or otherwise.

"You know I'm here for you, don't you? Whether it's ice cream at midnight or a shoulder to cry on. I'm all yours."

She's so damn sweet. Her large brown eyes glisten with unshed tears. After years of feeling invisible to everyone around me, it comes as no surprise that the one person who has consistently stood by my side is here for me now.

"Thank you," is all I can think to say. "How are things with you?" I ask, eager to redirect our conversation.

As much as I love that she's here for me, I feel terrible for making Imarah feel like this. She doesn't deserve to suffer on my behalf.

"I'm alright," she says curtly, making it abundantly clear she isn't finished with me yet. "Look, if you won't go to the police, you should at least see a therapist."

She's clearly not going to let this go. I'm surprised she hasn't delivered the 'but what if he does this to someone else' lecture yet.

"But Maisie, you really do need to consider going to the police. What if he does this to someone else? I know you – you won't be able to live with the guilt."

And there it is. The one argument I can't easily fight against. I take a deliberate sip of my tea to buy time.

Imarah continues. "I can see you're uncomfortable. Just think about it, yeah? This is your trauma, you get to dictate how it's handled. But we're here for you every step of the way."

If I truly get to dictate how this goes, why is she here pressuring me about it? I hold back a scoff.

"I got you these," she announces, grabbing her hand-bag from the floor and rummaging inside. She produces a stack of leaflets and printouts for victims of abuse.

This time I can't suppress my groan.

"Sorry, but you need help," she insists. "And I need to know you're getting it. You might think you're coping well, but that doesn't mean you're okay deep down. Trust me, I know."

Ah, shit. She's using her father's violence as leverage now. The man who beat her mother so severely she was hospitalised for a month while Imarah was taken into foster care.

"I'll read through them," I mumble in surrender. I have absolutely no intention of reading them, though I will strategically place them around the house so Caleb believes I have.

Perhaps then they'll finally leave me in peace.

This wasn't what I anticipated when I told the lie. I expected Caleb to remain home and be the devoted boyfriend, solidifying our relationship with promises of marriage and undying love. I never imagined he'd be out with his friend, likely getting drunk somewhere, while my friend sits here lecturing me like I'm a disobedient child.

No, this isn't right at all.

My cheeks burn with indignation. I need to regain control before my well-meaning loved ones drive me insane, and before the lie takes on a life of its own.

"I'll get help," I reassure Imarah. "I promise. But you must understand, I'm just so ..." I pause deliberately for dramatic effect. "Scared."

Her bottom lip juts out in sympathy. "Oh, Maisie, I'm so sorry." She springs from her chair and rushes to my side. She loops an arm around my shoulders and rests her head against mine. "I've gone straight into telling you what to do. I'm such a shit friend. You must be terrified, and all I'm doing is making it worse."

She cradles my head against her, and I exhale into the comforting warmth of her shoulder. This is exactly what I needed. This moment. This reassurance. I wrap my arms around her waist and pull her into a proper hug. "You're an amazing friend, Imarah. I know you care. I just need to handle this in my own way, you know?"

"Of course! I'll stop pushing you. Do you want to talk about what happened?"

I shake my head firmly. "Not yet."

And so we spend the afternoon in front of the television, indulging in snacks and laughing at Teri Hatcher's antics on *Desperate Housewives*.

It's perfect.

Now, I just need Caleb to come home and remember how to be the boyfriend I deserve.

Chapter 9

Imarah's a good friend, there's no denying that. But she's so attentive that I know she's never going to let this go. She'll keep pushing me for answers and pressuring me to report the attack, all in the name of her misguided mission to 'help' me.

If I'm going to get through this, I need to deepen my own understanding of what I'm alleging happened to me. I need to make myself more convincing. Even to myself.

Besides, curiosity is gnawing at me.

The moment Imarah's car disappears down the street, I pull my laptop close. I need more ammunition if I'm going to win this battle.

To enhance my performance, I've joined several online groups dedicated to supporting victims of sexual assault. The women in these forums share gut-wrenching and profoundly disturbing stories; tales that often break me into pieces as I read them. But as sorrowful as I feel for these women, their experiences provide material I can use when speaking to Caleb and Imarah.

While Caleb is out, I venture deeper into this virtual world of trauma. There are literally thousands of forums dedicated to victims of assaults like mine. Or my fabricated one, anyway. It's truly appalling what men put women through. And it's devastating how these women allow it to happen.

Many describe freezing with terror, unable to fight back. But I know that's not me. I would have fought back fiercely. That's how I escaped relatively unscathed.

Or that's what I keep telling myself, anyway.

The comments in these forums overflow with sweetness and support. There's a strong sense of solidarity and compassion pouring through the replies. It's beautiful to witness.

And I want a piece of it.

I click 'New Message' and let my fingers dance across the keyboard, creating my own post.

I know I shouldn't do this. It's foolish. Dangerous. But as I watch the words materialise on my screen, a twisted sense of satisfaction warms my chest. It feels like finally – *finally* – someone truly sees me and what I've been through.

I erase the last sentence. Rewrite it. Make myself sound more … helpless. The way they expect me to sound.

I need some support. I was attacked a few days ago somewhere near Branton Ridge. It was truly awful. My boyfriend was supportive for a little while, but has since forgotten all about me. He's out with his friend now. How dare he choose getting drunk with his friend over supporting me?! I'm devastated. What do I do?

And then I wait.

Seconds blend into minutes as I frantically hit the refresh button. I even close the browser and reopen it, just in case it's frozen. After twenty-two excruciating minutes, I surrender and slam my laptop shut.

How dare they ignore me? Am I not worthy of their sympathy, too?

My phone buzzes and I lunge for it, praying it's a message from Caleb.

Imarah: *Just checking in. Love you! xxx*

I send a quick response, assuring her I'm fine, then slump down in my armchair. The room feels unusually warm tonight, and I realise Imarah must have switched on the heating before she left. A thoughtful gesture.

It's snug as the sun dips below the horizon, and the gentle hum of the radiator lulls me into drowsiness. Before long, I'm sound asleep.

***

A rattling sound at the door followed by a dull thump jerks me awake.

My attacker! I panic and edge cautiously towards the door, before remembering he doesn't actually exist. I'm still scared shitless – the clock on the wall reads 2.00 am. Who would be trying to enter in the middle of the night?

I spin around, desperately searching for something to use as a weapon. Then, there's a tinkling sound of keys hitting the doorstep outside, and a voice calls out, "Ah, shit."

Caleb.

I rush to the door and yank it open. Caleb stands swaying against the fence, a lopsided grin plastered across his face. "Ah, Maisie, you gem. I couldn't get my key to work."

He's absolutely hammered. I step back to let him in, giving him a wide berth to stumble past me, and watch as he wobbles dangerously up the stairs. Halfway up, he leans backwards at such an alarming angle I fear he'll tumble down headfirst. Thankfully, he regains his equilibrium before I can reach him. Soon, he's sprawled across our bed, fully clothed, including his muddy shoes.

"What did you do?" I gasp. "How did you get in such a state?"

"Had a few drinks with Troy," he slurs happily. His eyelids are already drooping, and his mouth stretches into an infuriatingly contented smile.

"You left me to get this drunk? What's wrong with you?"

"Sorry, Maisie. I didn't mean for this to happen. But I think I might be a little bit drunk." His eyes are closed now. I have mere seconds before the snoring begins.

"Caleb!" I cry out sharply. He mumbles something unintelligible but doesn't open his eyes. "Caleb!" I whack him on the arm this time, but my efforts go completely unnoticed as the snoring commences.

The bastard! The selfish, inconsiderate bastard. I cannot fathom the insensitivity of it. The sheer cruelty.

And it's all Troy's fault. He undoubtedly plied Caleb with alcohol. And because Caleb's so inherently lovely, he couldn't refuse.

There's no way I can budge his unconscious form to make space in the bed, so the sofa will have to serve as my bed tonight. I gather up the extra blanket and a pillow and head downstairs. Fuck Caleb – he can sleep in his damn shoes. I hope he's uncomfortable.

I've already slept for hours, and now my body stubbornly refuses to drift off again. Besides, each of Caleb's thunderous snores pierces the ceiling and sets my teeth on edge. I toss and turn, frustration building inside me until I'm ready to explode.

Screw it.

I open my laptop, hoping to distract myself from the rusty chainsaw sounds emanating from our bedroom upstairs. The browser immediately loads the last page I visited – the assault support forum. To my surprise, there are over fifty responses to my post.

You deserve better hun. Leave him.

Talk to him. He needs to know what you're going through. xx

We're here for you. You don't need him.

The support manifests in countless forms, yet all make my chest swell with satisfaction. It's like having multiple friends who understand my 'suffering'. Like they truly see me.

I continue scrolling, reading and responding to every single comment. Then one stops me cold: *Branton Ridge?! OMG I live like two minutes from there! What are the police doing about it? I haven't seen anything on the news?*

My stomach plummets. My fingers hover uncertainly over the keyboard. For just a fleeting moment, I allow myself to consider the truth. To acknowledge the fear I'm instilling in these genuinely vulnerable women.

Before I can formulate a response, someone else replies to that message: *I live in Stasbridge, this is terrifying. OP—Have they caught the guy? Are you ok?*

My fingers dance nervously, ready to type, but the words won't come. How do I extinguish this fire without making the situation exponentially worse? I need to alleviate their fears while simultaneously protecting my lie.

Okay. I've got this.

The police have been amazing. They think they know who it is so they'll be arresting him straight away.

Yes, that should work. My stomach unclenches and I lean back, satisfied. But perhaps this was a mistake – I shouldn't have shared my story online. Everyone knows nothing good comes from the internet.

A tiny notification sound chimes through my laptop speakers, recapturing my attention.

The police are so good there. They really helped me a couple of years ago. Who is in charge of your case?

That's it. This is getting out of hand. I'm done. I shut my laptop and shove it to the side. I'm not engaging anymore. That nosy bitch can leave me alone. How dare she question me? Who does she think she is?

***

I take great pleasure in pushing the hoover around the house, fully aware that as it inches closer to our bedroom, Caleb's hangover headache intensifies.

Pressing my ear against the bedroom door, I can hear him groaning. I burst in, radiating energy and a deep desire to clean our bedroom from top to bottom in the noisiest manner possible.

"Maisie, please!"

I switch the hoover off and put on a sickly-sweet voice. "Sorry, babe. You not feeling so good?"

Rolling over, he attempts to look at me, but the sunlight streaming through the window – after I've deliberately whipped the curtains open – causes him visible discomfort.

Good.

"I feel like shit," he admits, finally surrendering and rolling over, burying his face beneath the pillow.

"Maybe that's because you were out getting pissed last night with your friend instead of at home with me. Me, your girlfriend, who is going through hell."

His voice emerges, muffled. "You had Imarah. I made sure you had someone. I wouldn't just leave you on your own."

I just snarl in response.

He revealed my darkest secrets to my friend. Then, after detonating that grenade, he went out drinking with his mate! Truly disgusting behaviour.

And he stinks. The stench in here is revolting. If the smell had a colour, it would be swamp-green – a nauseating blend of stale booze, sweat, and flatulence. I push the window open wider and restart the hoover, giving his side of the bed a damn good clean.

As I bend to collect the charger cables scattered across the floor, Caleb throws back the covers, leaps out of bed, and yanks the hoover plug from the wall. "Maisie, please. I know I've fucked up. Big time. I didn't leave last night expecting to get so hammered." He gesticulates emphatically. At some point during the night he must have stripped off, because he's standing before me completely naked, everything dangling freely. If the situation weren't so dire, I'd laugh.

Caleb continues. "I thought I'd be gone for a couple of hours, tops. But then one thing led to another, you know?"

"No. I don't know. But you know who does? That creep who attacked me. One thing certainly led to another that night, and if I hadn't stopped him, it probably would have led to me being killed."

He winces, his shoulders sagging in defeat. He collapses onto the edge of the bed, head cradled in his hands. "I'm so sorry, babe. You have no idea."

I'm torn between reaching out to offer comfort and leaving him to wallow in his well-deserved guilt.

"But Mais, things here have just been so ... *intense* this week. You know? What happened to you has been going around and around in my mind. What would have happened if you hadn't fought back? What could I have prevented if I hadn't walked away that night?"

He drags a hand across his face, his skin pallid and damp with sweat. "I can't stop thinking about it, Mais. About what could have happened." His hands clench into fists. "If I find him, I swear to God—" He sucks in a ragged breath, his entire body shaking with rage.

I press my fingers gently to his lips. "You don't have to think about it anymore," I whisper. "It's over. I'm okay."

Caleb shudders, and I realise he's crying now. As much as I ache for him, I'm also gratified that the seriousness of the situation is finally sinking in.

He raises his gaze to meet mine, his eyes wide and glistening. "Then after I'd had a beer or two yesterday, everything just felt a little lighter, you know? And I chased that feeling – it felt good to shed it all, just for a while. And I lost control. I got silly. But you know what, Mais?" He doesn't wait for my response. "It was selfish. I was a complete wanker. And you've got to believe me – I am so, so sorry. I won't ever treat you like that again. I swear to you. I—"

I silence him with a gentle "shh" and kneel before him. I stroke his hair, tenderly nudging him to look up at me. "Caleb, it's okay. I get it."

He shakes his head as heavy tears roll down his cheeks.

"I forgive you," I say. I repeat it, over and over. His raw honesty has breached my defences, and compassion overwhelms me. I want to pull him into my arms and never let him go. This beautiful man belongs to me, and that recognition now dissolves my anger.

His tears subside, and he pulls me up into his embrace so we're lying together on the bed, with me nestled in the crook of his arm. He plants a soft kiss on my forehead. "I'll never hurt you again," he promises. "I've been an awful boyfriend."

"I know you won't hurt me," I whisper back. "And you're an amazing boyfriend."

A thoughtful silence follows.

"This is too much," he groans. "I want to kill the bastard who did this to you. And I'll make it fucking painful. And slow." With each word, his grip on my waist tightens.

I wince involuntarily. I can feel Caleb's anguish pouring out of him. His frustration at not knowing the identity of my attacker lies buried in every taut muscle. And the torment in his voice cannot be denied.

I did this to him – I've buried him beneath too much pain, and he's beginning to suffocate. I owe him some solace now. Guilt sits heavily in my stomach, making me nauseous.

"I'll speak to the police," I hear myself say. The words feel alien on my tongue; wrong. But then I think of the women I've frightened in the forum. I owe them some sense of security too. If they believe there's a predator at large, they'll feel safer knowing there's police involvement. Besides, if the authorities are searching for my attacker, perhaps the real predators lurking out there will behave themselves. At least for a while.

Yes, I'll be helping everyone. Especially Caleb. He deserves that. Now that he's learned the proper way to love me, I should do this for him.

It's not *entirely* a lie. I was genuinely frightened that night. I did feel abandoned. If I just adjust a few details. If I make it convincing for them, maybe they'll understand me. Maybe Caleb will, too.

I need to push forward so that I can reach the end of this. I will go to the police for him. For me.

This is how I make it real.

Chapter 10

Storm clouds gather overhead, heavy with unshed rain. An omen, as if the universe itself senses the seriousness of what I'm about to do.

I linger at the bottom of the stone steps, watching people hurry past on the street, heads down, desperate to reach shelter before the heavens open. A uniformed officer approaches and my stomach seizes. But he merely dips his chin in casual acknowledgement and continues on his way, presumably giving me no further thought.

I cannot believe I'm actually doing this. What a catastrophically stupid idea. I should have allowed everything to run its natural course. But no, I opened my big mouth and now here I stand, outside the police station, poised to multiply my lie by a thousandfold.

Each step towards the imposing building feels like a betrayal, not just of truth, but of myself. I shouldn't be here. I should turn around and flee, but my traitorous feet propel me forward, dragging me toward the point of no return.

Imarah presses a gentle hand against my back. "You ready?" she asks, her voice laced with concern. Her tenderness is unbearable.

I insisted to Caleb that I needed to do this alone, pretending I couldn't bear him hearing the sordid details. But he was adamant I shouldn't face this ordeal unaccompanied, so purely to appease him I reluctantly agreed to let Imarah come with me. She's here to offer a supportive hand, pass tissues, perhaps buy me a consolatory glass of wine afterward.

Despite her being witness to the lies I'm about to weave, there's comfort in having her beside me. Her familiar, loving presence soothes my frayed nerves and anchors me.

She reminds me that I can do this.

I head through the automatic doors to the reception desk. I was expecting plastic chairs bolted to linoleum. Bulletproof glass protecting the desk officer. So I'm pleasantly surprised to discover plush seating and a welcoming oak counter. Behind it sits a rotund officer with frazzled hair and rosy-red cheeks.

"Yes? How can I help you?" she enquires, directing her question at Imarah – the more attractive, more approachable one.

Imarah nudges me forward, but I remain mute, paralysed. So she speaks on my behalf. "My friend would like to report a sexual assault."

The officer finally shifts her attention to me, and cocks her head to the side. "Of course, dear. Fill in this form and hand it back to me when you're done. I'll see who's available to speak with you." She hands me a clipboard before rising from her swivel chair with noticeable effort and disappearing through a door behind the desk.

We settle into the waiting area. "It's surprisingly nice in here, isn't it?" Imarah observes, in an attempt to break the tension. Her effort falls flat; the butterflies in my stomach have transformed into rampaging elephants. "All they need is a scented candle and it'd be like a spa."

I scoff derisively. "I don't think we're here for a facial, Imarah."

"Well, no." She shifts uncomfortably at her blunder. "We could go for one afterwards?" She throws me a grimace masquerading as a smile.

I begin filling in my personal details – name, phone number, address – everything I'm reluctant to divulge.

"Perhaps this is just what police stations look like nowadays?" Imarah persists in filling the silence.

"Doubt it. We just live in a nice town. I can't imagine they deal with much trouble here."

"Yeah, maybe you're right."

The silence between us expands, becoming a living thing. The longer we sit here, the more profoundly I realise the magnitude of what I'm starting.

The local news in Stasbridge reports on businesses closing, graffiti on school walls, and shopping trolleys abandoned in the stream behind the church. Sexual assaults simply aren't part of this community's narrative.

I feel like I'm about to drop a bomb, and the thought makes my temples throb. But I'm committed now. There's no turning back. Not without exposing myself to the ones I love.

The desk officer returns and watches through narrowed eyes as I complete the form. When I approach, she takes the clipboard from me with unnecessary firmness. "Thank you, dear. Someone will be with you shortly."

Before I even rejoin Imarah, a door at the side of the room opens and a friendly-looking man says, "Maisie?

Would you follow me, please? Sergeant Campbell will join us shortly."

We follow the young man, who introduces himself as Constable Dharva, down a corridor painted in a nauseating shade of institutional blue. The warmth of the reception area proves a cruel trick. The deeper we venture, the more it feels like entering another world, where walls bear ancient stains and the air hangs heavy with stale sweat and regret.

Perhaps Stasbridge harbours more darkness than I imagined. I find this thought strangely reassuring.

We enter a small interview room with a large window overlooking the river and seat ourselves at a small round table. Twenty excruciating minutes pass before the door swings open. "Sorry for the wait. I've just switched to part-time hours. Still adjusting to these extended periods sitting at home away from the desk."

Evelyn.

The last time I saw Evelyn she was a wreck, red-eyed and quivering in the dairy aisle at the supermarket. Now, in uniform, she's transformed. Composed, professional. Formidable. She studies me with penetrating eyes, as if she can see straight through me.

The moment recognition dawns, her posture softens to one of utmost sympathy. "Maisie," she says, the compassion in her eyes almost too intense to bear.

"You know each other?" Imarah enquires, failing to recognise Evelyn from their brief encounters.

"We're distant friends," Evelyn smiles. "I didn't expect our paths to cross again so soon. And in the worst possible circumstances."

I grunt noncommittally and glance out the window, wishing I was out there, free from this hell. What options do I have? Run away? Dissolve into tears and refuse to speak? Both seem equally plausible at this moment.

"How are you?" I ask instead, keen to deflect attention.

"Getting on with things," she replies, though I notice she averts her gaze. She shakes her head as if trying to dislodge painful memories. "So, you're here to report an attack?" she continues, settling into her chair and removing the cap from a ballpoint pen. "Can you tell me what happened?"

I take a heavy breath, and Imarah squeezes my hand beneath the table. When words fail me, she prompts, "Start at the beginning, Maisie. When did this happen?"

"Last Tuesday. Around eight in the evening."

"Good. Now, walk me through the events."

And so I do. I describe my argument with Caleb, eliciting sympathetic glances from both women. I feel instantly validated. I explain that I went for a drive and wasn't paying attention to my surroundings, and ended up lost on an unfamiliar track. I feel foolish recounting this, but Evelyn's encouraging nods propel me forward.

"We've all done unwise things when it comes to men," she jokes gently, attempting to ease the tension and keep my narrative flowing.

It works.

"I was sitting in my car, trying to call Caleb. But I couldn't get through to him. Then I looked up and this man was just ... there." I gesture toward an imaginary window beside me. "Staring in at me."

"What did he look like?" Evelyn asks, her pen momentarily pausing.

"Dark hair. Dark eyes. Big mouth."

"Skin colour?"

"White." I aim for generic details. Tossing a needle into the proverbial haystack. Tension is rising in the back of my neck. What am I doing here? What have I done?!

"Any other distinguishing features? Height? Clothing? Tattoos?"

"Nothing!" I blurt. "I wasn't paying attention." Suddenly, uncontrollable ugly sobs wrack my body and tears cascade down my cheeks. This was a big mistake. A stupid, horrible mistake.

"Alright, we'll return to that. Please continue. What happened next?"

I inhale deeply. Tears cascade down my cheeks, uncontrollable, ugly sobs wracking my body.

This was such a stupid idea. I never should have agreed to this.

Everyone waits patiently. Imarah strokes small circles on the back of my hand with her thumb. Constable Dharva maintains a mask of professional detachment. Evelyn remains poised, pen at the ready, her posture impeccable, the embodiment of procedural professionalism.

"He, um, he opened my door," I finally manage.

"So the door wasn't locked?"

"I didn't know that was going to happen, did I?" I snap defensively.

Evelyn carefully sets down her pen. "I apologise, Maisie. I simply need to ask these questions. You understand I'm not assigning blame."

"You're trying to make me look like a liar."

She dips her chin slightly. "Not at all. I just want to find the bastard who did this to you."

Our eyes meet, and I perceive the determination and righteous anger burning behind her professional exterior. I nod in acknowledgement. "He dragged me."

"By the arm? Hair?"

"Arm."

She makes a note.

"He dragged me from my car and shoved me onto the ground."

I pause, anticipating another question, but this time she remains silent, allowing me to continue at my own pace. "He started pulling at my trousers."

Imarah gasps beside me and her grip on my hand tightens painfully. I disengage from her grasp, and she withdraws, giving me space to breathe.

"He broke my jeans," I continue. "I still have them if you need to examine them."

Evelyn nods. "Have they been washed?"

I nod casually. But my stomach constricts violently. *DNA.* Of course she's thinking about forensic evidence. "I'm so sorry."

She frowns but dismisses my apologies with a wave and encourages me to continue.

"Everything after that is a massive blur. But I remember fighting back. I just kept hitting him. I resisted. But he wrapped his hands around my throat." I mimic my own actions from that night, acutely aware of the irony in demonstrating my fabricated strangulation.

"How far did it go?" Constable Dharva interjects.

I'm startled by his voice and irritated by the intrusion. "He didn't rape me," I clarify hastily. Some lies are simply too enormous. I refuse to cross that boundary. "He, um, he put his hands on me." I mime my area hidden beneath the table.

"You mentioned he strangled you? And you fought back?" The young constable asks.

I nod in affirmation.

"So, how did he manage to assault you sexually?"

A spike of panic courses through me. I hadn't considered this inconsistency. I grasp for a plausible explanation, but nothing fits. My throat constricts. "I don't know," I whisper; then louder, with mounting desperation, "It's all such a blur!"

"Would you like a break?" Imarah offers.

I shake my head vehemently. I just want this to be over with. "I don't really remember what happened next. I must have either got him off me or something spooked him because the next thing I remember, I was crawling back to my car. I got in and locked the doors. Then I called Caleb."

Evelyn poses several more questions, which I answer with an increasing number of 'I-don't-knows' and 'I-can't-remembers'.

"I think we should leave it there for now," she eventually announces, and I exhale a deep sigh of relief. It's over. I can leave and anticipate the inevitable call informing me they have insufficient evidence to proceed and the case has been closed.

Then we can all get on with our normal lives.

"Thank you for coming forward today," Evelyn says. "Now let's discuss the next steps."

Next steps? No. No, no, no. My pulse roars in my ears as Evelyn's words dissolve into unintelligible noise. The case was supposed to just fade away, not escalate.

"The next course of action is to refer you to the Sexual Assault Referral Centre."

"What?"

"Please don't look so worried. They're specialists in this field and will provide comprehensive support. They'll review everything you've shared today and, if you consent, collect forensic evidence."

"But there isn't any!" I exclaim. "I've showered every day since it happened."

"You'd be surprised what they can still uncover. Besides, I can see bruising around your neck. They'll want to document that. Any evidence that might lead us to your attacker is invaluable."

I nod reluctantly. "You said 'if you consent.' Does that mean this is optional?"

Evelyn sighs with resignation. "Maisie, you will never be forced to do anything against your will. However – and I'm being candid with you now, woman to woman – if you can assist in any way possible, it's far more likely we'll apprehend this criminal and ensure he's incarcerated, preventing him from harming others. At least consider it."

She glances at Imarah, who nods enthusiastically, poised to pressure me into something I desperately don't want to do.

"Do you have any questions?"

"Who will handle the investigation?" I ask.

"You'll be assigned an officer who specialises in these cases. But, Maisie, I promise you this – I won't rest until he's behind bars. I owe you that."

Chapter II

They're whispering in the kitchen, their voices hushed yet sharp, slicing through the stillness like razor blades. They converse as if I'm not there, as if I've become a ghost. Words like 'attacker' and 'arrest' drift toward me, each one twisting my stomach into knots.

I sit in the living room sipping sweet tea, contemplating the choices that led me here. To say I regret going to the police would be an understatement. I never expected things to snowball quite so much. Yet, that regret coexists with a peculiar certainty that if this were actually true, then I've done what's right.

Our relationship needed a jarring shock to propel it back onto its proper course. At least one of us has to fight for our future. To take necessary risks. And that person, by default, is me.

Caleb suddenly raises his voice, clear and deliberate from the doorway. "Maisie, why didn't you do the exam?" His tone is carefully measured, as if he's conscious of treading on thin ice.

Imarah responds with an emphatic "shhh," bustling in behind him. They exchange intense eye contact, unspoken words ricocheting between them.

I've had enough of this. I set my cup down with excessive force, sloshing hot liquid onto the coffee table. I pivot to confront them directly with a fierce gaze and they both appear immediately ashamed. "First, if you're going to talk about me, at least have the decency to move out of earshot," I say, my tone icy. "Second of all, don't you dare bombard me with your questions – don't you think I've endured enough already?"

Imarah's eyes widen with horror. Caleb rushes toward me, but I shrug him away and he retreats, palms upraised in surrender. "I'm sorry, babe. Imarah was just getting me all caught up on what happened with the police. I didn't want to force you to relive it all again."

I'm grateful for that small mercy. The last thing I want is to recount today's events to Caleb: how the compassionate officers at SARC guided me through unbearable procedures; how they made me repeat my story over and over; how they treated me with such delicacy I feared I might shatter into tiny pieces.

My shoulders slump in defeat. I just want to sleep now. Today has been overwhelming, and I wonder how I entangled myself in this mess of lies to begin with.

"But Maisie, you didn't do the physical exam." It's not phrased as a question, yet he regards me expectantly, eyebrows raised as if he's entitled to influence this decision.

"I didn't have to. No one forced me," I counter petulantly. "Or are you suggesting I should have allowed someone else to invade my body against my will?"

He blanches visibly. "No! Of course not. I just thought you'd go to any lengths to catch this guy."

And if it were real, I would. But how can I go to every length when there's nothing there to grab hold of?

"Maybe you should go back and ask them to—"

I erupt. "Go back there? You think this is easy for me? You think going to the police and reliving everything was what – a fun day out? Caleb, every time I go over what happened that night, something inside me dies a little. I'm terrified that if I have to tell even one more person, there'll be nothing left. Please, will you stop forcing me to do something that feels like another assault? You're just as bad as he is."

It's a low blow, but my anger has swelled so huge that the words escape unfiltered. He looks heartbroken as

I storm away, leaving him to contemplate what I said. They need to stop interfering. This isn't their story – it's mine – and only I determine its ending.

I climb into bed and glance at my phone, noticing an email from a strange address with lots of random symbols and nonsensical letters. I open it, fully expecting some generic scam. My fingers go cold. The words blur together as my vision narrows, and I fight against rising nausea. My phone slips from my grip, landing on the bedcovers with a soft thud, but the message remains seared into my consciousness.

What did the police say? Be careful, liars always get caught.

What the fuck?

I collect myself and look back at the email. There's nothing revealing the sender's identity. I even search the address online, but nothing materialises. No one knows about my attack except Caleb and Imarah, and they're downstairs discussing me behind my back, not sending threatening emails.

The support forum is the only place I've shared my story. Regret engulfs me. Why did I broadcast my lie? It was foolish – a pathetic bid for attention. What the fuck is wrong with me?

I type the forum's address into my browser with mounting dread. I don't know if I want to do this. I'm scared of what I might find. Sure enough, there are over one hundred notifications for my recent post. I struggle to make sense of what I'm seeing.

I scan the comments, finding multiple supporters defending me, offering their presence if I need someone to confide in. Telling people I deserve a break. But why? Why are they jumping to my defence?

Then I see them: people slagging me off, hurling every conceivable insult. Calling me a disgrace to women and a mockery to legitimate victims. How do they know the truth?

I keep scrolling, eager to locate the root cause of this backlash. Someone must have detonated an explosive accusation among the comments.

And there it is: *This poster is a liar and a disgrace. She was never attacked. She's just an attention-seeking whore.*

Is that all it took? Wow, it's disturbing how easily people are influenced. How can one anonymous internet voice cast aspersions that immediately take root in others' minds? It's genuinely worrying.

Whatever. These women have no idea who I am. I refuse to let them affect me when I have two people who genuinely care about me, who believe my story and are suffering because of it. I'm not going to let this bother me.

Oh, who am I kidding? I'm trembling, despite reassuring myself that their opinions are irrelevant. For every message of support, there's a corresponding message of doubt and hatred. And if I'm honest, that's killing me.

It hasn't escaped me that this entire situation is self-inflicted. I'd be delusional to pretend otherwise.

I force myself to remember what started all this – the argument, my uncertainty about our relationship's survival. Can I allow a few anonymous strangers to negate the good I've accomplished? I've salvaged my relationship. We're stronger than ever.

A little suffering for substantial gain.

No. I must forget about these online strangers and concentrate on the end goal. Now that Caleb has remembered how important I am to him, he'll never abandon me again.

Providing he never discovers the truth.

I move to delete the email, wondering how many more I should anticipate while my post stays active. My email address isn't even publicly visible, so this particular bitch is unnervingly clever.

My finger hovers over the delete button, but my common sense falters, and before I realise it, I'm hammering out a reply: *Thanks for your concern. The police were fantastic and the rape team were very understanding and helpful.*

That should shut her up.

The response arrives almost instantaneously: *But you lied to them. Didn't you?*

This time I delete it immediately. I was stupid to engage. This person has no idea what they're talking about. Probably projecting their own issues onto me.

Well, I have more important matters to attend to, and if they keep this up, I'll report *them* to the police for harassment. Then they can eat their damn words.

I hear Imarah leave, and I snuggle up in bed, waiting for Caleb to join me. I listen as he potters about downstairs, washing dishes, tidying the living room. I feel a surge of pride – this ordeal has genuinely changed him for the better. I smile to myself in the cosy dim light.

But then, all goes silent. There's no creak of stairs as he makes his way up to me, no flush of the toilet, no rustling of bedcovers as he slips in beside me to hold me close.

Pissed off, I tread carefully along the landing and peer down the stairs. I spy Caleb stretched out on the sofa, lit only by the soft glow of the lamp. His back is turned to me, so I watch him silently, waiting to see what he's doing.

Then I notice his shoulders trembling violently, and I realise he's crying. Sobbing quietly to himself in the waning evening light.

My guilt is so monumental I want to launch myself down the stairs and throw my arms around his neck. I want to tell him everything is going to be okay. I want him to know I love him unconditionally.

Because this is all my fault. The last thing I wanted was to cause him pain. The suffering was meant to be exclusively mine. Caleb was supposed to be the hero. Instead, I'm destroying him.

I wring my hands together. All this chaos is worth it – isn't it? Caleb is finally giving me his undivided attention. Imarah treats me as if I matter. That has got to count for something.

I long to go to him, to reach out and tell him I'm fine, and so is he. But I don't. I stand watching him tremble with quiet sobs. Something sharp and cold – something that feels an awful lot like regret – pierces my chest.

With a weary sigh, I return to bed.

Alone.

Chapter 12

I practically had to drag myself into the office this morning. After taking a week off, I couldn't further postpone facing my colleagues.

My supervisor, Alec, had been surprisingly accommodating – at first. "Take whatever time you need," he'd said. But his follow-up email yesterday had made it crystal clear: either return to work or provide medical proof that stress is rendering me unable to work.

I felt the weight of every stare as I settled at my desk. The stationery industry is hardly exciting at the best of times, but now the monotony feels like a blessed sanctuary. I just need to keep my head down and let the whispers gradually fade.

The team is tolerable, I suppose. There's Jan, who perpetually finds someone to moan about, and part-time Penny who somehow manages to cut her contracted hours in half. Then there's Alec, my creepy boss who can only seem to hold a conversation if he's staring at my breasts.

By the time five o'clock mercifully arrives, I've made a solemn vow to myself that I will find another job. I'm hideously bored and with everything happening lately, I've decided I deserve better. I owe it to myself to discover more stimulating work, something with actual substance. My relationship has finally blossomed into something wonderful; Caleb even woke me with tea and a tender kiss this morning. My friendship with Imarah is stronger than ever. Now I feel compelled to complete this picture of personal transformation.

My family remains a lost hope, but you win some, you lose some. Tonight, I'm determined to walk into Mum's with my head held high. No one will walk over me anymore, especially not my family. This is my life, and I refuse to be their doormat.

I'm the first to arrive. It's Rainy's due date, and Mum wanted to mark the occasion with a little get-together, but I'm secretly terrified her waters will break while we're nibbling on cake. There's no way I'm involving myself in the messy business of birthing her child. My shoes are new.

"Alright, darling? Can you keep an eye on the hob for me while I set the table?"

Not even a proper greeting. I poke at the bolognese sauce with a spatula. Mum has never been particularly skilled in the kitchen, and this concoction looks horrific. Still, I'll smile and push it around my plate to spare her feelings.

She breezes back into the kitchen. "How are you then, Maisie?" she asks without actually looking at me.

I open my mouth to respond, but then the front door bursts open, and my sisters' voices drift down the corridor, immediately stealing Mum's attention. "Hello! How's Mummy-to-be doing? Ready to drop yet?" She vanishes to greet them, already forgetting about me.

"Oh, Mum, don't. I feel bloody awful. I swear this baby is clinging to my bladder so they don't have to vacate."

Mum offers a sympathetic groan, guiding them into the dining room. "Dinner won't be long. Spag bol. Though maybe I should have researched labour-inducing foods."

I hear Faith chime in. "Orgasms! I read about it online. That apparently works."

I grimace. I feel for poor Steve. Imagine having sex with a sweaty whale? Rainy hasn't got a chance in hell of expelling that baby through her own efforts.

"Where's Maisie?" Faith inquires. "Late again?"

"I'm in here. Cooking your dinner," I snap.

She pokes her head around the doorframe. "Hardly *cooking* it. You're just poking it about a bit."

She's not wrong, so I keep quiet and reach for the oregano. Maybe I can breathe some life into this meal. Mum seems to think seasoning begins and ends with salt.

I get roped into serving, and by the time I finally sit down, I'm even more disgruntled and moody. I'll sit, eat, endure their fawning over Rainy's enormous belly, then leave. Caleb is probably missing me, anyway.

I'm nearly finished when they finally acknowledge my existence. "So, how's the envelope factory?" Faith asks, her contempt barely disguised.

I shrug dismissively. "Stationery, not just envelopes. And there's nothing to report."

Rainy raises an eyebrow and leans forward as far as her protruding belly allows. "No? Nothing you want to share with your family?"

My stomach tightens painfully. Does she know about the attack? Surely not. Caleb and Imarah wouldn't have betrayed my confidence. And I haven't received any threatening emails since that night a week ago. She must be alluding to something else. Still, I don't like the way she's looking at me like she's bursting to spill some scandalous tea.

"Maisie, sweetie. I've been biting my tongue all evening, but don't you think we should address the elephant in the room?"

Carefully, I set my cutlery down. "I don't have anything to tell you." I push my plate away. "Though perhaps it's time I head home. Caleb will be wondering where I've got to."

Rainy giggles at his name, so I'm sure now that she knows nothing about my attack or she wouldn't be laughing at me. Relief floods me. But curiosity overwhelms caution, and I foolishly ask, "What is it, Rainy? Spit it out."

"I bumped into Caleb a few days ago. Outside the old Blockbusters."

Something sharp and electric pulses through me. What was Caleb doing on the other side of town?

"I asked him when he's planning on dropping to one knee." She waves a dismissive hand. "Don't worry, I didn't let on that you'd found a ring. I was all casual, you know? *Discreet.*" She emphasises 'discreet' with infuriating pompousness.

I'd completely forgotten I'd told them I'd found a ring. Bollocks. How utterly stupid of me. I want to run away.

Need to escape. But I remain frozen, simply hanging my head in shame.

"He looked *very* confused. In fact, I'm pretty sure he has absolutely no intention of proposing. And you know what else I think? I don't think you ever found a ring."

No shit, Sherlock. Tears burn the back of my eyes. "Yeah, well, you know nothing about my relationship with Caleb."

"I know enough. And I can read people like a book. I'm an *empath*."

Oh, please. "Leave me alone, Rainy. Stop trying to ruin everything just because you're jealous."

"Jealous?!" She presses a hand to her chest in exaggerated shock. "Me? What on earth would I have to be jealous about?"

Maybe the fact that your husband views you as nothing more than a breeding machine. Maybe because you have no life beyond your children. Maybe because you're a grade-A bitch.

But I don't say any of that. My mouth refuses to cooperate, and to my absolute mortification, my tears spill over.

"Oh, honey, there's nothing to be embarrassed about," Mum soothes, draping an arm across my shoulders. "Naturally, you're eager to move your relationship forward. After so many years together, you're bound to feel a little impatient."

"I didn't lie though, Mum."

"I know," she says kindly. "Maybe you found a ring, but it was meant for someone else?"

Stunned by her suggestion, I shove my chair back, rattling the crockery. "I need to leave."

"Oh, don't go. This just got really fun," Faith smirks.

I round on her, jabbing my finger accusingly in her direction. "Do you have any idea what I've been through recently? If you did, you wouldn't dare treat me like this."

"Oh, please. Talking bullshit as always. You've always pretended you're above this family. Well, I hate to break it to you, Maisie, but you're really not."

"I was attacked, Faith!" The lie bursts from me once again. "While you were sitting around lording your superiority over me, some bastard nearly raped me. But do you care? No! Because the only person you care about is yourself!"

Silence crashes over the room like a tidal wave. My chest heaves with the adrenaline of lying so brazenly. Rainy and Faith sit motionless, mouths agape. Rainy clutches her ample chest, while Faith grips the edge of the table.

Mum's mouth hangs agape. "Oh, darling. Why didn't you tell us? Don't you think we deserve to know?"

My jaw locks at her audacity. The absolute nerve of this family! My trauma isn't theirs to own. What relevance is it to them? It's not as if they love me. I doubt they even care.

"Are you okay?" Rainy asks, her voice so faint I barely hear it. Her eyes are panicked; whether for my wellbeing or her own, I don't know. But at least I know she feels *something*.

The fight drains out of me, and I drop back into my chair, utterly defeated. "Yes," I admit. "I am now."

"Did you report it to the police?"

I nod. "Yes, but there's limited evidence for them to go on."

"Oh, well, that's just disgusting. You'd think in this day and age there would be all sorts of forensic evidence they can use. Like they have on the telly," Mum says.

Rainy ignores her completely. "What did he look like?"

"I'm not sure. Everything blurred together, you know? Because of the shock."

They all nod as if they understand (they don't), and we each bury ourselves in our own thoughts. I notice that no one offers me a hug. No one gives words of comfort. All three are probably considering the implications for them, without giving me an ounce of consideration.

"So, what actually happened?" Rainy finally asks.

I tut disapprovingly and shake my head at them. "I'm not going through the details again."

"Why not?"

"Rains, leave the poor girl alone," Mum interjects.

"What? I think we have a right to know what kind of evil is prowling our streets." She gestures towards the window as if my fictional attacker might parade past at any moment.

Mum offers the slightest shrug before they collectively return their attention to me.

I shake my head firmly, casting them a defiant glare. "I'm not talking about it."

I shouldn't have said anything. Divulging my 'attack' was a massive mistake. Last year Faith visited A&E for a verruca, and Rainy cries when fictional characters die on *Coronation Street*. They're hardly well-versed at keeping things in perspective, and I just know they'll turn this into a massive spectacle.

"Look, I should go now. Happy due date, Rains."

"Oh, don't leave! I've bought us chocolate cheesecake," Mum says, jumping up to block my exit.

"No, I want to get back to Caleb now. He'll be waiting. Worrying. You know?"

"Waiting to propose?" Faith jokes lightly, but thankfully no one finds it funny. It's too soon for that. I'm too fragile. She winces apologetically, and I turn away from them. "Sorry! That was a stupid thing to say. Just trying to lighten the mood."

"I'll see you soon, yeah?" I'm already at the front door, freedom tantalisingly close.

But then, Faith gasps dramatically and her chair clatters backwards as she stands. "I know what you should do!"

Oh no. This cannot possibly be good news. Faith's thinking never ends well. I'm tempted to pretend I didn't hear her brainwave, but given the volume at which she announced it, feigning ignorance would be pointless.

When I reluctantly turn to face her, she's staring at me with wide, excited eyes, clutching Mum's hand as if she's about to perform some miraculous healing. "You should speak to Peters!"

"Peters? As in multiple guys called Peter? How many are there?"

Faith laughs, waving dismissively at my apparent silliness. "No, no. Peters. One guy. As in the radio host at Shine FM."

Oh, fuck no.

Rainy gasps, mirroring Faith's excitement. "Yes! That would be brilliant! Tell everyone what you've been through. Give a description of this psychopath. It can only help, right? Everyone can keep their eyes out for him."

"She's right, darling," Mum concurs. "It can't do any harm, and think about it – if people are more aware, they can exercise greater caution. You might save a life, Maisie! You'd be a hero!"

"No, I—"

"I bet someone out there recognises this creep. You might have this entire situation resolved before bedtime," Rainy interrupts. "Oh my God, Faith, you're a genius."

"And Peters would be thrilled to have you on," Faith adds brightly. "His show has nearly forty thousand listeners apparently."

I wince. "That many?"

"It's gone national lately, too, they stream it online now. He interviewed that minor celebrity last month, and the segment went viral." She retrieves her phone. "Look."

The figures displayed make my stomach twist. Thousands upon thousands of followers.

"It would help people understand what happened to you," Faith continues, oblivious to my mounting panic. "Put a human face to the story."

"Story? This is my life, Faith. You make it sound like I'm making it up."

She waves dismissively. "You know what I mean. These things spread so fast nowadays. Better to control it than let others do it for you."

Her reasoning makes sense, even as something within me recoils at the prospect of thousands of strangers learning about my attack. Perhaps this is my chance to be believed. To be truly heard. To be someone.

But when they all turn to me with expectant expressions, the intensity of the situation makes my stomach churn violently. "Absolutely not."

They have the audacity to look confused, but it's Faith who speaks up. She looks downright offended. "Why not?"

"You think it was simple for me to endure this ordeal? Then repeatedly recount the details to law enforcement? You believe I want to share my experience with some stranger called *Peters* and have it broadcast all over the world? Hell no. Absolutely not."

"It's hardly worldwide, is it? It's a local station with national interest. And Peters is lovely. He'll treat you really well."

"Your friend could be the nicest guy on the planet – that doesn't mean I wish to reveal my darkest moments to him."

"Oh, he's not actually a friend. I just slept with him once. He's really nice though."

Mum rolls her eyes and turns away from her eldest daughter in exasperation.

"Faith, please. Just promise you won't tell him about me. In fact, all three of you, complete silence about this, yeah? This is *my* business to tell, not yours."

No one says anything.

"Please?" I implore.

They need to understand. I cannot have my private life broadcast. Faith is incredibly popular, always has been. If any of this gets out, the entire town will know within hours.

"Alright," Mum finally concedes. A light weight lifts from my shoulders, but I recognise my secret remains precarious, on the cusp of being shattered to pieces.

"You hear me, girls? We'll keep Maisie's secret, won't we? We support each other in this house."

I trust Mum's word. She may have been a rubbish mother, but she's not malicious. She's my mum. But I know my sisters' nods are utter bullshit.

As I finally escape the house, I notice blood trickling across my hand where I've picked the skin surrounding my nails. My nerves are so frayed it feels like I've completely disconnected from my body.

All I want to do is bury myself beneath the duvet and wait for this nightmare to end. Because it can't possibly go on forever.

Can it?

Chapter 13

"Maisie? There's someone on the phone for you." Caleb places his phone in my hand, and I glance up at him quizzically. He merely shrugs, kisses me on the forehead, and retreats to the living room to keep playing some thunderously noisy video game.

I speak tentatively into the receiver. "Hello?"

"Is that Maisie Tallow?"

"It is."

"Hi Maisie, my name's Peters, I'm a host at Shine FM. It's an *absolute* pleasure to speak with you."

I'm going to kill Faith.

An uncomfortable silence threatens to stretch between us, but it's promptly filled by Peters who, to his credit, does sound incredibly professional. He has a captivating voice. I just wish he weren't using it to speak to me.

"Sorry to catch you on this phone. I couldn't get through on your number."

So Faith took the liberty of providing him Caleb's number as well? Oh, her death is going to be slow and excruciating.

"Are you still there?"

I nod. "Oh, yes, sorry. But you're going to be disappointed. I'm not speaking on the radio."

"No, no, that's perfectly fine. Faith has already conveyed your sentiments on the matter. If you don't wish to go on air, I understand completely. But if you'd consider giving an interview, I believe it would be tremendously valuable to share your story. Warn people of the potential dangers."

"No, sorry, I'm not going to do that." I move to hang up the call.

"Wait! Please don't hang up. What if you remained anonymous? Come meet the team, see what you think. The girls on makeup might even give you a little makeover if that's your thing? It could boost your confidence."

"Makeup artists for a radio station?"

I practically hear his shrug through the phone. "Radio is streamed online these days. We have to look presentable, conceal the bags under our eyes." Cue nervous laughter. "So, what do you say? If we protect your anonymity, would you consider it?"

"Oh, I don't know. Talking about that experience is horrible."

"It's a chat between us – just you and me. No pressure whatsoever. If you become uncomfortable at any point, just say the word and we'll terminate the interview immediately. Absolutely no risk involved."

I chew pensively on the inside of my cheek. Peters is very convincing. If I remain anonymous, what harm could possibly come from this? And I've always been curious about behind-the-scenes operations at television studios. I suppose this is the next best thing.

"Alright, I'll come meet with you. But I'm making no promises."

***

"Wow, look at that photo!"

Imarah gazes at me as if I've lost my sanity. It's only a picture of the radio hosts arranged in awkward poses, but it's been magnified to such proportions that they tower over us like giants. Their dazzling smiles showcase perfect teeth and cheerful eyes.

I shrug, dismissing her judgy look. "It's just big, that's all."

I'm beginning to regret asking Imarah to accompany me today. Because she works at the theatre, she's been 'warning' me about the entertainment industry all morning: how people might appear lovely, but they're nasty behind your back; about how one should always treat makeup artists respectfully, as they're not beneath us.

Does she think I emerged from the womb yesterday? As if I'd behave rudely towards anyone here. I'm not a rude person!

Now I'm contemplating how to tactfully drop her.

We're escorted to a small room featuring a bowl of sweets on a low table and bottled water arranged in a glass-fronted refrigerator. The entire space is painted a shade of blue that instantly makes me feel claustrophobic. It reminds me of the police station.

"Peters will be with you soon," a young assistant informs us, throwing me the warmest smile. "There are refreshments in the fridge, please help yourselves." And then she's gone.

Imarah perches elegantly on the sofa and hugs a cushion against her midriff. "So, you're staying anonymous, right?"

"Absolutely. I really don't want to be recognised for this. It just feels so wrong."

She nods understandingly. "I get it. And with that in mind, you're sure about doing this?"

With some persuasion from Peters, I've agreed to a pre-recorded interview on the condition that he won't disclose my identity and I remain off-camera. We've chatted on the phone daily since our initial conversation. His charisma is otherworldly, and his kindness genuine. I truly feel we're developing something approaching friendship. I've been excited all week about meeting him.

And now I'm here.

"I'm sure," I say, though not entirely convinced myself.

Naturally, I've researched Peters online, and he's super hot in his pictures. The whole package. I can't believe that Faith managed to attract someone with such defined abs. With her loud mouth and brash personality, I would have expected him to have better taste.

My phone vibrates in my pocket and I pull it out to read the text: *Now you're lying on the radio? Tut tut tut.*

My face burns as I stare at the screen, willing the message to just disappear. A cold shiver travels down my spine. I turn my phone over repeatedly in my hands, resisting the urge to scan the room nervously. They know I'm here. They know I'm lying. *But who are they?*

I pray this is a figment of my imagination. But the message remains there, sitting on my screen and propelling me towards a nervous breakdown. My pulse accelerates and sweat breaks out on my brow.

"Everything alright?" Imarah asks, her expression full of concern. "You look like you've seen a ghost."

I smile weakly and push my phone into my bag. I'll ignore it. Whoever they are, they can message me all they like; they can't hurt me. "I'm fine," I whisper. "Just nervous, I suppose."

"You don't have to go ahead with this, Maisie. Just say the word and we'll walk straight out of here. No questions asked."

Imarah: beautiful, inside and out. Her support strengthens my resolve. I reach out and gently squeeze her hand. "What would I do without you?"

She beams back at me. "Right back at you. Best friends for life, you and me."

"Damn right."

Imarah's concern is simultaneously touching and induces panic, but I force a smile. I can't deal with her protectiveness at this moment. I need to *breathe.*

"Maisie Tallow?" a masculine voice calls from behind me. I turn and find myself immediately blindsided by Peters' good looks. If someone were to ask me to imagine a hot guy, Peters would pop into my head. Perfectly chiselled features, a blinding smile revealing perfectly straight white teeth, thick blonde hair styled with effortless sophistication. His Wikipedia page says he's six foot five, a colossal height compared to my own, with shoulders so broad he could enfold me in the biggest hug, protecting me forever.

I rise and with a smile, offer him my hand. "Nice to meet you, at last."

He clasps my hand firmly. "The pleasure is all mine." He locks eyes with me, as if Imarah has ceased to exist. I notice he doesn't rush to release my hand, and warmth floods through my entire body.

I feel seen. I feel attractive. I feel *alive*.

"Please, come with me. Don't worry, I'll look after you."

Imarah stands behind me, but I motion for her to stay where she is. "I've got this," I assure her with a smile.

Her eyebrows crease. She looks alarmed.

"It's okay. Just wait here. I won't be long."

She sits back down as if scolded. Peters acknowledges her with a nod and a wink. "We won't be long. Feel free to help yourself to anything in the fridge."

He guides me down the corridor and up a staircase, where we reach the studio. 'Shine FM' is emblazoned across the wall in spray paint, and the lighting is subdued and soothing.

"And this is where the magic happens," Peters says playfully. He pushes open another door, and we enter a room equipped with microphones and countless buttons. Some blink up at me, performing their own little disco.

"I'm not going on air!" I panic.

He raises his hands reassuringly. "No, no, Maisie, don't worry. I don't broadcast until later. I'm reserved for peak times," he smiles. For a moment I think he might wink again; thank God he doesn't. This isn't the time to flirt. "We'll just record our conversation here. Just you and me. Is that okay?"

I nod, though still unsure. I wring my hands as I take in my surroundings.

The text message keeps taking up space in my head. They know I'm lying. They know I'm here.

But does that matter? They can't get to me. Whatever intimidation tactics they employ cannot affect me;

they have no evidence. If I repeat this to myself enough times, perhaps I'll eventually believe it.

Peters gestures to a seat beside him and I sit down, savouring his cologne with a deep breath in. He leans forward until we're unbearably close. "So, Maisie, I'm going to press this button to record, and this light will come on. If you need to stop, you can press that button to turn it off. You're in complete control here."

"Okay," I whisper, readying myself. His soft voice is pulling me in. I feel seen. Truly seen. And I lap it up greedily.

"This is going to be great," Peters declares, his smile perfect and rehearsed. I notice how his eyes repeatedly dart to the producer behind me, seeking approval.

I thought we were going to be alone.

For a second, his expression changes – calculated, almost hungry – before his charming mask slips back into place.

"You're being very brave," he continues. "Stories like yours need to be heard." There's something in his emphasis on 'stories' that gives me pause. Is it skepticism? Or something entirely different?

The red light begins to blink. My voice trembles initially, but as I continue speaking, something shifts within me. Perhaps I can do this after all.

***

"Well? How did it go?" Imarah asks as I re-enter the green room.

"Really well," I gush. "Peters is *so* nice. He was understanding and incredibly sweet. It was actually quite fun."

"Fun?!"

I backpedal quickly, painfully aware of how that sounded. "Well, maybe not quite *fun*. Cathartic, you know? As if speaking to Peters has released some of the pressure building inside me."

We make our way outside, where I blink against the harsh sunlight.

"You didn't feel like that when you spoke to me and Caleb? Or your mum?"

"Well, yes, of course!" I lie. "But Peters is a stranger, you know? It was just different somehow. He had no preconceived notions about me."

She looks at me as if I'm speaking a foreign language. "Right," she drawls. "Want to get a drink?"

"You know what? I think I'll walk home, get some fresh air."

"Sure. I'll come with you."

"No, no. You should go home. You must have better things to do than escorting me everywhere."

She wrinkles her nose at me. "It's not like that and you know it. I just want to be here for you. You must be going through absolute hell."

"Yeah, well, you can take a break. I'm doing okay."

"Sure?"

I want to scream at her to just go away. I want to reflect on the past hour with Peters. I want to revisit every minute detail before I start to forget things. To recapture the sensation of his hands enveloping mine, the way he gently dabbed at my tears when I began to cry. His gentle voice when he shushed away my pain.

Don't get me wrong, he's no Caleb. I love Caleb with every fibre of my being. But a harmless fantasy never hurt anyone. In fact, it probably reinvigorates a relationship to add a little spice.

That's what I'll keep telling myself, anyway.

"See you soon." I kiss Imarah's cheek and walk away.

The moment she's out of sight, I search for Peters online, simply to admire him. He gave me his number, but I have no intention of using it – surely he wouldn't want to hear from me? He must have more important matters.

As soon as that thought enters my head, my phone vibrates in my hand. It's him. I nearly drop my phone in excitement.

Peters: *Great to meet you today. You did really well. Call me sometime, I'd like to take you out for a drink as a token of appreciation.*

Holy shit. Has Peters just asked me out on a date? I push away the sickening thought that he's slept with my sister. It's not as if I'm planning to jump into bed with him, anyway. A drink, as friends, is harmless.

Before doubt can creep in, I reply: *How about tonight? x*

Maybe the kiss was too far. Oh well, the message has been sent now, and it was only one. Hardly flirtatious.

I wait for his response, but when it doesn't come, I pop into Boots. A woman deserves a small indulgence after sharing her harrowing ordeal with a stranger.

Ten minutes later, I emerge with a new perfume and a smile on my face.

Peters has texted back. We're meeting tonight.

Chapter 14

I've just discovered that the best thing about Caleb never asking about my job is that it makes the perfect excuse.

"So what's this Jan like?" Caleb asks me now. He's perched on the edge of the bed, watching me slick on lipstick.

He's just got back from work – late – and acting weird. It's as if he's taken some kind of stimulant; he's jumpy and excitable. Though when I told him I was going out with my 'friend from work', his face immediately fell. Now he looks so on edge I almost feel sorry for him. Maybe if he hadn't arrived home from work so late, I might have changed my mind. But now that I know he's feeling abandoned, I am secretly enjoying giving him a taste of his own medicine.

I've arranged to meet Peters at The Crooked Pot, a pub in a neighbouring village. I've already Googled the menu and it's expensive.

"Maisie? What time do you think you'll be back?"

My phone rings, saving me from this awkward conversation. It's Evelyn.

"We've got him," she says, voice taut with barely contained excitement. "A suspect. In custody."

The world tilts beneath me. "You— What? How?"

"The trail wasn't as cold as we thought. A man matching the description you gave us was spotted near the area that night. We pulled his car on an unrelated violation and found some ... concerning items."

"What kind of items?" My mouth has gone dry.

"I can't discuss specifics of an ongoing investigation, but enough to bring him in for questioning." Her voice softens. "We'd like you to come in, Maisie. See if you can identify him."

The room spins. A real person. A real man who will be punished for something that never happened. "Is that— Is that necessary? I told you I didn't see his face clearly."

"Even the smallest detail might help. The shape of his jaw, his posture – anything could be the piece that helps us build our case. And you'll be surprised what comes back to you when faced with the perpetrator. You'll be given the utmost support."

I want to throw up. Caleb is looking at me confused; I turn away. We make arrangements. I can fix this. I can help this poor guy.

Eventually I hang up and turn to face Caleb.

"What was that about?"

"Nothing."

"Maisie?"

"Caleb, what's your problem? You're bothering me. I never go out with my friends and now you're acting like Miss Fucking Marple. In fact, you're always pushing me to have a life outside this house. And now I am, you're all butt-hurt."

"No, it's not that. I just want to know what's going on, that's all."

"Why? You're acting really shifty. Spit it out."

He sighs. "I made reservations at One tonight. I was just looking forward to treating you, that's all. I wanted it to be a surprise."

One. The most exclusive restaurant in town. Where the fish is supposedly on a whole new level and the chef personally welcomes the guests. The Prime Minister himself has been known to dine there when visiting this part of the country.

"How did you manage that?! I thought One booked up months in advance?"

"I made the booking months ago."

My mouth hangs open. Caleb has never displayed this level of romance before. He's more of a take-away-pizza-in-front-of-the-football kind of guy. "Oh, Caleb!" I squeal.

Right now, I have a choice to make. Meet Peters to satisfy my need to feel special and beautiful; or go out for dinner with the man I love, but who usually lets me down.

I realise now, though, that Caleb *has* been there for me lately. And despite Peters being incredible during the interview, he's not the one who's supported me throughout this entire ordeal.

I can't lose my head here. No – I'd be mad to choose Peters over Caleb, no matter how special I feel around him.

I pick up my phone. Despite knowing this is the right decision, I can't suppress the feeling of regret and sigh as I type out the message. As much as I love Caleb, Peters made me feel sexy again and I've been clinging to that feeling all day, quivering with excitement. And now it all comes crashing down.

"What are you doing?" he asks, hope illuminating his face.

"Cancelling Jan."

"Really?!" He's like a puppy who's just been told he's going for a walk. He jumps up and waits eagerly for me to finish texting before pulling me into his arms. "Yes! Maisie, you're going to love it. I've already looked up the wine options and paired them with the food I think you'll choose. Of course, I might have ballsed it all up. But at least I've tried, eh?" He laughs nervously.

I'm stunned. That's a level of thoughtfulness I never knew Caleb was capable of. Why does this feel like so much more than just dinner?

Then it dawns on me. If Caleb is this excited about dinner, maybe it's more than just a meal out. Maybe he's proposing! At long last.

My heart leaps into my throat at the prospect, and I rush to get changed. Tonight deserves my classiest dress, the best makeup, and more time spent styling my hair.

"Wear your navy shirt," I instruct Caleb. "We should match."

He looks confused but goes along with it. Half an hour later, I'm wearing my finest navy blue dress and ready to take our relationship to the next level.

***

We're having dessert, and Caleb *still* hasn't proposed. I've rummaged through the chocolate mousse that Caleb selected for me, expecting a glistening diamond to be nestled at the bottom of the dish. But there's nothing, and the mousse no longer appears appetising enough to eat.

I glance around uncomfortably. As the evening has drawn on, I've felt increasingly uneasy. Like someone is watching me. I suppose that's what lying to people you love does to you – makes you paranoid.

"Everything okay?" Caleb asks with his mouth full, spraying me with chocolate mud cake.

I nod, forcing a cheerfulness I don't feel. "This has been truly wonderful. The food ... wow. The company—"

He looks at me expectantly. I was going to criticise him for not having proposed, but that wouldn't be fair. And the night is young. Perhaps he has something planned after this. A romantic stroll along the river? Or maybe something extra special like hiring a rickshaw. I've seen couples doing that in London and it looked so romantic. Do they even have those here?

"Maisie? Is everything okay? You seemed to really enjoy your dinner, but now you've completely shut down. Did something happen? Did you not like it?"

"No, nothing happened," I snap.

"Oh?"

I exhale forcefully, forcing myself to calm down. "Everything's great, Caleb. The food was amazing. The company is even better. Tonight's been wonderful. I just ... didn't expect this."

"Well, after everything that's happened lately ..."

The insinuation hangs between us. I really don't want to discuss my attack, and I'm furious at Caleb for mentioning it. "Please don't, Caleb. Don't ruin this."

He waves dismissively, and I realise he's slightly drunk. "No, no. I just wanted to do something special for you, you know? After everything you've been through, you deserve to be spoiled a little."

That doesn't make sense. "I thought you booked this months ago?" If he arranged this because of my attack, how did he book it beforehand?

He blushes. "Well, it was, just not by me."

I lean back, stunned. "Who made the booking, Caleb?"

"Why does that matter? We're here, aren't we? Enjoying ourselves?"

"Who made the booking?"

He sighs and looks away. "Troy. He booked it for Evelyn's birthday. He didn't want it to go to waste." His eyes return to mine. "But their loss is our gain, right?"

It feels as if the bottom has dropped out of the entire evening. This was never a proposal. It was just Caleb piggybacking on his friend's romantic plans. And worse, plans that were cancelled because that friend cheated on his girlfriend! "Oh, Caleb!"

"What?"

"I thought you were doing something nice for me."

"I am! I'm making an effort, aren't I? Who do you think is paying for all of this?"

I can scarcely believe what I'm hearing. All the magic has been stripped away and I feel exposed. A fool. Bollocks to this.

My chair scrapes across the stone floor as I stand, drawing all eyes to me. I throw my napkin onto the table and storm out into the pouring rain. I refuse to be humiliated like this. I came here believing this would be an extraordinary, life-altering event. But we are just Troy's sloppy seconds. And that makes me, by extension, just Caleb's afterthought.

I cancelled a night with Peters for this.

"Maisie, wait!" Caleb comes running after me, his feet splashing through puddles. "I'm sorry!" He sounds bewildered, as if he's completely unaware of what he's apologising for.

I don't turn around, but my heels impede my progress, and he catches up with me effortlessly. "I didn't mean to cast a shadow over tonight. I really just wanted a special evening with you, you know! Everything has been so shit lately, and I needed some quality time with you. And we had that, right? It was wonderful to just pause and really talk to you. I feel closer to you somehow. I loved every second of it."

He looks so determined to make me understand, so horrified by my reaction, that my icy exterior begins to thaw. Despite madly anticipating a proposal all night, he's right – I have thoroughly enjoyed spending time with Caleb. We've laughed, flirted, and truly connected for the first time in ages.

"I've loved it, too," I admit. "And I love you." As the words leave my lips, they've never felt more true. What was I thinking earlier when I agreed to meet Peters? What was that about? I was blinded, captivated by a handsome face.

I think, because everything has been so intense recently, I've made some silly decisions. I've been so distracted by the dramas surrounding me that I've pushed everything else, everything normal and familiar to me, away.

"Oh, Caleb, I'm sorry." He has no idea what I'm sorry for. He's blissfully unaware of the pain I've deliberately put him through. And for what?

It's as if someone has shone a light on me tonight. The extreme measures I've taken to feel acknowledged have overwhelmed me. I've forgotten who I am. What I do best.

And that's loving this man.

He pulls me against his chest and cradles my head in his arms. "Don't be sorry," he murmurs. "You have nothing to apologise for. I'm the one who should be saying sorry. I'm trying so hard, Maisie, I really am."

Oh, if only he knew. We stand there, the rain washing away my sins while I silently vow to put things right with Caleb. He's proven himself to me recently, and I've thrown that back in his face.

We stroll back to the car, hand in hand, lost in thought. He continuously swirls his thumb over the back of my hand, grounding me. And for the first time in a long while, I feel as if both feet are firmly planted on solid ground.

Even if he didn't tell me he loves me too.

***

The sex was fire last night. It was one of those sessions that started sensually and calm, but the slow and steady approach whipped us into a frenzy, and before I knew it, we'd fucked all over the house. Just like the good old days.

The proposal, or lack thereof, is a blow – make no mistake. But I know it's coming. If Caleb is willing to make an effort like he did last night, it only confirms how deeply he loves me. And with love comes marriage. It's simply the natural order of things.

I place Caleb's coffee on his bedside table and climb back into my side of the bed, clutching my own drink. Caleb immediately drapes an arm over me in his slumber and continues to snore softly into his pillow.

This is how mornings should be. Relaxed, peaceful, affectionate. My coffee is hot and sweet, my man is gorgeous and all mine. I snuggle down and decide to spend a few moments scrolling through my phone before Caleb's alarm goes off and we're thrown into our daily work routine.

As I'm settling against my pillow, a message arrives, startling me: *Well, did he propose?*

It's the same number as before. The arsehole who keeps messaging me. Tormenting me. I'm absolutely sick of it.

I hit reply: *Who are you?*

As if I'm going to tell you, Maisie. Where's the fun in that?

I squeeze my phone so forcefully that I drop it onto the bed. Just ten seconds ago, I was on top of the world, and this stranger has dragged me back down. No, I won't tolerate this anymore.

I slip out of bed and head into the bathroom. I turn on the shower, hoping it drowns out my voice, and call the number.

It rings without answer.

I try again.

You really think I want to talk to you? I don't speak with liars.

Yeah? Seems to me like you've got plenty to say. Now fuck off or I'll go to the police.

Oh, you won't do that.

No? You're a freak. You're talking shit and you know it. I'll have you charged with stalking me.

Lol. I wouldn't risk that if I were you.

What do you mean?

No reply.

What do you mean?

A photo appears. Me, examining my dessert at One last night, peering into the glass bowl, clearly searching for something.

So, did he propose? You looked so disappointed.

I hear my teeth grind together inside my skull. This person was watching us at the restaurant. That creepy feeling I had was real. The thought of eyes following me, documenting my desperation, makes my skin crawl. Was it someone at a nearby table? A server? I mentally scan the restaurant but can't recall a single face. I'd been too focused on Caleb; on my own aspirations.

This is far more serious than I initially thought.

You're not going to reply? But I was having such fun.

Leave me alone.

Maybe. Maybe not. I've got so many pictures to show you yet. I can prove you're a liar.

A cry works its way up my throat. I feel so exposed. Like this person possesses far more ammunition than they've shown so far, and it's all aimed directly at me.

I turn my phone over in my hand. How does this person know how to find me? Have I inadvertently clicked something I shouldn't have? Granted access to my camera without realising? Technology terrifies me sometimes, all the invisible ways people can slip into your life.

I could ignore them, but they'd still take up too much space in my head. They'd still have access to me. If I go to the police, it would significantly complicate matters that are already so messy, so precarious. I don't want to continue drawing their attention to me when I'm already walking a tightrope.

No, I need to flush them out. I need to discover who's sending these messages and end them for good.

So tell me … Do you have the same sexual connection with Caleb as you did with Peters?

Shit!

Chapter 15

"Maisie! How are you?" Mum sounds particularly chipper today. Without waiting for a response, she reveals why. "Rainy has had the baby. A girl! Nine pounds exactly, can you believe?"

"Wow, that's great news. What did she call her?"

"Bluebell-Rose."

"Oh. Well that's *pretty*." It's a lie. I hate the name.

"Isn't it? She's going to be gorgeous, I just know it. Like a Disney princess."

I can see that. With a name like Bluebell-Rose, I fully expect to see her talking to birds and rodents in a few years' time.

"Anyway, the reason I'm calling is, can you give me a lift to the hospital tonight? Faith is on a flight somewhere and won't be back until tomorrow, so can you swing by when you're on your way there?"

I had no intention of visiting Rainy tonight. Until twenty seconds ago, I didn't even know she'd given birth, and I wanted to get home and listen to the radio. They're airing my interview with Peters tonight, and I wanted to listen in private. Preferably in the bath, wine in hand and surrounded by candles, in an attempt to soothe my nerves.

And even now that I know, I still don't plan on going. Would Rainy even want me there? I doubt it.

"Mum—" I start.

"Thank you, honey. Shall we say six o'clock? That should give us plenty of time to see her during visiting hours. I'll pop over the road and grab some flowers from the petrol station."

"Mum …"

"They usually have some lovely roses. Probably no bluebells. But that'd be a nice touch, don't you think? I'll go over there now in case someone else snaps them up."

"Mum!"

She finally shuts up. "Yes, Maisie?" She has the audacity to sound annoyed at *me!*

"I'm not going to the hospital tonight."

I can hear the confusion and frustration in her voice. "But why not? Maisie, she's given birth!"

"I know. And I'll see her after work tomorrow. But right now, I feel like Rainy has enough on her plate. I'm sure Steven and the kids will be visiting her tonight; there won't be any room for me in there!"

"I'm sure they can vacate the room for five minutes. I have every right to see my newest grandchild."

I glance over at Caleb, who's looking at me sideways from the sofa with wide eyes and a grin – he thinks this is hilarious. I roll my eyes at him and shrug.

"Sure. But Mum, I'm not going tonight. Sorry, I have plans."

"Plans? Maisie, what could be more important than this?"

I wrack my brain. I have no concrete plans, and having a bath doesn't really feel like a legitimate excuse. "It's Imarah. She's going through something at the minute. She needs me."

"Oh?"

I turn my back to Caleb so he can't see my face while I lie. Like that makes it somehow less terrible. "Yeah, she, erm ... she's had her heart broken. I've promised her a girls' night, and if I let her down now, I'm scared she'll do something silly, you know?"

Caleb yells at his video game, and I hold up my hand to quieten him.

"Oh, darling, that's just dreadful. Give her my love, won't you? But are you definite you cannot reschedule? I mean, a baby surely trumps a tiff with a boyfriend."

"Mum."

"Okay, okay. I'll tell Rainy you can't make it and I'll get a cab. But, Maisie, she's going to be so disappointed."

"I'm sure she'll be fine." I doubt very much she'll even notice.

Aside from a couple of texts, my mum and sisters haven't bothered to check in on me after I told them about my attack. They couldn't care less about me, and the feeling is mutual.

Still, as blasé as I try to be about my family situation, it guts me that I've always been the odd one out. I don't know at what point my family wrote me off. Was it before my dad left, or after? I was too young to remember.

I remember at Christmas, Faith and Rainy would get matching pyjamas, while mine were always different – like an afterthought. I watched from the sidelines as Mum showered my sisters with love and offered me the tidbits when she remembered I existed.

Even as an adult, her love is conditional on my meeting her expectations. It's a flimsy kind of love. Like she can snatch it away from me at any second. I swear to

God if I disappeared, it would take them less than twen-ty four hours to forget me.

So, fuck them. I'm not going to the hospital. I don't care enough to take time out of my evening.

After I hang up, Caleb walks over to me and presses a hand on my shoulder. "Maisie?"

"What?"

"Rainy's given birth. That's a pretty big deal. You don't want to see her?"

"Not really." I walk away, determined not to get the third degree from him as well.

But he follows me. "But don't you think it would do you some good to spend time with your family? Meet the new baby?"

I laugh sarcastically. "I can't think of anything worse, actually."

He pulls a face of disbelief. "Oh, come on! You love them, really. Even if they can be a little difficult some-times."

"Caleb, don't."

"And what was that about Imarah? Is she okay?"

"She's fine," I sigh. "I just said that to shut Mum up about going to see Rainy."

"You lied?!" His look of incredulity is almost comical. Like I've committed the worst transgression known to mankind. He's such an innocent darling.

"It's no big deal. Mum was rabbiting on. I had to tell her something just to get rid of her."

"Lies have a way of catching up with you, Maisie." He shakes his head at me and pulls back, and I take the opportunity to head upstairs to run the bath. The interview is being broadcast soon, and I want to hear it from start to finish in the warm cocoon of lavender-scented bathwater.

As I'm running the bath and piling my hair on top of my head, Caleb calls out as he climbs the stairs. "I'm going out!"

I pause. "Oh?"

He joins me in the bathroom, his eyes roaming my naked body in approval. "Yeah, meeting some of the lads. I won't be late."

I lick my lips, hoping to persuade him to stay. "You never told me."

"I only got the message just now. Not a problem, is it?"

I sigh. I can hardly ask him to stay while I'm hanging out in the bathroom. I'm not a psycho girlfriend. "No. You go and have fun."

He smiles at me and takes my hand, pressing a kiss to the back of it.

I have noticed lately he's kissing me anywhere but on the lips. Does he think I'm disgusting since the attack?

"You're amazing, Maisie Tallow. And don't you forget it."

"Don't *you* forget it, Caleb Rush," I poke at him. "You're a lucky boy." I kiss him on the cheek, lingering at his neck, letting my lips brush his sensitive skin ever so slightly.

He groans but pulls back. "I wish I could stay a little longer. You're very tempting, Maisie Tallow."

I giggle like a little girl. "You owe me."

"Deal." He wiggles his tongue suggestively and disappears out of the bathroom.

I quite like the idea of him missing me while he's out. Maybe I'll take some photos in the bath and send them to him.

***

Hello everyone, and welcome back to Shine FM. Now, I've got a story for you all that should probably come with a trigger warning. I recently secured an interview with a young lady who was attacked up on Branton Ridge on Tuesday,

15th September. This young lady's story has gone unnoticed by the media so far, and I felt it important that I give her a voice and warn you of what lurks out there in our community.

I feel a rush of excitement. Here's my moment in the spotlight. Where everyone gets to hear my story, my words broadcast into thousands of homes across town. My story will be on people's lips. I can't believe I didn't want to do this! I feel famous! It's a meagre sliver of fame, but I bask in it nevertheless.

I'm introduced as 'Jane Doe', Peters making it clear that my identity will not be revealed in order to protect my privacy and safety. I hear myself say hello, and I almost melt with embarrassment. Though the more I hear myself speak, the more I like it. My voice sounds husky, sultry even. Probably because I was flirting.

Peters does a wonderful job teasing the facts out of me without making me feel accosted: how my attacker leered at me through my car window; how he grabbed me by the hair and yanked me out of the car; how he then pulled my jeans down only to be spooked by something in the woods and run off.

I tell my story with restrained detail. A woman caught between wanting to bury her secret and needing to warn the world. A woman in pain and denial. A woman who is brave and frightened, yet warm and likeable.

I hug my soggy knees to my chest.

I know Jane's story was hard to hear. We should all feel safe in our neighbourhoods, and yet Jane has shown what evil is out there. Probably living amongst us. If anyone has any information, please contact the police directly. Remember, we're looking for a man in his mid to late twenties, short brown hair, blue eyes. Wearing a black jacket and jeans. Let's catch this guy before he does this to someone else.

Next, Peters introduces a celebrity guest brought on to speak about my story. I don't know the celebrity', apparently, it's someone from a nearby town who has briefly appeared on *Love Island* and has been a victim of sexual assault a few years back.

They talk about how sorry they feel for me. What measures people should be taking to stay safe. What the police should be doing to catch this guy.

I don't want people to approach the police. I have already wasted so much of their time. Though I am interested to hear what they've been up to since I made the report. The guy they arrested turned out to be innocent, but I hear from Evelyn regularly. She wants to keep me in the loop, though she never has anything of substance to tell me. Just that they're 'making progress'. Whatever that means.

I refocus on Peters' voice and listen in horror.

Driven by sympathy for Jane, I have, in fact, spoken to the police myself. My contact there gave this statement: 'We are making steady progress in this case, and our investigation is advancing as expected. Our officers are following up on multiple leads and continue to work diligently around the clock. We encourage anyone with additional information to come forward.'

But here's the thing. After I got this official statement, they said something that got me thinking. They said, and I quote: 'We also must stress that when claims like these are made, the validity of the claim should be investigated alongside the reported crime.'

There's a moment of silence before Peters continues.

Don't you find that a little odd?

His guest replies. *What, how they're checking the validity of the claims? I'd say that's really weird.*

Exactly. It made me see things a little ... differently, shall we say.

Peters turns back to the mic and addresses the listeners in a more vibrant voice.

So, there you have it, folks. I'll leave it up to you to read between the lines here. Myself? I believe Maisie's story. But, and it's sad but true, we must remember that not everyone speaks the truth. So, what do you guys think? The phone line is open.

I slam my index finger into my phone, turning off the radio broadcast, and sink back into the bath, fully prepared to drown myself. How dare they?! They're currently sitting in that studio discussing the truthfulness of my claims, and I want to just die.

And he said my fucking *name!*

After all his promises of anonymity, of protection. The whispered reassurances. "Trust me," he'd said, his hand lingering on mine. "I'll take care of you."

What a fool I'd been. Peters wasn't interested in helping me – he wanted ratings born from controversy.

The heat of the bath suddenly feels suffocating, and I scramble to get out; the water is heavy, pulling me down. My pulse races, and I can't breathe as I stumble out of the bath. I leave a trail of drips on the carpet as I drag myself into the bedroom.

As I'm burying myself under the duvet, still soaking wet, my phone buzzes. I don't want to look. But my sick curiosity compels me to pull my phone close to my face, and I look at the screen through squinting eyes.

Did you hear my little police tip-off? I won't let you get away with this, Maisie.

Chapter 16

"Maisie?" Caleb's voice slices through the darkness, gentle but searching. Testing to see if I'm awake. I've never been further from sleep.

Two hours have passed since my interview played on Shitty-Shine FM. I prayed that no one listened to it and I could brush it under the carpet as a regrettable experience, but when my phone started incessantly beeping, I knew that dream was dead in the water.

"You awake?" He sits on the edge of the bed and presses a cold hand on my upper arm. I can smell the booze clinging to him, but his words are steady and coherent, his movements controlled. He's back earlier than expected, which only confirms it – he heard the interview. And now he's here to check on me.

I shift to look up at him, tears swimming in my eyes, making his face blurry. Does he believe the nonsense Peters was spouting about me? How the truthfulness of my police report is apparently up for debate? Has the interview planted seeds of doubt in his mind?

"What are you doing home so soon?"

"I came to check on you."

He sounds so serious, and for a second, I think he believes I'm a liar. The thought compresses my ribs, making my breath come in shallow gasps.

But then: "That was brutal. So fucking horrible."

Relief floods in so fast, it's dizzying. He didn't believe them. He still believes me. The relief knocks me back, and I dissolve into tears, throwing myself into his arms.

"I'll fucking kill him, you know. That Peters can rot in hell. What he said about you ..."

I don't want to think about what he said about me. After turning off the broadcast and breathing through the panic, my masochistic side compelled me to turn it back on. I had to know what they were saying about me.

They had sat there, cool and detached, providing a 'balanced argument' and dissecting the problem of women lying about sexual assault. How false accusations destroy innocent men's lives; how liars make it harder for genuine victims to be believed. They didn't explicitly state that I am a liar – but they didn't need to.

I was the fodder who launched the debate. I was the liar being discussed.

I want to scream. I didn't do any of the things they're accusing me of. No one has been falsely arrested. Or even accused. No one else, anyway.

If anything, my account will surely embolden women to speak up. *I'm* not making a mockery of the women who need to report these crimes, that damn show is! As if anyone will come forward now, when they're afraid they'll be accused of fabricating stories by a local radio host with turkey teeth and some D-list celebrity.

"You'll stay away from him," I tell Caleb. But his body is so tense, I know he cannot hear my plea right now. "Please, Caleb. Don't make this about him."

Make it about *me!* That's what all this started with in the first place, a desperate bid to get the attention I deserve. Oh, how things have changed. How they've exploded out of my control. I've got the attention I craved, but from all the wrong people and for all the wrong reasons.

I wish I could take it all back.

"I really need you right now," I tell Caleb, and he slides into bed beside me, pulls the covers up to our chins, and wraps his arms around me. I feel safe.

"Oh, Maisie, I really thought you were doing better. Why did you do this?"

"I don't know!" I say with a wobbly voice. And it's the truth, why on earth did I do this to myself? What did I hope to achieve?

I had to turn my phone off. Every second, the screen lit up with comment after comment, tagging me in threads dripping with vitriol. *Liar. Disgusting whore. You deserve to die.* They claim I'm an evil bitch. That I'm a disgrace to women and a terrifying threat to men.

Internet sleuths have done their research and my full name and picture is already everywhere. My face. My life. I'm being eviscerated by people who don't even know me.

All because of some trivial throwaway comment made by a police officer. They never actually stated I wasn't telling the truth – Peters just transformed it into something bigger, more sinister. The police just said they're being thorough, which is the entire point of an investigation, is it not? It's astonishing what people can infer when reading between the lines. Then they run with it.

This is my life they're ruining. Can they not see that? Do they not recognise the real person behind their vicious remarks? A person with feelings, a conscience. Someone with a potentially fragile mental health and terror lurking beneath it all.

"I'll call the police in the morning," Caleb whispers into the darkness. "Get all this straightened out."

"What?"

"They need to take your case seriously, not talk nonsense to the local media. They need to do their fucking job and find this guy. He needs to get what he deserves."

"You're not calling the police, Caleb."

I feel his head turn to look at me in the dark. I'm grateful he can't see my face.

I just want all of this to go away. I've already emailed Alec at work, requesting time off. Given his swift acceptance of my request, he's undoubtedly heard about the radio show.

My plan is to hide in bed and not venture out until the public finds something else to talk about. I understand how these things work. One minute they'll be dissecting me, the next they'll be condemning some celebrity caught cheating on their pregnant spouse.

Fickle. That's what they are. Fickle and pathetic.

I'm exhausted. Exhausted and broken. I know I've created this mess, but I never anticipated it would grow like it has. Like a malignant tumor. Out of control.

Of course, my plan of letting it blow over depends on one critical factor. It all hinges on whether the vindictive arsehole who keeps messaging me can let it rest.

Surely I've suffered enough? They suspect I'm lying, but they can't know with certainty. That uncertainty will presumably force them to restrain themselves. Or are they so deranged they'd destroy my life based on nothing but speculation?

Or is it speculation? Maybe they *do* know something. My breath catches at the thought.

I'm damn sure no one else was there that night. I was in the middle of nowhere. No one witnessed anything; I know it, and doubting myself can only lead to trouble.

But then, whoever sent those messages has got my phone number. They're technologically savvy. I've Googled myself, and my number doesn't appear anywhere online. They must have hacked something. And if they're that clever, who knows what evidence they could conjure up.

False evidence can appear compelling when you're already villainised.

Or maybe they didn't have to track down my number. Maybe they already had it. Maybe ... they know me. The room tilts violently. My stomach heaves. I lurch toward the bathroom, but I'm too slow and I vomit on the carpet, Caleb shouting panicked cries behind me.

Whoever it is, they're out there, watching, waiting, on the brink of ruining my life. And there's nothing I can do to stop them.

Chapter 17

My plan to stay in bed all week is interrupted the very next morning by a hammering at the door. I'm in the bathroom when the knocking begins, and I freeze until I hear Caleb stagger down the corridor, zipping up his shorts.

I tread quietly out of the bathroom and lean over the banister, careful not to be seen.

My first thought is that it's Imarah. She's been trying to contact me since the radio interview, but, feeling ashamed, I told her I'm just too sick to meet. She knows I'm lying, of course, but she's giving me the space I'm too embarrassed to explicitly ask for.

The voice downstairs is male – not Imarah then. I don't catch what the visitor says, but Caleb's voice rings loud and clear. "Fuck off, will you? You really think she needs this right now?"

"But, sir, we want to get her side of the story. We think Maisie deserves a chance to have her say."

Shit. It's the press. I crouch down, wanting to avoid any shred of media attention.

"You heard her story last night. Before it was shot to shit by that nasty piece of work radio presenter. All this needs to stop. Right now! You need to get the fuck away from my house. The police need to be doing their fucking job. And I need to be getting to mine."

The door slams shut.

I creep over to the window where I can hear voices outside. I count six people, all milling around, Mrs. Jennison among them, speaking into a damn microphone. No doubt more neighbours will be joining her to gawk at the woman who allegedly lied about being sexually attacked. A tall man with glasses looks up at me, and I squat down out of sight.

Before Caleb comes back upstairs, I crawl back to the bedroom, not wanting him to see me squatting on the floor like a weirdo. He joins me and I notice, even in his anguish, he can't resist running his eyes up and down my body. I don't know whether I find that flattering or disturbing. I choose the former; there's no more room for negativity right now.

"Who was at the door?" I ask.

"Oh, no one."

He turns away from me, always a sure sign that he's lying. I'm grateful for it. I love that he's trying to protect me, and a rush of affection suddenly overwhelms me. I run to him and loop my arms around his waist. He hesitates before bringing his arms around my shoulders. He places a gentle kiss on top of my head.

"Please stay with me today," I whisper.

He sighs. "I just need to go in this morning. I've got a job I really need to finish. But I'll have a word with Malek about taking some time off."

My heart sinks. If I could hold on to him and never let him go, I would, but I just don't have the strength. I feel like there's so little of me left. "You promise?"

"I promise I will ask," he says noncommittally. He pulls away and holds me at arm's length. "Just promise me you won't answer the door today."

I smile up at him. "I heard what you said to that reporter, Caleb. And thank you."

He just shakes his head. "Vultures. The lot of them. But do you promise me?"

I nod. "I promise. I won't even open the curtains."

"That's probably a good idea. I swear to God if anyone upsets you, I'll ..."

"You'll do nothing, Caleb. Don't go making this worse than it already is."

He runs his tongue over his top teeth. "Fine."

He busies himself getting ready for work while I settle on the sofa, piling up blankets and snacks. I open the back door for fresh air. If it weren't for the perpetual dread of everything, this might actually be really cosy.

Not long after Caleb has gone, I hear the letterbox rattle.

Groaning, I force myself up to see what it is. Maybe it's just the postman, and I'm being paranoid. I'm bound to be a bit shaky with everything going on. But I hesitate, and when the rattling continues, I jump back in shock.

A male voice calls out, "Miss Tallow! Are you in there? We just want to talk to you!"

Fucking press. Caleb was right; they're all vultures, feeding on pain for entertainment, poorly disguising it as news.

"Fuck off!" I shout.

"There's no need to be like that. We're on your side."

For a fleeting moment, I'm tempted. I long to fight back, prove my innocence. But common sense quickly prevails. If I've learned anything lately, it's that every-one is only on their own side. And I'm not deluded enough to think they'd present me as a victim – viewers will want to see me slaughtered. I know that from the online reaction to my interview.

"Please. Please, just leave me alone," I inject more fear into my voice, playing the damsel in distress.

He sighs and before finally retreating drops a blue business card through the letterbox. "Here's my card. Call me."

I have to fight the urge to spit on it.

When I re-enter the living room clutching the card, something feels off. Something I can't put my finger on. It's as if something has been moved, but I can't figure out what it is. Trepidation makes me pause. What is it?

Slowly, I edge towards the sofa, and spot something white tucked under the edge of my blanket.

A piece of card. It's blank, just plain white and folded in half.

Someone has been in here.

Blood rushes through my ears as I stare down at the piece of paper like I'm waiting for it to jump up and bite me. Just like the first time I got one of those texts. That same cold, creeping sensation runs down my spine.

Jumping into action, I rush to the back door and slam it shut, ensuring it's double-locked before heading back into the living room and scooping up the card in shaking hands. I hold it out in front of me as if it's about to explode.

All kinds of scenarios flit through my mind. My more positive side thinks maybe this is a note of support. Just what I need right now. But my more realistic side tells me I'm being stupidly optimistic.

It's most likely hate mail, and I'm half-tempted to throw it straight in the bin. No good can come from reading words of hate.

And they were inside my house.

Of course, I know who it is – that goddamn stalker.

I have repeatedly called their number, but it just rings out; it doesn't even go to an answering machine. Then they'll text me: *I don't talk to liars.* And I end up throwing my phone down in frustration, feeling lost and power-less.

As desperate as I am to know who is doing this, I don't know where to start in trying to find them. How do you find someone when you have no idea who you're look-ing for? Besides searching the internet for their phone number, I have absolutely nothing to go on.

Maybe I should hire a private detective? But then, my money only just about covers my share of the bills as it is. And I'd be lucky to find someone to help me, now that I am public enemy number one.

I've also toyed with the idea of speaking to Evelyn in a non-professional capacity, but I really don't want to add fuel to the fire. I don't know her that well, and I can't be certain she'd help me as a friend and ignore her role as a police officer. I don't want police involvement in this, not when they might just arrest me for wasting police time.

So, I'm stuck.

Gritting my teeth, I force myself to unfold the card. It's a screenshot. It takes me a few seconds to figure out what I'm seeing. It's all just words and numbers.

I cry out as realisation smacks me in the chest. It's my search history.

On the bottom is a date stamp showing the date and time of my attack – when I was waiting for Caleb to come and get me.

Whoever this is has hacked my phone. And has evidence that'll confirm what everyone is saying about me. Evidence that'll end my relationship with Caleb and friendship with Imarah – the only two people on the planet I love.

There's a note scrawled across the bottom of the photo in thick black marker. CAN'T WAIT TO SHOW CALEB WHO YOU TRULY ARE. *LIAR.*

***

My foot is practically pressed to the floor as I race through the centre of town to get to the garage where Caleb works, before this psycho stalker does. Why isn't he answering his damn phone?! The petrol light blinks an angry, insistent warning, but I can't stop now. I need to get to him before they do. I don't know what their intentions are, but I sure as hell don't intend to find out.

I park with a screech of tyres and fly through the garage, ignoring the calls of greeting and confusion from Caleb's colleagues, and I eventually spot Caleb through the window of his boss's office. I burst through the door, and they both spin around to stare at me, mouths open, neither of them knowing what to make of the crazy lady interrupting their meeting.

"Caleb," I say through heavy breaths. A crippling stitch in my side knocks more air out of me, and I fall against the doorframe, clutching on for dear life. My eyes scan the room in search of that same telltale piece of card that will destroy everything I have fought so hard for.

Did my stalker deliver here too? Did I get here in time?

Caleb comes to me and holds both of my hands in his. "Maisie, what happened?" he says, dipping his head to try and get me to lock eyes with his. "Maisie! Speak to me!"

If I could, I would. I can't breathe!

He hasn't seen the screenshot; that's for sure. He wouldn't be looking at me like that if he had. He wouldn't be looking at me at all.

He turns back to his boss. "I'm going to go, Malek. Thanks for that, mate."

Malek nods at him and waves us out of his office, probably pleased to be rid of the liability who just disrupted the entire workplace.

Caleb's colleagues watch, frozen to the spot, as we head out. My eyes flit around the workshop, but there's no sign of that innocuous piece of white card. And my shoulders relax, just a little.

He leads me back to my car, gripping my hand tightly in his and ignoring the questioning glances from his workmates.

"Come here," he says, pulling me into a tight hug. "Oh, Maisie, what happened?"

"I just got scared. There were people outside the house, and I didn't know what to do ... I needed you." The words stick in my throat for half a second. It's not really a lie, is it? I *was* scared. And I did need him. Just not for the reasons he's thinking.

He breathes in deeply and pulls back just a little. "Well, you've got me now. Malek just gave me two weeks off work."

"Really?!" I can't disguise my glee. Having Caleb at home with me – just me and him – is simply perfect. It's just what I need right now. It's all I've ever wanted. It's the dream that started all this.

"I'm going to look after you, you hear me?" Caleb says, smiling down at me, his eyes comforting, if a little distant.

I kiss him on the lips, and as a testament to how serious this is, we don't get one jibe from his workmates. Usually, they bark like dogs if a 'missus' turns up and shows a little affection.

Boys will be boys.

With one final kiss on the head and a quick check-in, Caleb jumps in his van, and with my heart rate finally steadying, I follow him in my car out of the garage car park and head home.

We're halfway there when my dashboard makes a jarring beeping sound, and the petrol light flashes at me, forcing me to turn in at the nearest petrol station.

Car now full of fuel, I drive home a little faster than legally acceptable, eager to see how Caleb intends to make good on his promise to look after me.

I find him standing in the living room, his cheeks red and his eyebrows dipping into a deep frown. The room feels too quiet, too still.

"Caleb? What's wrong?"

But his eyes don't meet mine.

He's gripping something in his hands so tight I can see the effort in his tense arm muscles. And then, finally, he holds it out.

I left it behind. In my panic, I did the one thing I ran off to prevent.

A piece of white card folded in half. Inside, a screenshot from my phone, proving I lied.

Chapter 18

"What's this?" he asks, confusion rather than anger etched across his face. "Why have you got this?"

"Oh, it's just something silly," I laugh, snatching it from him and crumpling it into a ball. "It can go straight in the bin."

I glide over to the kitchen like nothing untoward is happening. Like my heart isn't thumping so hard I fear it might push its way out of my chest. I've done plenty of stupid things in my life, but leaving physical evidence of my deception lying around surely tops it off.

Caleb follows me and tilts his head, studying me. Maybe I wasn't as nonchalant as I'd hoped. "Let's see it again."

"Why? It's just rubbish."

I bury the card deep in the bin, tucking it into yesterday's leftovers to deter him from pulling it back out. He slowly returns to the living room and I switch on the kettle, every nerve ending on fire with anticipation as I wait for it to boil. I've just finished stirring my tea when Caleb re-enters the kitchen and performs his ritual of staring at the fridge's contents.

I've got away with it.

But then, he says, "Hang on, what was the date on that picture?"

Shit.

Despite the knot in my stomach, I grab some biscuits from the cupboard to avoid making eye contact. "Oh, I don't remember. I didn't think it mattered."

He leans against the counter, watching me carefully as I arrange biscuits on a plate – something I've never done in all my life. "Maisie, why are you acting weird? Did someone push that through our door today? Was it a journalist? Christ, what a vile thing to do."

Yes, that's it! I nearly collapse with gratitude that Caleb has unwittingly provided the perfect cover.

"No wonder you were so frightened, Mais. It's sick, that's what it is."

I sip my scalding tea, my hand shaking visibly, dangerously sloshing the hot liquid around. I nod. "Yeah, it just freaked me out, that's all. But now you're home, I feel so much better. It almost seems silly to have let it bother me so much."

"No, no. It's completely understandable." I want him to pull me into his arms, but that questioning look doesn't wane.

"Should we order takeaway tonight?" I ask, desperate to change the subject. "My treat. Indian or Chinese?" I waffle on as I return to the living room, still avoiding his eyes.

"Indian," Caleb responds, distracted.

"Perfect, I'll order now so it's all sorted for later." I pull my phone from my bag. "Caleb, sit down. Why are you standing there like that?"

But he doesn't move a muscle, frozen in the middle of the room, thoughtfully scratching his chin. "September fifteenth," he states with sudden clarity.

My heart sinks. "What about it?"

"That was the date on that image."

"Was it? I can't remember."

"Maisie, that was the night you were attacked."

My phone slips from my grasp, bouncing across the carpet toward Caleb's feet. Heat rises from my chest, and creeps upward. "It was," I confirm. "And I'd prefer to forget it now, please. It's too painful to talk about." I feign wiping dust from the windowsill.

"Maisie, you're being really weird."

"Am I? Can you blame me with everything that's happening?"

His expression wavers between sympathy and suspicion, a man torn between his heart and his instincts. "Something isn't right here," he says, instinct winning.

I instantly jump into defence mode. "What exactly are you suggesting?" And immediately curse my stupidity.

I shouldn't have said that. Why would I encourage him to pursue this line of questioning? I should be moving him away from this conversation, not drawing his attention to the evidence. I've just made myself look fucking guilty.

But Caleb, ever the gentle soul, recoils and raises his palms in surrender. "Nothing! Nothing at all. Sorry, Maisie."

I pray that's the end of it. That we can move on.

But as I absentmindedly scroll through nearby Indian restaurants, Caleb breaks the silence. "I'm sorry, but I *have* to know, Maisie. Was that screenshot taken from your phone?"

"Oh, Caleb, give me a break, yeah? I'm so tired of all this."

"No, sorry, but I need to get to the bottom of this. Was that your phone? Did you search how to strangle yourself? Why would you do something like that?"

"It must be photoshopped!" I shout, a little too loudly. "Someone's probably trying to provoke me into giving an interview. Well, they can go to hell. I refuse to play their games."

"It looked pretty real to me."

"Caleb, you thought Katie Price's boobs were real! Now stop this, will you? You know exactly what happened that night. Why would I search for something so disturbing?" I pick nervously at the skin around my nails until I tear it off completely, drawing a bead of blood.

"You're a shit liar, Maisie."

I laugh then, a full-throated, maniacal sound. *Oh, is that right?*

I quickly compose myself. "This isn't happening. I can't believe you're calling me a liar. Caleb, I thought you loved me. If you did, you wouldn't be treating me like this."

He recoils, his eyebrows knitting together as he lowers himself into a seat.

I wait, struggling to maintain my mask of indignation rather than letting it slip into guilt. How can I claw this back? I silently implore any God who might be listening to make this all go away.

"Let me see your phone," Caleb says, his voice so quiet I pretend not to hear. "Give me your phone, Maisie!"

"Absolutely not. You either trust me or you leave. I won't tolerate these accusations from you. You're supposed to trust me."

"I want to trust you," he pleads, his voice cracking. "I really do. But you won't look at me. You refuse to meet my eyes. Something is going on."

I force myself to look him dead in the eyes. But it's too late to prove anything.

"Phone, Maisie."

"I can't," I whisper, the fight draining from me.

He studies me, eyes narrowing. "Why not?"

"I just can't."

He crosses his arms, leans back, and scrutinises me. "I listened to your interview," he says determinedly. "At the time, I put it down to nerves. I imagined talking about your experience to that radio host must have been really difficult." He swallows hard, his Adam's apple bobbing up and down.

I squeeze my fists so tight my nails dig into my palms. I'm dreading what comes next.

"But now I'm not so sure."

"I don't know what you're talking about," I say, but my voice betrays me, breaking mid-sentence. My eyes widen as my mind races. What is he talking about?

"I remember it, clear as anything. You told me that night your attacker had a bald head. Yet you told that radio guy he had brown hair. I understand details might blur, but that's a pretty big difference. Where are you going, Maisie?"

He springs to his feet and captures my wrist, preventing me from leaving.

But I can't stay here and listen to this. I don't have the words to fight it. Everything I might say would only sink me deeper into the hole, and I desperately need time to think this through.

"I need some air," I tell him. "I can't believe you're doing this to me."

"Me doing this to *you*? Maisie, we need to talk about this. The lies you've been telling *everyone*. Please, tell me what's happening because right now I'm imagining the worst possible scenario, and I don't want to think that of you. I really don't."

He sounds devastated. Uncertain. Desperate. Words fail me.

He continues softly, "You used to make me laugh. Remember our road trip to Wales? You entertained us for hours with those ridiculous stories. I'd never met any-one who saw the world quite like you did – everything was an adventure waiting to unfold. What happened to that woman, Maisie?"

I want to heal his pain. I want to fix everything, but I just don't know how. "Caleb," I begin. "I didn't mean ..."

"You made a mistake, right? You didn't intend to con-fuse the descriptions of the guy?"

I watch a single tear trace down his cheek. My shoul-ders slump as my conscience finally awakens. I can't do this anymore. "I didn't mean to hurt you."

He takes a step back, shaking his head in disbelief. "No, Maisie." More tears fall as he raises his hands to cradle the back of his head.

The truth surges within me with mounting pressure, making me dizzy and disoriented. I need to be close to the exit. I need an escape route before I open my mouth again.

"I wasn't attacked that night, Caleb." I daren't look at him. I wonder if I'll ever have the courage to look into his eyes again. "I just needed you to hear me. You weren't listening. And I was terrified of losing you."

"Maisie, I ..." He fumbles for words. "What the fuck?!"

"Look, I know what I did was really shitty, but it worked, didn't it? Look at how close we've become."

"No! You can't possibly suggest that what you did was okay. That it was somehow justified. No, that's absolute rubbish. It's twisted. And it's fucking cruel!" His voice escalates with each syllable. "Seriously! What could I possibly have done to deserve this?"

"What happened?" My own voice rises to match his. "You abandoned me, Caleb. I thought we were over."

His expression shifts from fury to bewilderment.

I explain. He *has* to understand. "The whole situation with Evelyn and Troy. You treated me like shit that night, Caleb. And then you walked out. I needed to get you back. I needed you to see exactly what you were throwing away."

He raises his hands to silence me. "Wait. You did all of this because of a simple argument? Oh, Maisie, no." His face flushes crimson, his mouth contorted into an expression of pure rage.

My tears fall freely now, pooling at my collarbone. I'm afraid to wipe them away. Afraid to move at all.

He strides into the kitchen before immediately returning, gesticulating wildly. "This is too messed up. I need you to leave. Now."

Panic overwhelms me now. "No, Caleb! We need to figure this out."

He turns away. "You know what hurts the most?" he asks without facing me. "I actually defended you to everyone. When Peters questioned your account on air, I telephoned the station and gave them hell. Made an absolute fool of myself." His laugh is empty, hollowed of all joy. "I stayed with you. But it was all lies."

"Caleb, I love you! That's not a lie. I love you and I have always loved you."

He makes a dismissive sound. "Just get out."

"Please." I fall onto my knees, begging him, my dignity completely stripped away. "Don't send me away. We can figure this out if we can just talk."

"GET OUT!"

I disregard his demands and crawl towards him. I cling to his ankles, imploring him, my words garbled and wet through my sobs. I don't even know what I'm saying anymore. I don't know the words that could possibly make this better. I just know I have to do something. *Anything.*

"Please, just go. You're making this worse," he says, tears streaming unchecked down his face, giving me a flicker of hope.

I sense an opportunity here; I just need to discover how to wedge myself into it. "No, Caleb. I'm staying so we can fix this. We belong together. I know it."

He roars then. Reaching down, he grabs my shirt at the shoulder, hauling me upright. Keening sounds escape me as he drags me forcefully towards the front door. "You know what, Maisie?" he demands, compelling me to face him. "I really wish I had left you that night. Our relationship was a farce, Maisie. You were always so needy, so suffocating. But I never imagined you were capable of this! I'm done with you."

With that declaration, he shoves me out of the house. I stumble forward. I could catch myself and retain some dignity, but what would be the point? I allow myself to collapse into the flower bed.

He doesn't reach out to help me as I'd hoped he would.

The crowd surrounding my house collectively gasps. I shut them out; I can't deal with that right now.

Caleb looks down at me, his eyes brimming with sorrow. His pain keeps that spark of hope within me. He doesn't truly want this. I know him too well. He's one of the good ones. He wouldn't kick me out like this.

"You were such a waste of my time," he pronounces, before pivoting sharply and slamming the door with devastating finality.

Chapter 19

"You and Caleb? I thought you two were solid!" Imarah says, shaking her head in disbelief.

So did I. Until I massively fucked up.

After leaving home, I came straight to Imarah's, where she's been tending to me like I'm a wounded animal. I haven't stopped crying, and snot keeps trickling into my mouth. She hands me yet another tissue, and I wipe my face again.

Taking a deep breath, I draw my knees beneath my chin and squeeze my eyes shut. I haven't told Imarah what the fight was about, and she's been gently probing for details since I arrived. I've messaged Caleb repeatedly, but he remains stubbornly silent. Right now, I just want to wallow in misery without explanation or justification.

"I'll put the kettle on," Imarah says, walking away. I exhale with relief. I know she means well, but her solicitude feels suffocating. Too nice. Far nicer than I deserve.

My heart aches for Caleb, but my shame burns hotter. The humiliation of being found out, of watching my lie unravel before my eyes, is unbearable. The thought of everyone learning the truth, especially those who've been throwing me shade, sends a spike of fear through my spine. I cannot stop shaking.

And now it just feels like a waiting game. When Imarah discovers the truth, I can kiss goodbye to our friendship, too. I'll lose everything.

My phone vibrates against the sofa cushion, and I snatch it up. It's him! He ignores my pleas for conversation, my apologies, my begs for forgiveness.

His response is brutally concise: *Your stuff's outside. Don't bother knocking.*

My heart plummets. He hasn't even checked that I'm okay. For all he knows, I'm wandering the streets homeless. And judging by the thick, black clouds gathering overhead, a downpour is imminent.

I can't just sit here. I can't lose my belongings along with my entire life and future.

Imarah approaches with two steaming mugs just as I'm heading for the door. "Where are you going?" she calls after me.

"Stay here," I tell her. "I won't be long." I'd like to take her with me. I'll need her help loading the car. But I can't risk bringing her close to Caleb. I can't have him telling her everything.

But she sets the drinks down and grabs her coat, falling into step beside me. "I'm not letting you drive in this state."

"Imarah, no ..."

"Tough. I'm coming with you."

I'm too exhausted to argue and we leave her apartment. "Just stay in the car, yeah?"

The journey passes in what feels like mere seconds, and as promised, everything I own has been unceremoniously dumped onto the lawn in black rubbish bags, packed without the slightest care. There's no sign of Caleb or his motorbike, and after loading Imarah's car, I sit for a while, gazing up at what was once my home. What I believed would be my happily-ever-after.

I contemplate the gravity of my situation. How much I've sacrificed because I became obsessed with controlling circumstances. With lying to get my way. I'm nothing but a foolish, selfish child.

"You okay?" Imarah asks softly, as if any sound above a whisper might trigger another breakdown.

I slam my palms against the dashboard, over and over, taking my frustration out on the poor car.

"Maisie, stop! You'll hurt yourself."

A flicker of movement in the rearview mirror. I twist around abruptly. A shadow? A trick of the light? My pulse stutters. I pivot in my seat, scanning the empty street, but there's nothing. Just the steady glow of street lamps. Then why does my skin prickle as though I'm being watched?

"What is it?" Imarah sounds perplexed now, probably regretting her decision to accompany her crazy friend.

But what was that? I continue staring into the mirror, trying to make sense of what my gut is telling me. Someone was there, I'm sure of it.

There's no one watching me, I tell myself.

Then why does it feel like there is?

Shaking off my unease, I instruct Imarah to drive away, leaving my profound discomfort behind us.

***

"You ready to talk about what happened?" Imarah asks as we settle down to watch a recording of Saturday's

Britain's Got Talent. "I mean, you don't have to. But I've got to admit, the suspense is killing me."

I can't suppress a small smile. I'm surprised she's lasted this long before asking directly, to be honest. I arrived at her apartment hours ago, and this is the first time she's truly pressed me. Another reason to cherish this woman.

I study her as she looks at me with wide, expectant eyes. I'm at a loss for words. We're lounging in our pyjamas. Imarah has just prepared a delicious lasagne, and we're tucked up in her bed, ready to eat. Everything feels so warm and comforting, and I'm not prepared to go and find somewhere else to stay. So I can't tell her the truth. She would never let me stay after learning what I've knowingly put her through.

"I think Caleb has been seeing someone else." The lie comes from nowhere. At this point it's as though lying is so deeply ingrained in my character, I've forgotten how to be honest.

Imarah gasps and covers her mouth with her hand. "No fucking way!" she says through a mouthful of food. "What makes you think that?"

"I found makeup on his shirt." The most clichéd excuse imaginable.

"Wait – are you sure? Caleb doesn't seem the type. Maybe there's another explanation?"

I shake my head emphatically. "I know what I saw, Imarah. The evidence was dead clear."

She bites her lip. "Yeah, you're right. Sorry." She takes another bite of food. "That bastard! What was it, lipstick on the collar?"

"Foundation," I say. "Just here." I gesture at my chest before turning my attention to the food, but my appetite is suddenly gone.

"Oh, Mais, I'm so sorry. But surely you two can work through this, can't you?"

"I don't know," I respond, truthfully this time.

"Well, you can stay here as long as you need."

I don't know how that arrangement could possibly work. Imarah's one-bedroom duplex apartment barely accommodates her, let alone the both of us. And, although I adore Imarah, sharing a bed with her doesn't have the same appeal as sharing a bed with Caleb.

"Thank you," I say. "I just need time to figure things out, you know?"

But she doesn't get the chance to respond.

A thunderous crash reverberates from below. Glass shattering. Imarah yelps, and my fork slips, leaving a trail of slimy pasta across the sheets.

Silence follows. My breath catches in my throat.

We're not alone.

"What was that?!" Imarah wheezes.

I shrug, too terrified to speak out loud.

Imarah whispers, "Did you leave a glass balancing on the draining board?" There's a hint of desperate hope in her voice, as if she's praying for a mundane explanation.

I shake my head.

"A window open? Perhaps it was just a strong gust of wind."

I shake my head again. She's clutching at straws now, and we both know it.

She grabs my hand. "Come with me? I don't want to go down on my own."

With excruciating slowness, we tread down the narrow staircase that leads to the open-plan living area, gripping each other's arms. The scenario resembles a horror film where the women invariably die first, usually due to their own foolish decisions.

Imarah peers around the corner, and we hover at the threshold. I wonder why we lacked the common sense to arm ourselves before venturing downstairs. All I have is my phone, ready to call 999. My only hope now is that Imarah possesses some hidden martial arts skills.

We quickly determine that the living room appears empty, and we edge around the wall to investigate behind the sofa to confirm. My heart pounds so violently I worry it might burst through my ribcage and splatter across Imarah's cream rug.

From where we stand, the kitchen seems deserted, too. But the pantry door is wide open – and obscures our view inside it. My stomach drops. Imarah glances at me questioningly, and I shake my head. Her eyes widen. Neither of us left it open.

My fear now merges with a primal urge to fight. There's no room for weakness. We either confront this fucker or become victims, and I'm not prepared to give up just yet. I scoop up a knitting needle Imarah left on the sofa and grip it tightly as we approach the kitchen.

Broken glass is scattered all over the floor. We tread carefully and position ourselves behind the open door, bracing for attack. With a surge of adrenaline, I charge into the pantry, yelling like Tarzan and brandishing the needle above my head. I leave Imarah behind, yelling at me to be careful.

But the pantry is as empty as the rest of the apartment. There's nothing in here but tins of beans and bags of pasta. And there's nowhere else to hide.

"How did the glass break, then?" Imarah asks, looking to me for answers.

"No idea. You sure you didn't leave it out while cooking?" Watching Imarah prepare dinner had been chaotic. I think she used every pan and utensil she owns.

But she shakes her head, looking down at the glass fragments glittering on the tiles. "That glass? I shoved it away at the back of the cupboard years ago. It was a commemorative one, you know? Mum gave it to me when I qualified, and I've never actually used it."

We turn on all the lights and look through the cupboards to determine if anything else has been disturbed. Then my heart sinks when I realise we hadn't even locked the front door. Idiots.

Imarah tries to dismiss it as one of life's inexplicable mysteries. I know better.

As I sweep up the glass, something else on the countertop catches my eye – Imarah's laptop is partially open. She never leaves it like that; she always keeps it closed when she's not using it.

"Did you use your computer earlier?" I ask her.

She frowns at me. "No, but it's been doing strange things lately. Sometimes it powers on by itself."

I close it firmly, a chill running through me. Someone has been here, and not just to shatter glassware.

They're messing with my head.

To confirm my point, my phone lights up.

You can't hide from me, Maisie. I'm not done with you yet.

Chapter 20

Imarah watches in horror as I hurl my phone across the room, where it makes a sickening crack against the wall before clattering to the floor.

"Maisie! What the fuck?"

"Sorry. I didn't know what to do. I panicked and I was stupid. I—"

"Whoa, slow down."

I'm gabbling utter nonsense. My words tumble out in incoherent sentences, and I can't organise my thoughts into any semblance of order. I'm trying to tell Imarah about my stalker. About my helplessness. About how I can't do it anymore.

"Stalker? Wait. What? Maisie, slow down, will you?"

I take a deep breath as Imarah guides me gently onto the sofa, forcing me to sit. She fetches me a glass of water, pressing it into my hands. "Right, now talk."

A flurry of thoughts races through my mind, from the stalker to my lies to Caleb, to the shattered glass. How much should I tell? Can I trust Imarah? What else might spiral beyond my control?

But ultimately, I must confide in her. I need her to understand at least a fraction of what I've been experiencing; and I have to ensure her safety, too.

"Someone has been stalking me."

Her eyebrows shoot to the ceiling in astonishment, but she waits patiently for me to continue. She's always possessed a remarkable talent for knowing when to just listen.

I take a few moments to gather myself and determine which path to take. "It started soon after my attack. They said they didn't believe me. About what happened."

Imarah emits a sound of indignation. "You didn't pay any attention to them, did you? Like all the other arseholes doubting you at the minute, just ignore them. You'll soon prove them wrong."

"I ignored them at first. But Imarah, they won't leave me alone. They're texting me all the time. And ..." I look directly at her, hoping my expression conveys my sorrow. "I think they're the one who was in your apartment just now."

Her eyes widen in disbelief and she holds that pose for just a second before leaning back in her chair and shaking her head. "No way. You're telling me this stalker knows where I live and just walked right into my home? Honey, I think the stress of everything is making you paranoid. There must be some rational explanation for the broken glass, but an intruder isn't it."

I tell her about the text I just received. The sensation of being observed outside my house. How they likely followed me here. By the time I finish, Imarah is leaning forward, her cheeks flushed, face buried in her hands.

"Oh, Maisie. Why didn't you tell me this before? Does Caleb know?"

I shake my head, eager to steer the conversation away from him.

"You should tell him."

"Why? He doesn't want anything to do with me anymore."

"Perhaps he would if he knew what you're going through. I mean, I wouldn't even care to take him back, cheating bastard; but I know you. You're more forgiving, more willing to put up a fight for what you want."

"What, and have him stay with me out of pity?"

"I thought you left him?"

Silence engulfs us. We regard each other intently, each waiting for the other to make the next move. I surrender first. "Actually, he left me," I admit quietly. And I might as well go the whole hog. "When I confronted him about his cheating, he ended things, not me."

Okay, maybe not quite the whole hog.

"Oh honey, I'm so sorry! Who would have thought he could be such a wanker. I've always liked Caleb."

That's exactly what concerns me. Caleb and Imarah were friends up until now. Not intimate friends, but their relationship was solid. Now I just pray they don't talk about me behind my back. But Imarah is loyal; she wouldn't contact Caleb without me knowing. And I suspect that Caleb, being a good guy, won't divulge my lie to others. He would hate to cause a disturbance. He likes a quiet life.

Besides, I've already received my punishment when he ended things. He knows that. I don't think I'll be found out.

But I want to make sure. "Please, don't talk to Caleb, will you? I don't want you two talking about me."

She looks puzzled. "Of course I won't talk to him without telling you first. You know I've got your back. Even if I do want to give him a piece of my mind."

"Imarah, no! Just leave it, yeah? I want to handle this my way. No offence, but outside involvement might just complicate things."

She nods in understanding. "You can trust me, Maisie." Reaching for my hand, she adds, "You'll be okay, you know. You will figure this out."

"I hope so."

And I really do. I cannot bear losing Caleb over this. It was just a silly mistake. Once he's over the initial shock, he'll recognise I did it for him. For us. He'll appreciate the measures I took to strengthen our connection. Won't he? Or is that my delusion talking?

"And I'll try my best not to chop off his balls in the meantime."

I laugh, but my heart isn't in it. Her faith in me feels like a crushing weight on my chest. If she knew the truth, would she still support me?

"Right, what are we going to do about this stalker? Do you really think they were in my apartment?" Her face goes a faint shade of green at the thought.

"It's the only explanation that makes sense. And considering that text ..."

"But what would they gain from doing that? It seems a bit risky, don't you think?"

"I don't think they care anymore. They're obviously unhinged."

Imarah gets up and heads to the door, double-checking the lock is secured. When she returns, she asks, "So, what did the police say?"

"About what?"

"The stalker, Maisie! Keep up!"

My cheeks flush.

"You haven't told them?"

"I wanted them to concentrate on investigating the attack. They haven't gotten any further since the false arrest, and I didn't want to burden them with this."

"Fucking hell, Maisie, you do make some stupid decisions. This lunatic came to my home! They could be dangerous."

I refrain from telling her that I suspect they are indeed dangerous. This person harbours intense hatred for me. They despise what I've done. And they refuse to let the matter rest. Earlier today, on my way to Imarah's, I had naively hoped that once they knew Caleb had discovered the truth, they would cease their torment. But evidently, they're determined to destroy me completely, which means I must find them before they tell anyone else my secrets. And before Imarah gets another unwelcome visit.

"Any idea on how I can trace a phone number?" I ask her.

"So, what? You're going to play police officer now?"

"Look, I'll contact the police tomorrow, okay? I just thought I could help out. You know how understaffed they are. It's all over the news."

She presses her tongue against her upper teeth – her characteristic thinking face. "There's a guy at work who's a bit ... eccentric. Really into computers, you know? When he talks about technology it's like he's speaking a foreign language. I could ask him?"

"How do you even know someone like that?"

"Maisie, *everyone* knows someone like that. Apparently, this kind of thing is actually really easy once you've been shown. It's just that most of us have a strong enough moral code not to do it."

"I don't know anyone like that."

"That's because you don't talk to anyone outside of your little bubble."

I can't deny that.

"So, want me to speak to him?"

"Yes! Please!"

"I'll do it tomorrow."

And for the first time in a long time I've been offered a glimmer of hope. It's small and tenuous, but it's there.

I might just be able to pull back from this. If I can't keep Caleb, I can at least keep my friendship with Imarah. And maybe my dignity.

I dare to hope.

"And Maisie?"

I look up at my best friend.

"No more secrets, yeah?"

"I promise," I lie.

Chapter 21

Imarah breezes in the next day, her eyes scanning the apartment. "Any sign of them?" she asks, prowling around like an FBI agent. She means my stalker, of course. She's frightened, and after yesterday's break-in, she has every reason to be.

"Nothing today," I tell her from my position on the sofa, where I'm inserting my SIM card into a new phone. After my temper tantrum yesterday, my old phone was completely destroyed, forcing me to dip into my meagre savings to buy myself a new one.

Imarah tosses her bag onto the floor and collapses next to me. She kicks off her shoes and props her feet up on the coffee table with a huge sigh.

"Good day at work?" I ask, though I don't really care all that much. I'm still on sick leave, completely unable to summon the motivation to return to a workplace I don't remotely miss.

"Yes! Oh and I spoke to Davide, the IT geek I told you about?"

I shift eagerly to face her. Could this Davide hold all the answers I desperately need?

"He thinks he can trace the number. I just need to forward it to him. I did text you earlier – did you not get it?"

"I've only just set up my new phone," I admit. I don't tell her that I've been sitting here staring at it, too afraid to turn it on.

"Ah, okay. Well, let me have the number and I'll pass it on to Davide. He said he can at least get a name, possibly an address. Hey, wouldn't it be funny if we turned the tables and stalked her instead?"

"Her? What makes you assume it's a woman?"

"Because women are more psycho than guys," she shrugs.

"Might be a man," I counter. I now picture a male figure, enraged by my false accusation against one of his sex. But maybe Imarah's right. It could be either – craziness isn't gender-specific.

"Show me the messages when your phone's working. All of them."

"Why?" I snap defensively.

"Because I want to see them," she replies, visibly confused by my reaction. "I want to know what we're dealing with here."

"Oh, well, I deleted them. They freaked me out, you know?"

She rolls her eyes at me. "Maisie, you idiot. That's *evidence*."

I wince, dreading her inevitable follow-up question.

"What did the police say, by the way?"

And there it is.

"Erm, well, they took my details. But like you said, there wasn't much to show them, and they seemed reluctant to delve any deeper into it."

"Surely they can recover your deleted messages?"

"Perhaps, but they're not going to."

Because, one, I haven't actually told the police, and two, the messages are still on my phone. I clamp my mouth shut.

"Shit," Imarah drags out the word, distressed by my admission. "So what are we going to do now?"

"Catch the bitch?" I suggest.

She looks at me as though I've lost my mind, but the moment passes swiftly and she nods. "Damn right we are. You've been through enough. I'll get Davide to hurry up with tracing the number."

I power on the phone and watch the logo dance across the screen. A sickening sensation blooms in my stomach as I contemplate what awaits me. I should have changed my number, but Imarah persuaded me otherwise. Despite the psychological torture, the messages provide insight into my tormentor's thoughts, offering some messed-up form of preparation.

Besides, Caleb might have called, begging me to go back. He couldn't have done that if I had got a new number.

A girl can dream.

My phone starts beeping, and Imarah leans in curiously.

"Just emails," I tell her, scanning through the irrelevant updates. Nothing interesting.

But another alert follows. Another message. From her.

Clock is ticking, Maisie. It's time you told everyone what you really are.

What clock? I don't understand. Shifting away from Imarah to hide my screen, I open my message history and discover previous texts sent yesterday.

You've got twenty four hours to publicly confess or I will tell your friend myself. Who do you think she'd rather hear it from?

You shouldn't have lied, Maisie. Lying is a dangerous game to play.

"Who is it?" Imarah asks, trying to glimpse my screen. I quickly press the power button.

"Just Caleb. Reminding me about the gas bill."

"But you're not even living there right now!" Imarah gapes.

"I'll be back there soon enough."

I disappear into the bathroom, panic mounting inside of me. Twenty four hours. That means less than three hours left. She (since Imarah suggested it, I can only imagine this person as female) has already threatened to expose me to Caleb.

But she didn't go ahead with it. The threat proved empty. Or did I just beat her to it by foolishly leaving that screenshot where Caleb could find it? It was *my* carelessness that betrayed me. Maybe she never truly intended to tell him. But who can say what she'll do this time?

What do you want from me?

The stalker just replies with a laughing emoji. I'm trembling uncontrollably, tears building along my lower eyelids. I have the irrational urge to claw my skin off just so I can feel something other than this constant state of raw panic. I feel utterly hopeless. Completely desperate.

What do I do now?

I can hardly issue a public apology. I saw the reaction when mere speculation about my deceit circulated. Once speculation transforms into confirmation, I'll be crucified.

I tap my foot anxiously, searching frantically for solutions that just don't come.

I've already lost Caleb. If I tell the truth, I can only hope that Imarah might eventually forgive me. There's a possibility my mother and sisters won't even notice. If I bury my head in the sand for a while and delete all of my socials, I might emerge relatively unscathed.

But where would I live? What will the police do to me? Would they arrest me for wasting their time?

Maybe that wouldn't be such a bad thing. At least I'd have somewhere to stay.

Tick tock.

Fuck you! You think you're better than me? Treating someone this way is cruel and psychotic! FUCK YOU.

...

My outburst provides no sense of relief. I feel a huge sense of dread while I await the next message. I watch those dots with mounting anxiety.

That wasn't very nice. Time's up.

Immediately, Imarah screams my name through the door. "Maisie! What is this?"

My body jerks violently, nearly causing me to drop my phone, and I'm too terrified to leave the sanctuary of the bathroom. A true coward.

I can already picture Imarah's look of disappointment. Her pain at my betrayal. I can't face it. I don't want to be that person.

"Maisie!" Her voice sounds panicked rather than angry, but I emerge with my head lowered in shame, just in case. She thrusts her phone at me. "What are these?"

Screenshots. Messages between Caleb and me.

"Who sent these to you?"

She shrugs. "No idea. Unknown number. What's going on, Maisie?"

I read through them with growing dread. They display the messages I've sent Caleb since he dumped me. Begging for forgiveness. Asking whether he intends to reveal what I have done. Apologising for lying about the attack.

Shit.

"They must have photoshopped them!" I exclaim, staring at the damning evidence that exposes what a horrible person I am. How I invented my assault, lied about my break-up with Caleb. They reveal exactly what kind of friend I am. What sort of person I pretend to be.

Surely it's game over now. I feel as though I'm clinging to the remnants of my life by a threadbare rope, a pit of fire beneath me.

"Who?" Imarah questions, looking dubious.

"My stalker! She sent you these solely to cause more trouble. To intimidate me. None of this is true!" I cannot disguise the desperation in my voice, and I press my lips together before making myself appear even more guilty.

She snatches her phone and scrutinises the messages again. "They appear so genuine, Maisie!"

My face flushes red hot. It feels like the walls are closing in around me.

I go for the jugular. "Ims, she knows your address and now has your phone number. Doesn't that terrify you?"

She looks from me to the phone, then back again, uncertainty clouding her features. "This is too messed up."

"I know, right?" I flounder. I don't know what to say. "She's really got me now. She knows too much!" The stalker feels oppressively close to me, a constant shadow.

She *must* know me. I wrack my brains. Could it be someone from work? I doubt it, they barely know how to turn their computers on. So who?

"Well, she's certainly got the way you text down to a fine art." She shakes her head in disbelief and retreats a step, still examining the messages intently. I observe her expression transform as she processes my suggestion that the messages might be fake. Though skepticism lingers in her eyes, her faith in me proves stronger.

Her unwavering loyalty feels unbearable now. I'm disgusted with myself, but my love for this woman swells inside me.

She continues to stare at her phone as though it contains all the answers, and I have to resist the urge to snatch it out of her hand. "Imarah, I don't feel safe. This has become too much now. Heard anything back from Davide yet?"

"Damn right it has. Maisie, this is *weird*. And no, not yet."

I drum my fingers against the small dining table, wondering how to position myself so I don't look guilty. Imarah remains fixated on the screenshots.

"How did they get my number?" she eventually asks.

That question has been going around my mind, too. Whoever this is, they possess intimate knowledge about me and those I care about, yet I remain clueless about their identity. It creates a sense of insecurity that makes me feel dirty.

"At least we've got some evidence now," Imarah says with forced optimism. "We can go down there now."

Police! Why does she keep going on about this? Why is she so hell-bent on making this more difficult for me? The exhaustion from everything that has happened lately suddenly overwhelms me, manifesting as an ugly rage.

"Will you please just stop, Imarah?!"

Her eyes dart to mine, shock glistening behind them.

"Stop telling me what to do and give me a minute to think for one goddamn second! You've been in on this for a couple of days. This has been my life for *weeks*. Let me handle this my way and get off my fucking back."

Her mouth falls open, but no sound comes out. I stand panting at her, my defiance overpowering any semblance of shame I should rightfully feel.

"Mais …"

To my horror, tears well in her eyes. If she cries, I genuinely fear what I might say next. I can't take this. I can't take *her*. This is all just too much.

"I need to get out of here," I gasp. I can't breathe. I try to suck air into my lungs, but it's too much effort, as though my lungs have been filled with concrete. The panic that has lived inside me these past weeks threatens to burst out of me with catastrophic consequences.

"Maisie?" Imarah's voice sounds distant, as if filtered through layers of fabric. "Maisie, breathe!" She grabs my shoulders, shaking with such force that my feet momentarily leave the ground. But somehow I remain upright. My vision blurs and I lose all sense of direction and understanding. My body doesn't feel like mine, disconnected, and I struggle to understand what's happening.

Then suddenly everything shifts upward. I'm falling. The fall seems eternal until I hit the floor.

I glimpse my phone illuminating on the coffee table. Another message.

Then everything goes black.

Chapter 22

I can hear voices. Then someone is dragging me into a wheelchair. Imarah shouting at them to hurry up. I want to yell at her to stop, that I can hear everything she's saying, but my mouth feels like it's made of rubber.

An older woman with a husky voice tells Imarah to calm herself. A silly mistake. Imarah yells louder at her, saying that if they don't admit me now, the lady will really see her kick off.

It seems Imarah has met her match when the woman shouts back, "Do not lose your temper with me, or I will call security. Now, your friend will be seen as soon as someone is free. She's doing okay."

"Okay?" Imarah replies, quieter now, almost defeated. "Does she look okay to you?!"

"Her heart rate is high, but she's conscious and breathing. Her case isn't urgent."

"She blacked out!"

"And now she's back with us." Footsteps retreat. The woman is leaving, probably to attend to more critical patients.

"Please! She's my friend. She needs help."

But the stranger doesn't respond. She's already moved on.

Imarah tuts loudly before squatting down next to me. "How are you doing now?"

I just look at her. My breathing has returned to normal, but it's as though my body has completely given up. I simply cannot summon the energy to handle anything anymore. I'm utterly exhausted by it all.

The smell of disinfectant is cloying. The noise of chatter and machines beeping overwhelms me. My eyes drift shut, and I fall asleep.

***

"Yes, your friend experienced a severe panic attack."

"But she's going to be okay?"

"Oh, yes! She'll be fine. I have some exercises that she should work through now, so if this happens again, they'll be accessible. Simple breathing techniques can make all the difference."

"Okay," Imarah tells the doctor. She glances at the leaflet, absorbing the information. "I'll help her with this. But doctor, I think there might be more to it …"

The silence sits between them and I imagine the doctor waiting with increasing impatience.

"Oh, never mind," Imarah says.

"Excellent. Now, Maisie will be discharged within the next hour or so."

"Already?"

"She's healthy. We cannot keep a bed for her. I'm sure you appreciate how busy we are."

Given that they took three hours to see me, I'd say they're pretty manic.

"But *look* at her, does she look okay to you? She can't even speak!"

"Do you want me to ask psych for an assessment? Might be a long wait."

Imarah glances at me as if contemplating the offer, and I meet her eyes, silently pleading. *Don't do that*, I beg. She understands and turns back to the doctor. "No, don't do that. She just needs to rest at home."

"Good. Someone will return shortly. If this happens again or you're concerned about anything, bring her back in." His tone suggests otherwise.

Imarah huffs as the doctor withdraws. "Fat lot of good they are here! They didn't give a shit." She turns to me and perches on the edge of my bed. "I care though. Okay? I've got you."

My cries begin small, pitiful. I don't deserve Imarah. Not only have I lied to her about ... well, everything; I've also endangered her. I can't do this to her anymore.

She strokes my hair as I weep into my hands, and that's how we remain until I'm discharged.

***

Car headlights are blinding as we head back to Imarah's. I pretend to sleep to avoid conversation and by the time we arrive at her apartment, dawn is approaching. Imarah fusses around me, despite my protests. Checking if I need anything, bringing me water, and offering food. Finally, we settle into her bed. I'll let her sleep a little before I tell her everything. She at least deserves that much.

I wait until her breathing becomes steady and her body relaxes before I slip out of bed and head downstairs. I check the door is locked and quickly survey the room for any sign of intrusion. Finding nothing, I feel marginally lighter.

Now I just sit and wait for Imarah to wake up. I wonder if I should delay my confession until we hear back from Davide. He might hold the key to all this. Perhaps it can all be resolved before the truth needs to be disclosed.

There's that dishonesty again. Where did it come from? My mum is straightforward – what you see is what you get. I was too young when my father left to remember what he was like; maybe I inherited this trait from him?

No. I draw my legs closer to my body. This is just *me*. No excuses. I'm to blame, and I'm being punished for it. It's only fair.

The sun is forcing its way through the curtains when a tap at the door startles me so violently that I send the cushion on my lap flying across the room.

I approach the door cautiously. My stalker wouldn't knock, I reassure myself. Perhaps Imarah is expecting someone. She was scheduled to work today, so maybe someone is checking on her.

They knock again, more insistently this time, and movement comes from upstairs. "It's okay! I called them," Imarah calls down, her head appearing at the top of the stairs. "You're safe."

I release the breath I have been holding and open the door, bracing myself for whatever lies behind it.

"Evelyn?"

She's in full uniform and wears a grim look on her face. "May I come in? It's freezing out here." She doesn't wait for an invitation and steps inside, offering me a warm smile. "Are you alright? Your friend mentioned you've been struggling lately."

"She really has. Thank you for coming over," Imarah says, securing her robe around her waist and rushing to the kitchen to busy herself with making drinks.

Evelyn turns to me. "You okay, Maisie? You're very quiet. Pale."

I nod and lead her to the living area, where we sit opposite each other.

"She had a major panic attack last night. I had to take her to the hospital," Imarah explains.

"Oh, darling, I'm so sorry. All this has taken its toll on you, hasn't it? And Troy tells me you and Caleb have broken up?"

That jolts me. Does that mean Evelyn is back with Troy? Despite my deep-rooted disgust that Evelyn could forgive a cheater, it also kindles hope. If Troy can be pardoned for the unthinkable, perhaps it shows

Caleb that love can flourish even when the light has dimmed.

"Why are you here?" I ask, my voice strangled in my throat.

"Your friend called us. I got the report when my shift began, so I wanted to check on you personally. She mentioned you have a stalker?"

My eyes widen as I turn to look at Imarah, who's busying herself inside the fridge, the back of her neck flushed red.

"She shouldn't have called you," I say. "I didn't want the police to get involved."

"But why not, Maisie? We are here to keep you safe."

"Yeah? Well then, tell me, how much progress have you made in finding my attacker?"

Imarah snaps to attention, clearly shocked by my hostile attitude towards a police officer.

"Well, actually, that's another matter I came to discuss. I thought it would be better coming from me. Woman to woman."

I notice dark circles beneath her eyes, poorly concealed with makeup that's slightly too pale for her complexion. Her uniform, typically immaculate, bears a coffee stain near the collar.

I wait to hear what she has to say, distracted by my pounding heart.

Evelyn clears her throat as Imarah settles beside me on the sofa, taking my hand.

"As you know, we haven't made much progress with your case. There's very little CCTV in the area to examine and we found nothing significant on cameras from nearby roads. We have no witnesses and found no evidence on you to work with."

I gulp. There was no evidence to begin with, so this hardly comes as a surprise.

"So – and I'm truly sorry, Maisie – they've decided to close your case."

My shoulders slump as I take a deep breath. It feels oddly liberating to know that chapter has ended. One less thing to worry about. I have an alarming urge to laugh and I stifle it forcefully, making me cough.

Imarah grips my arm tightly. "Are you okay?" she asks, not waiting for a response before turning to face Evelyn. "How dare you do this to her? How dare you let that monster roam free? You call yourselves protectors? It's fucking disgraceful!"

She's outraged. And it dawns on me that I should be showing the same emotion.

But Evelyn speaks first. "I understand. And I'm sorry." Turning back to me, she continues, "Look, you can appeal this decision. Bring us more evidence and fight for reopening the case. There must be *something* we can use to reignite it. *Think*, Maisie. What have we missed?"

Both women look expectantly at me but I have nothing to say, so all I can do is shrug.

Evelyn sighs. "I wanted to tell you ..." She hesitates, glancing around. "I believe you. Even if some of my colleagues have their doubts. Don't be afraid to speak up."

"Thank you," I respond, genuinely touched, though the thought of them discussing the validity of my claims makes me uncomfortable. Still, at least they haven't pursued my lies.

She moves closer, her eyes hardening momentarily. "Men like that – predators – deserve whatever comes to them. Chop off their balls is what I say." There's something deeply personal in her tone, something raw and unfiltered. Before I can respond, she straightens her uniform, and her professional demeanour returns. "We'll do everything possible to find him," she says, her voice normalised. Her gaze shifts between Imarah and me. "Now, tell me about this stalker."

Imarah opens her mouth, but I cut her off. "You think I'm going to report that when you've shown me how grossly incompetent you are?" I don't want to file a report. I don't want police involved when I'm perilously close to being arrested for wasting their time. It feels dangerously like tempting fate.

"Maisie, wait ..." Imarah says, placing a hand on my leg.

I shove her away. "No, Imarah, what's the point? The police are clearly useless." I stand abruptly. "You can leave now, Evelyn. Thanks for nothing."

But she remains seated, and I fight the impulse to physically drag her out. If she sees the messages on Imarah's phone, she might question the truth behind them. I can't let her see those messages. She might contact Caleb. I feel sick at the thought.

"Maisie, you should reconsider. Your stalker might seem like a stranger hiding behind a screen, but that's the danger. You have no idea what this person might be capable of."

"I know what you're capable of," I spit venomously. "Nothing. Now, I'd like you to leave."

A tense silence follows as Evelyn thinks through the situation. Imarah is practically vibrating behind me, desperate to interject, but loyalty holds her back. I just want the earth to open up and swallow me whole.

Seconds feel like hours before Evelyn sighs and rises. "You have my number if needed. But Maisie, think about this: don't let things spiral out of control before seeking help."

"I'll be fine," I assure her. "I have to be."

And I watch with immense relief as she leaves.

Chapter 23

"What are you doing?!"

Imarah is standing right behind me. I didn't hear her creep up on me – I was too absorbed in trying to break into her phone.

Busted.

"Shit, Imarah, you made me jump!"

"Why are you looking through my phone?"

After Evelyn left earlier, I told Imarah I needed some space and retreated to her bedroom to figure things out. When I crept downstairs later, I found her fast asleep on the sofa, her mouth inelegantly hanging open. I took the opportunity and snatched her phone from the sofa, tiptoed into the kitchen, and turned my back on her to focus on working out her passcode.

"I just wanted to reread those messages," I tell her. It's the truth, partially. I also wanted to delete them and check whether Davide had responded to her yet. I accomplished neither of those things.

"Why didn't you just ask me?"

"You were asleep. I didn't want to wake you."

She frowns, studying me. "You figured out my passcode then?"

It wasn't exactly hard. A birth date hardly requires MI5-level intelligence to crack. I just didn't have enough time to access anything before Imarah woke up.

"Sorry, Ims. I didn't think you'd mind."

She looks at me with arms crossed before her shoulders relax and an uncertain smile appears on her lips. "No, it's fine. It's not as if I have anything to hide." She laughs nervously and plucks her phone from my hands. "Want me to forward those messages to you?"

I notice she's clutching her phone protectively against her chest, keeping it out of my reach. She's secretly pissed at me, and I can hardly blame her.

"Yes, please." Although it doesn't resolve the problem of removing them from Imarah's phone before she sends them to the police. I'm clinging to the lie that the images are fake by the thinnest of threads, and each mention feels like I'm tugging on it dangerously.

Imarah's phone suddenly vibrates and her expression immediately brightens. "Hey! Davide texted me back."

I rush to her side, instantly forgetting about the screenshots of my confession.

Sorry it's taken so long. It was my boyfriend's birthday and I got sidetracked. Anyway, that number is untraceable, sorry.

Exasperated, I groan and stomp away from Imarah, who watches me with her phone still clutched tightly in her hands.

Will I ever get closer to this prick? I toy with the idea of telling everyone I lied. Of releasing a confession video online. After all, what I did wasn't that bad. I didn't hurt anyone. Only Caleb, and he's already suffered. Imarah would be okay ... eventually.

But then I recall the reaction when people merely *suspected* I was lying. The abuse. The death threats. I shudder to imagine what would follow if the complete truth were to come out.

And how would my mum react? My sisters? My colleagues and friends? Can I afford to lose Imarah's friendship? Can I kiss goodbye to a reconciliation with Caleb for good?

No. I can't. It's all too overwhelming. My life is already so small; I cannot throw what little I have away. Where would I live? My income isn't sufficient to support myself – and that's if Alec would even keep me on.

"Mais? Are you okay?"

The sympathy in her voice makes me want to tear out my heart and offer it to her. A gesture of atonement. An apology for being the worst friend.

I reflect on our friendship. I remember the time in school when I told her Trisha Gibbons had called her a 'poopoo head', because I wanted Imarah all to myself. It wasn't true – I just didn't want to share.

Then, when we were sixteen, I made out with her boyfriend to split them up. I blamed him, engineered a scenario where he appeared to be coming on to me just as Imarah walked in on us.

How I neglected to tell her that Caleb initially requested her number, not mine. My jealousy prevented me from passing it along, so I gave him mine instead. A silly mix-up. I called it fate at the time. Now I'd call it bullshit.

Is anything in my life real? Have I lied so much that I deserve nothing?

No, I *had* to lie. To protect. To serve. To determine the course that would benefit everyone. It all stemmed from a place of love. Surely they can see that. I never intended to be malicious.

Maybe it is time I faced my truth. Imarah will understand. She has a heart of gold. She'll see.

Wow, this constant flip-flopping between decisions is so tiring.

"Mais?" Imarah repeats. But her phone vibrates in her hand, drawing her attention. Her focus shifts to whatever she's reading. Her eyebrows draw ever closer together as her eyes skirt across the screen.

As I open my mouth to ask if she's okay, my phone erupts with a chorus of alerts and beeps. Notification after notification floods in, the sheer number difficult to take in.

I open one at random. A private message from a Kirsty Mancin: *I knew you were lying. Whore.*

Then another. Adrian Reynolds: *Women like you deserve to be raped.*

No. This cannot be happening. They know.

Anita Ellen: *Why did you do it? You know there are real victims out there, right? You have no idea what you've taken from them.*

I keep reading message after message, comment after comment. All hating me. All wishing terrible things to happen to me. I feel disconnected from my body, detached from the entire situation. As though I'm observing from the sidelines.

"Maisie?" Imarah cuts through my dissociation, pulling me back to reality. "What is this?"

She shows me a news article. 'LOCAL WOMAN LIED ABOUT SEXUAL ATTACK'. My face, taken from my Facebook profile, smiles beneath the headline, oblivious to the hatred generated, the pain inflicted, the terror provoked. Oblivious to how much she would come to despise herself.

Because I do. I have never loathed anyone with such intensity in my entire life. I want to rip my shame out of me, to shred my skin and expose my innermost self in a desperate bid to demonstrate how truly sorry I am.

"Tell me this isn't true. It's rubbish, right? They've got it wrong."

I watch her carefully. Even in her distress, she's breathtaking, her large brown eyes wide with concern, her lips in a perfect pout. But who is she concerned for? For me, facing extreme hostility? Or for herself, confronting my betrayal of her loyalty and trust?

I shake my head slowly. "It's all true," I whisper. "I lied about the attack."

Imarah's jaw drops. She stares at me for a fraction of a second before taking a step backwards. "I knew there was something off about you. I *knew* you were keeping things from me. But this? Fuck no. You're talking a load of crap. No offence, Maisie, but you're not that good an actor."

I don't tell her I've had years of practice. "I'm so sorry, Ims," I gasp. "I never meant for it to get so out of control."

She shakes her head, tears welling in her eyes. "No, you couldn't have. Maisie, I was so worried about you. You wouldn't do that to me." Her voice fractures as the truth penetrates her disbelief. "Please, Maisie, this isn't funny." She continues to stare with widened eyes, taking in my confession. Then she paces the living area, moving up and down the room several times before returning to her spot by the kitchen counter.

I reach towards her, but she pulls back. "I never wanted to hurt you. I love you so much, Imarah. I never wanted to cause you pain."

She steps back further. Her face contorts, her expression morphing from horror to absolute fury. "Why?!" she shouts. "Why would you do this?!"

"To get Caleb back! Ims, I thought he was going to leave me. I had to do *something*. I just never expected it to evolve into something so massive. If it wasn't for that stalker, we would have moved on by now."

"Seriously? This was about Caleb? You lied about an assault because you and Caleb had a row? And don't put all the blame onto that stalker. This was all your fault! Maisie, what the fuck?!"

I shouldn't have confessed. It was foolish. Imarah was so much happier living in ignorance. How could I inflict this on her?

"I know it's messed up and the second I said it, I wished I could take it back. I *told* you I didn't want to go to the police. But you wouldn't let it go. I wanted it all to just stop so we could forget it ever happened."

"So this is somehow *my* fault?"

"No! Absolutely not. I just didn't expect it would go this far."

"Then why did you go on the radio, Maisie? Because to me, you seemed to be enjoying yourself."

She's got me there. The radio interview was a moment of madness. A foolish need to feel significant. Famous. How was I to know it would spur a witch hunt?

I stare at the floor, unable to meet Imarah's gaze. "I don't know what possessed me," I admit.

"No shit, Sherlock." She turns away, running her hands over the back of her head. "I need you to leave."

"What?"

"You heard me! Go, Maisie, before I say or do something really regrettable."

"But, Ims. Please, I didn't mean ..."

"You never *mean* to do anything, Maisie. That's always been your excuse." She stands, gathering up her bag. "Fuck this, I need space. I cannot keep doing this."

As she reaches the door, she turns back. "I care about you. I've always cared. But I don't know how to help you."

Chapter 24

The rain lashes down as I pull up to Mum's house. I can't believe it's come to this, but my options are severely limited. Mum seemed like the lesser evil compared to my two sisters.

Still, I remain in my car, forcing myself to muster up the courage to knock on her door. The rain has transformed the windscreen into a blurry shield, granting me blessed anonymity. No one can see me here. My doors are locked, so no one can reach me. My phone is powered off, its silence bringing me a moment of profound peace.

I could sit here forever. Except I need to use the bathroom.

What if I just disappear? Go somewhere far away and never return. Adopt a new identity. And start all over again. I allow this fantasy to dance through my mind for a little while. A smile plays across my lips as I surrender to the dream.

But then, I think of Caleb. How devastating it would be to never see him again. How I cannot simply write us off just because he has. Then there's Imarah, the only person I know intimately. My confidante. My ride or die.

I can't start over; too much of myself is in this town and in the people I love. It would be like exorcising a piece of my heart.

I look at Mum's house through the downpour. It's a nice modest house, located in an undesirable part of town, but it's proof that you can polish a turd. Delicate pink flowers bloom beneath the bay window, offering a cheerful pop of colour even through this miserable weather. She's painted the door a rich emerald and added gold accents that give the house some elegance.

It's charming. And the funny thing is, I've never truly noticed it before. Maybe I've been so preoccupied with my own life that I've failed to look at Mum properly. Maybe it's time I did.

I have no idea if Mum has learned the news yet. She avoids social media, so she won't have encountered the online vitriol directed at me, but my face is plastered across local news outlets. Plus, my sisters adore gossip.

Who am I deceiving? Mum always knows everything.

I sigh and grasp the car door handle, but nerves make me hesitate. Mum isn't particularly engaged at the best of times, so why would she take me in now, even if it's my hour of need?

Panic intensifies. Where will I go if she refuses? I can't face Faith or Rainy, so I'll have no more options. I'll be forced to sleep in my car. I glance around me. It's so small in here. I can recline my seat, but it doesn't flatten completely, and all my stuff is piled in the back, so I couldn't move the chair anyway. And where would I brush my teeth? Go to the toilet?

Mum is my only option, tragically. My bladder protests – I'm out of time. I dash from my car and sprint through the rain to Mum's doorstep. She takes an age to answer, and when she does she just stares at me with that look of disappointment that pulls at my heart. The look that only a parent can deliver. The one that breaks you apart.

"Mum?" I whimper, rain dripping from my nose.

Her expression softens, and she opens the door wide, gesturing me inside. "Come on in, love."

She guides me upstairs, where she provides a towel and warm pyjamas. "Dry yourself off. I'll make you a toastie. You like them."

I could cry. Mum's cheese toasties taste of my childhood. She always made them when I stayed home sick from school and they're my ultimate comfort food. I feel nurtured. Protected.

Home.

The kitchen smells of burnt cheese when I wander back downstairs. I find Mum elbows-deep in a sink filled with soapy water. My food awaits me on the dining table, accompanied by a steaming cup of tea.

"Thank you, Mum," I murmur, settling down to eat.

We remain silent until I've finished my food, while Mum wipes surfaces and arranges the spice rack in alphabetical order. I feel restored, warm, and comfortable in Mum's pyjamas.

The Stasbridge Gazette lies on the kitchen counter, its front page staring up accusingly. 'LOCAL WOMAN'S ATTACK CLAIM QUESTIONED' blazes across the top in bold black lettering.

My stomach convulses as I scan the text. There are quotes from 'sources close to the investigation', all suggesting inconsistencies in my story. The radio interview features prominently, complete with extracted quotes from callers who challenged my story.

"Mum, why have you got this?" I ask, my voice quavering.

She grimaces. "It's not just the newspaper, love. It's appearing on the websites, too. And people are talking about it at the shops."

I sink further into my chair, reality crashing down on me. This isn't just online chatter now. It's penetrated traditional media and infiltrated conversations among people who've known me throughout my life.

"Someone from the *Midlands Today* programme called me," Mum reluctantly adds. "They want to produce a segment on false reporting and its impact on police resources."

The room seems to spin around me. A regional news programme. How many additional viewers would that reach?

"I told them to sod off," Mum says firmly, placing a protective hand on my shoulder.

I glance back at the newspaper. A sidebar article titled 'False Reports: A Growing Problem?' features statements from a police spokesperson regarding the serious implications of filing fraudulent reports. They don't identify me directly in that piece, but the insinuation is clear.

"It'll blow over," Mum asserts, but we both know she's lying. She lowers her voice to a whisper. "Why did you do it, Maisie?"

My shoulders slump. I wish the floor would open and swallow me whole. At the time it felt like such a good idea. Now I just feel like an absolute fool. My reasons are invalid and childish. "I don't know," I say timidly. "It was a stupid, stupid mistake."

"You can say that again!" But she doesn't sound angry. Just profoundly sad. "Oh, darling, where did I go so wrong with you?"

My hands fall limply to my lap, my mouth agape. What do I even say to that? Besides, she has a point. Where *did* she go so wrong with me, because I'm not exactly *right*.

Since I was a little girl, I've struggled with honesty. Lying came so naturally to me. Lying made me visible. It drew people closer. It made me feel substantial. Now, ironically, I wish I were invisible.

"Mum? I need help."

Her expression softens, and she reaches for me, enveloping me in plump, warm arms. "Oh, darling," she breathes into my hair. "Stay here until this blows over. You'll be tomorrow's chip paper before you know it."

I must push away the doubt. Doubt that I deserve this kindness and affection. I embrace her reassurance, and already my burden feels lighter. "Rainy and Faith ..."

"Are staying away. I've already cancelled tomorrow's dinner, and they're under strict instructions not to bother you."

I stare into her eyes with wonder. Who is this woman, and what has she done with my mother? "Thank you," I say sincerely.

"There's just one condition," she says, seating herself opposite me.

"What is it?"

"When we can all be together again, you need to engage with the family a little more. You come here and sit silently. You're so ... disconnected, Maisie. We know you look down on us, but is that really fair? You're no better than us, we are all just the same. And we miss you."

I'm astonished. I always assumed the three of them excluded me, but have I been the one severing ties?

Mum continues. "I've always made an effort with you. You wanted so much to be different, I understood that, but when I would get the things you asked for that allowed you to stand out, you complained that I treated you differently. If I attempted to include you, you'd pull away. We lost you years ago, Maisie, and I didn't know how to get you back. I feel awkward around you, like I don't know what to say to make you like me."

I break down sobbing.

She reaches across to me, clasping my hands in hers. "Let's use this terrible situation for good, shall we? Let's start again. Rebuild our relationship – baby steps. And I know your sisters will come around. I know they can be cruel, but that's because they don't really know you. Let them in."

I nod. "I'd love that," I admit. I long to be little again, to sit on Mum's lap while she brushes my hair. To be wrapped in a thick, fluffy towel, her arms encircling me to calm my chattering teeth after getting out of the bath. To know she supports me no matter what.

But she is supporting me. Even now. And I realise that's always been true. She's my mother.

"I'll offer to babysit for Rainy," I suggest brightly.

"Oh, I wouldn't go that far; those children are a handful."

We share a gentle laugh.

"So, you and Caleb?"

"Over."

"I'm so sorry. I knew how thrilled you were when you found that ring."

She believed me. By the disappointment on her face, I can see she was excited on my behalf. Over yet another lie.

"Caleb was never going to propose. I never found a ring," I confess. "I just said that to get Rainy and Faith off my back. I'm sorry."

Mum presses her lips together. "Why do I get the feeling I'm about to learn a lot about you?"

Because I've lied about my entire life? Because I've lied so much even I don't know who I am anymore? I don't say any of this and avoid her gaze. That action alone tells her everything she needs to know.

She sighs. "Go and get your stuff from the car. I'll make your bed up."

***

I go to bed early. So early that I hear the *EastEnders* theme tune floating up through the floorboards.

My phone sits on the bedside table, taunting me. I feel lost without having something to scroll through. I've attempted to read one of Mum's Josephine Cox novels, but quickly got bored and lost concentration. Now I'm twiddling my thumbs.

What is Caleb doing right now? It's Saturday, so he's probably out with his friends. Drinking. Talk to other women.

Jealousy smacks me in the stomach and I snatch up my phone, turning it on for the first time in hours. Thankfully, I had the foresight to put it on silent mode, or it would be chiming incessantly now with the hundreds of notifications flooding in.

Ignoring them all, I head straight to Caleb's profile. He rarely posts content himself; in fact, I doubt he even checks the app often. But occasionally his friends tag him in photos. And I've found that by checking the profiles of certain people, I can find more of Caleb that he hasn't been tagged in.

The most recent content on Caleb's profile dates back months, when I tagged him in a photo I captured of us standing on a hillside, our windswept faces displaying broad smiles and joyful eyes.

But Troy's profile is a little more up to date. A woman I don't recognise has tagged Troy in an image. He stands alone in a bar, smiling drunkenly. But it's the background that captures my attention.

He's unmistakable in his checked shirt – I remember ironing it for him the evening this photo was taken. I remember desperately hoping that by being super nice, then it might just persuade him to stay at home.

But Caleb didn't stay home that night.

And according to this photograph, he was kissing another woman instead.

Chapter 25

"Why don't you go for a walk, Maisie? The fresh air will do you good."

I grumble back at my well-intentioned mother and turn up the TV volume. I haven't slept a wink and my mood is foul. It's taking every ounce of self control not to snap at Mum and her incessant questions. She doesn't deserve my irritation. I know she's only trying to help. But God, it's exhausting.

"Well, you need to get out of my living room. I'm about to hoover the carpet."

I force a smile. "Okay, Mum."

I notice her grin as she turns away. The sly devil simply wanted me to get out for a while. I suspect she'll claim my spot on the sofa the second I leave, the hoover left forgotten in the cupboard under the stairs.

However, the instant I step outside, I'm flooded with gratitude for Mum. She was right, as always. The air immediately cleanses my lungs and the breeze caresses my skin, sweeping away my troubles. I wander aimlessly, relishing the sense of space and peace. There's a refreshing chill to the air, counterbalanced by sunshine. Who would've thought something so small could provide such serenity.

I find myself outside the corner shop and cannot resist popping in for a handmade samosa. But as I step back outside and unwrap the aromatic pastry, someone shouts. I scan my surroundings for the source of the commotion and am horrified to see a woman charging directly towards me. Her baggy jumper billows behind her as she raises her arm, revealing a tightly clenched fist. I duck just in time, dropping my food, which scatters across the pavement.

"You're that bitch, aren't you?! That lying whore?"

My pulse thunders in my ears as panic sets in. I've never had a physical fight in my entire life, and this woman is as broad as she is tall. I haven't the slightest chance of winning. And I *really* don't want my face rearranging.

"It was all a massive misunderstanding," I stutter.

A thick globule of spit lands on my cheek. It's warm as it slides downwards. "My boyfriend was arrested because of you. I kicked the bastard out because of it. I thought no smoke without fire, you know? Turns out you were lying and he just happened to be in the wrong place at the wrong time. He wasn't in those woods attacking you! He was … doing something else."

I notice people have begun to gather, phones raised. Recording. One woman provides running commentary, speaking directly to her camera. This isn't just one angry woman; it's evolving into a spectacle. Content for social media. More fuel for the fire already consuming my life.

Somebody initiates a slow clap from the edge of the crowd. Another joins in. The woman confronting me smiles, feeding off their approval. "You can't go around ruining lives and not expect consequences," she declares, loudly enough for her audience to hear.

"I'm so sorry. I told the police it wasn't him. As soon as I heard, I went straight there and fixed things."

But she disregards my pleas. "And now he won't come back to me. Says I should've trusted him. He's upped and left me, me and the baby." Her voice cracks at the end. This is a woman in pain. Because of me.

I bite my lip. I'm at a loss for words. All I've got are apologies, and something tells me they won't be enough and will only serve to enrage her further.

She's screaming at me now but I can't understand her words. She thrusts her face into mine and my vision distorts. All I can make out are her lips moving and teeth gnashing. Spectators hover nearby, chatting as though they're watching the latest episode of *The Kardashians*.

I can only cower pathetically, apologising repeatedly. The shame is overwhelming. Never before have I so desperately wished for the earth to swallow me up.

I resign myself to my fate. I close my eyes as she grasps the front of my shirt, pulling me toward her.

"Hey! Get away from her!" I know that voice. I love that voice.

Caleb. I dare to squint in the direction of his call and see him dismounting his motorbike in the car park, rushing towards me while pulling off his helmet. He pushes through the crowd that has formed around us.

My attacker stares at him too, her cheeks flushed crimson, a bead of sweat trailing down her temple. "Who the fuck are you?" she shouts at Caleb, though I notice some venom has stripped from her tone.

"A friend. Now back off, or I'll call the police." I note he already holds his phone, and I also note his use of the term 'friend'. Is that truly all I am to him now? I suppose it's better than 'ex.'

"Well, do you know what your 'friend' has done?"

"I know better than anyone. I also know there's nothing you can say or do to her right now that would make her feel worse than she already does."

She pulls away from me and snarls. "Yeah? We'll see about that." With that, she stalks away to a Mini Cooper parked across two parking spaces. She enters the driver's side, and I breathe again. Thank God that's over.

"You alright?" Caleb asks, blocking my view of the woman who sits scowling at me. I long to reach for him. Being unable to touch him feels unnatural. Painful.

"I am now. Thank you."

He shrugs. "I couldn't just watch you get decked. We may have broken up, but that doesn't mean I want to see you get hurt."

And there's the confirmation. We've definitively broken up. Until this moment, a flicker of hope had persisted, but that glimmer has just been blown apart by Caleb's words.

I take a step back, silently praying my legs stay strong enough to support me. My knees quiver, and I resist the urge to run away and cry.

Venturing outside was a terrible mistake. I'll never listen to Mum's advice again.

"Thank you, Caleb, but you should go now," I mutter. I cannot be around him anymore. Just having him here is killing me. "Take care, yeah?"

He goes to reach for me but withdraws as though scalded. "You're okay now, right?"

I nod, not looking up from the ground. I'm such a disaster. "Please go."

He hesitates, looking down at me one final time before placing a hand on my shoulder. "Take care, Mais."

And he's gone. I watch him get back on his bike and the engine roars to life.

I'm so fixated on watching him that I miss the figure rushing towards me. She's just a couple of metres away when I notice her. And this time, she isn't preparing to punch or spit – she's clutching a bottle.

It's as if time slows down, and I'm watching from outside my body. I see the woman raise her arm, clear liquid spurting from the container, directed straight at me. I see my arm rising to shield my face, my body recoiling in a desperate attempt to escape the assault. But my reaction is too little, too late.

I sense Caleb about to merge onto the main road. I hear the screech of tyres and the thunderous impact of a vehicle striking his bike.

Then the liquid washes over me.

The sound of my own screams fills my ears. So loud. So unbearably loud.

Chapter 26

Her laughter rings loud amidst the chaos. I watch as someone else crashes into her, knocking her to the ground. I stand drenched, waiting for the pain, the searing agony of melting skin. I realise I'm screaming and clamp my hand over my mouth to make it stop. Hands reach towards me, but I shove them away. I don't want others to be contaminated; I don't want them to get acid on their skin like I have on mine.

"You're okay! You're okay!" a young woman shouts repeatedly. She grasps my shoulders and forces me to face her. "Look at me!"

I do, but my eyes dart frantically, unable to focus. I can smell something. Fumes. Panic engulfs me in an overwhelming wave.

"You're okay," she insists. "It was water. You're okay."

Her words echo in my mind.

"It was just water," she repeats, her eyes filled with concern.

A young man appears at her side, breathless. "She ran off," he tells the woman. "Someone's called the police."

My attacker. She's escaped. Part of me seethes with indignation – how dare she leave without consequences? But a bigger part of me feels relieved. I never want to see her again.

Cautiously, I touch a damp patch on my neck. My fingertip returns wet, but painless. The liquid is clear and odourless. *It's just water.*

I repeat this to myself over and over, trying to make sense of what's just happened. But the panic persists, my stomach hurts, and my heart continues to pound.

But I'm okay.

"Quite the scare, eh?" The young woman asks kindly. "We all shit ourselves when we saw her throw that bottle at you. You must have been terrified. You see these acid attacks in the news all the time …"

She leads me to a bench where I sit and catch my breath. I'm surrounded by people gawking at me. I want to tell them to piss off, but I'm too panicked. Too frightened still.

I'm okay.

Thankfully, the young man who chased my attacker speaks for me. "Alright, nothing more to see here. Let's give her some space, yeah?"

Most disappear, grumbling. Some snap final pictures before walking away. A few remain, brazenly watching, likely hoping for additional gossip to spill to their friends.

Blue flashing lights capture my attention. No, I don't want medical attention; this is humiliating enough already.

But to my surprise, they stop before turning into the car park.

"Some poor bastard got knocked off his bike. It's all happening today."

Then it all comes flooding back. The horns sounding. The screech of metal as Caleb's bike falls and scrapes along the pavement. The cries of shock and dismay.

"Caleb!"

I dash towards the road, pushing through the chattering crowd. Two paramedics lean over Caleb and dig equipment out of their bags.

Caleb's helmet is still on. I can't see his face, but I know from his limp body that he's unconscious.

"He drove straight out of the junction," someone to my left remarks to no one in particular. "I saw it all.

He was looking back towards the shops and pulled into traffic. He wasn't paying any attention, the idiot."

Looking backwards? He was looking at me! He must have heard the commotion of my attack and glanced back. This is that woman's fault! If she hadn't pretended to douse me with acid, this wouldn't have happened.

But a voice in the back of my head speaks up. She wouldn't have done that if I hadn't ruined her life. No, this is entirely my fault. *I* did this. And the casualties keep mounting up. A sob escapes me as I rush forward.

"You need to step back," a paramedic orders. "Don't crowd us."

"He's my boyfriend!"

She throws me a sympathetic look before returning to stabilising Caleb's head. They work quickly and methodically, updating each other on his condition. I hover anxiously nearby. I need to see his face. I need to see he's okay.

Once his head is secure, the paramedics carefully remove his helmet. To my astonishment, he's conscious. He stares directly at me, his expression terrified.

They strap him to a stretcher and begin pushing him towards the ambulance. I hesitate for just a second before joining him. We might not be together, but that doesn't mean he should go through this alone.

I sit in the back of the ambulance in complete silence, allowing the paramedic to concentrate. She needs to focus on Caleb, not me. She offers reassurances that I dismiss. Until hospital doctors examine him thoroughly, I can't believe any of it.

"Sorry," I repeatedly whisper. But my apologies go unnoticed by the man I love.

A delay in the emergency department aggravates me. I keep asking when he will be seen, but the answer remains the same every time: 'He's in the queue. We have to prioritise more urgent cases.'

I try to take comfort in the fact he's not considered the most critical patient here. The morphine they've given him is taking effect, and by the time he's taken for X-rays, he's rambling about rising beer prices. I watch him go with sadness in my heart.

***

"Caleb is stable and doing well, considering the circumstances. Tests have shown he's sustained a fractured pelvis from the accident, but there's no immediate threat to his life." The doctor offers a gentle smile. "He's being assessed for a pain management plan and has been referred to orthopaedics, but his rehabilitation will be a long journey." He pauses. "Miss Tallow, Caleb is ready to see you now."

I jump up from my chair and hurry to his bedside. I reach for his hand, but he pulls away. "Caleb ..." I begin, but he shakes his head.

There's no life behind his eyes, as though he's lost within his suffering and pain. "Thank you for coming here, Mais. But you need to leave now," he states, breaking my heart in two.

"I can't just leave you here alone!" I gasp.

"Then call Troy. Ask him to bring me some stuff. But, Maisie?"

I look at him hopefully.

"I need you to go and not come back." He looks straight into my eyes, his words sure and definitive.

I go to speak, but he turns away, putting an end to our conversation.

I turn and walk away without so much as a backwards glance. Of all the terrible things to have happened lately, none are as painful as this.

It's over.

It's hardly surprising. All this is my fault. If I hadn't lied, we'd still be together. If we were together, today's events would never have happened. This is all my fault.

It takes three attempts to reach Troy. "Maisie," he states flatly. His voice contains no warmth or friendliness. He despises me, too.

I tell him about the accident, and he barks, "I'm on my way now," before hanging up.

I sit there in the waiting room, pressing my phone between my palms, unsure what to do now. Should I try to see Caleb again, apologise, and let him know Troy is on his way? Or should I wait for Troy and face his wrath? Should I simply leave and allow Caleb to recover without me here making him feel worse?

Because that's what I am to him. A parasite, draining all joy from his life. For so long we pretended to be happy. But I now understand that was impossible because Caleb wasn't capable of making me happy. My standards were impossibly high. The poor guy was fighting a losing battle all along.

My phone vibrates, alerting me to a text message: *Maisie, it's Peters. I've been trying to reach you. Please call me.*

The audacity! After what he did to me! I type furiously: *Don't you dare contact me! You destroyed my life.*

His reply arrives instantly: *I know you're angry, but you must understand it's purely business, nothing personal. We've achieved remarkable ratings since your story broke.*

I've seen what just happened to you today – eager to get your take on the attack.

You went back on your word! You told me you'd protect my identity. You can fuck off with your interview.

That's not very nice, is it? First rule of show business, Maisie – trust no one. And sign a confidentiality agreement.

I stare at the screen in disbelief. He just wants to profit from my misery. I can't believe I thought this slimy bastard was on my side. I have been the biggest fool.

I block his number and drag myself from the hospital, away from Caleb. He needs to heal in so many ways, and I'll keep my distance to help him do just that.

My phone vibrates again, and I look at it with dread. Is Peters using an alternative number? Is it my stalker? I can't handle her right now. She's taken up too much mental energy already, and I have nothing left to give.

But it's Faith: *Saw what happened to you today. Meet you at Mum's.*

My attack has already spread online – how humiliating. What's wrong with people these days? How can people post content like that just for a moment of satisfaction, while simultaneously destroying the person they're talking about? Have people lost all empathy? Do they not understand that strangers have feelings too?

It's time I face reality. Thanks to Mum, I've avoided interrogation from my sisters since the truth came out. It's time to confront it. I'm too raw to care now, anyway. Why not rub more salt in my wounds?

***

I find Mum and Faith in the living room when I return home. Rainy isn't here, thankfully.

"Rainy's looking after the baby. She has a cough."

"Rainy or Bluebell-Rose?"

"Blue. She's shortened it to Blue," Faith explains. "And it's Blue who's ill. You'd know if you checked in every now and then."

I hang my head and sit on the sofa, ready for my verbal bashing.

"I saw the video of your attack online," Faith tells me. "Maisie ..."

"I know, I know, I deserved it."

She gasps. "No, you didn't deserve *that*!"

I look at her and see she's regarding me with utmost sympathy.

"Maisie, you've been really stupid, but seeing that? Fuck me, I nearly had a heart attack." Tears run down my cheeks as she slides beside me, wrapping her arm around my shoulders. "You poor thing."

I rest my head against her shoulder and sob. Mum comes to sit on the arm of the sofa on my other side. She presses a hand on my shoulder and plants a kiss on top of my head.

We sit like this while I unleash all of my anguish. We're all crying, a moment of solidarity. United by my horrors. Horrors *I've* caused, and I've never felt more grateful. More loved.

"I'm so sorry," I blurt. "I'm so sorry I lied to you."

Faith shrugs. "Hun, you're always lying. You think we can't tell? We assumed it was just a stupid personality trait. We never imagined you'd take it this far. But what's done is done, right? Just promise me you won't do anything like this ever again."

"I never meant for any of this to happen. I ..."

"Just promise me, Maisie. This isn't a debate."

"I promise!" And I absolutely mean it. I'll never lie about so much as a surprise party ever again. "I've learned my lesson."

"The hard way, it seems," Mum says. "But we're here for you."

I nod. "Thank you," I whisper. "I love you guys."

"And we love you, too."

"They've already found the bitch who threw water on you," Faith tells me.

Water. It all seems so ridiculous now, my reaction so over the top. My cheeks burn with embarrassment.

"She's been arrested, apparently. Rumour has it she's angry with you, not because her boyfriend was arrested for your assault, but because once they discovered he was in the area, he had to explain why. He had to admit to her he'd been dogging just two miles from where your *attack* happened." She says 'attack' like it's vomit on the end of her tongue.

I'm surprised to feel compassion for this woman. Imagine watching your partner arrested for something he didn't do, then released only because he was actually engaged in promiscuous activities nearby? How mortifying.

"How's Caleb?" Mum asks gently.

"You know about that, too?"

"Everything is on that Facebook thing these days," Mum says matter-of-factly. "Faith showed me."

"There's a picture of you in the ambulance going viral," Faith adds. "You looked terrible."

"He'll recover," I say. "Broken bones. Lots of physio, I reckon." I don't mention he kicked me out. Given that I'm here rather than at his side, it's blatantly obvious we're broken up, anyway. I would never have chosen to leave voluntarily.

We sit and ruminate on Caleb's accident, our arms still entwined, in a relaxed atmosphere that warms me deep inside.

The letterbox rattles, and Mum wanders off, muttering about the postman's irregular schedule. She returns clutching a single envelope. "It's for you," she says. "Strange, though – there's no address. Must have been hand-delivered."

My name is written across the front in bold capital letters. My stomach contorts. I know exactly who sent this.

My stalker is back.

Chapter 27

IT SEEMS YOU'VE HAD QUITE THE DAY! WHAT A PITY. SORRY TO HEAR ABOUT CALEB. IT WOULD BE SUCH A SHAME IF SOMETHING HAPPENS TO HIM IN THE HOSPITAL. FOURTH FLOOR, ROOM THIRTEEN, RIGHT?

"I've got to go," I say, getting up abruptly.

"What is it?" Mum asks, trying to get a glimpse of the letter. But I pull it away from her view. She doesn't need to worry about this as well; I've caused enough trouble.

"Oi, no more lies, remember?" Faith snaps. "Maisie, come on!"

"I'll explain everything, I promise. But this is an emergency."

"Maisie!"

"Not now! I'm not lying, I'm just ... in a rush."

Faith huffs and slouches back into the sofa. Mum stands between us, her eyes imploring. I reach out to touch her hand. "I'll explain everything, I promise. No more lies, yeah?"

She smiles, though it's full of sadness. "See you later, darling. Call if you need us."

***

The hospital car park is completely full when I arrive, and by the time the lift reaches the fourth floor, I'm sweating profusely, my face flushed. My eyes frantically scan for any sign of my stalker. Have I arrived before her? Did I make it in time?

I have no idea what she intends to do. If anything. She's probably just trying to scare me again, like she did with the screenshot of my search history. She never actually sent that image to Caleb; he found *my* copy. I massively dropped myself in it that day. And I'm scared I'm about to do the same again. But I cannot walk away now. I *have* to know he's safe.

The blinds are drawn in his room, but I see movement behind them. Someone is leaning over his bed.

My heart slams against my ribcage as I enter the room, prepared for the worst. If she wants to torment me, fine — I've earned that. But Caleb? He doesn't deserve this. No more victims. Not him.

I find Caleb lying on the bed, a slender woman leaning in close to him. What is she doing?

I hover at the end of the bed, locked in place by shock. Her lips are pressed against his and he's responding passionately, his tongue sliding into her mouth.

They're oblivious to my intrusion as he brings an arm around and hooks it under her tiny, denim-clad arse.

My breath catches, a sharp pain spreading through my chest. I should leave, pretend I never saw this, but I know if I move now I will draw their attention. So I stand immobilised, not knowing what to do with myself.

I watch as this woman runs her hand over Caleb's head and withdraws slightly, smiling, looking into his eyes with profound fondness. "Calm down," she murmurs. "We don't want to cause you more damage."

"I'll cause you some damage," Caleb growls. They both laugh.

Then the woman pulls back and notices me for the first time, her eyes widening.

"Maisie!" she says, as though she already knows me.

Caleb nudges her aside to get a look at me. The fury on his face is scalding. "I told you to leave!" he barks.

Despite everything – the fear I felt when he was knocked off his motorbike, the terror of my stalker threatening to hurt him – right now all I feel is pissed off.

Yes, I lied, and I'll forever regret that. Yes, I've committed some truly reprehensible acts. But that doesn't mean I should just push Caleb's misdemeanour aside.

"You cheated on me," I snap. "Don't you think it's time you got off your high horse and tell me some goddamn truths yourself?"

His eyes narrow. "Steph, you should go," he tells this woman, his tone gentle.

She turns to him with wide eyes. "No, I'm staying."

"Please, Steph."

Steph doesn't move. Instead, she clutches Caleb's hands and perches on the edge of the bed, her gaze fixed on me.

Caleb sighs but doesn't say anything else. He returns his attention to me. "Fine, let's lay it all out on the table, shall we?" Caleb suggests. "I met Steph during a night out, quite some time ago."

I swallow hard. "How long has this been going on?"

"Initially, it was nothing. Just a random encounter, a passing moment. Steph will tell you, I told her that I was in a relationship with you, and we went our separate ways. But then we kept bumping into each other on nights out, and ... I don't know, Maisie. It just grew into something more."

He's speaking as though I'm some impartial observer rather than someone whose heart is breaking with every word. Steph at least has the humility to look ashamed. Caleb appears as though he's unburdening himself of an enormous weight, his words tumbling out of him, increasing in volume as he talks.

"Then, when you were attacked ..." He pauses to acknowledge the elephant in the room – it was a lie. "I told Steph we needed to stop. I tried, Maisie, I really did. I wanted to be a good boyfriend to you. And then when I found out none of it was true ..." He throws me a grim look.

"You jumped right back into bed with her?"

They glance at each other and no more words are needed.

"Caleb." I pause, attempting to piece together my thoughts. "You're a cheating piece of shit and a liar. So don't you dare come at me." I stride towards the door, but before exiting, I pivot sharply. "You think I'm the villain? You should look in the mirror, Caleb."

As I approach the corridor's end, Troy walks towards me, frowning. He sports an impressive bruise along the side of his face that makes me wince.

"What are you doing here?" he demands. "You shouldn't be here."

"Just saying my goodbyes." I attempt to push past him, but he seizes my wrist.

"I mean it, Maisie. You have no idea of the damage you've done to him."

"Did you know he was cheating on me, Troy? Did you encourage him? Are you partly to blame?"

His mouth opens, then snaps shut. He doesn't deny it. Doesn't even try. Guilt is written all over his face, but there's something else – frustration? Pity? It's as though he's trying to decide whether to defend Caleb or let me walk away with the last word. "What you did was far worse," he finally admits.

"You don't think I know that?! You want to know the difference, Troy? *Remorse.* I feel fucking awful for what I did. Whereas he's lying in there fondling her arse."

I wrench my wrist from his grasp and storm away.

I'm not taking any more shit. From Troy. From Caleb. From that trashy gossip-mongering stalker.

I'm done.

Chapter 28

The anger from confronting Caleb still simmers inside me as I drive away from the hospital, a strange mix of determination and unease coiling in my chest. I crank up Beyoncé, allowing the music to drown out the doubt creeping in.

The letter from my stalker rests on the passenger seat, its bold text screaming up at me. Traffic slows on the bridge, and I crumple the paper into a tight ball, hurling it out of the window. It lands in the river where the murky brown water soaks it, causing the text to bleed into a blur.

I'm almost at Mum's house when I deliberately by-pass the turn. I continue down York Street and head onto Langdale Close. Rainy's house. It's time I visited the baby. It's time I concentrated my efforts on what truly matters.

Rainy's husband, Steven, answers the door. He appears flustered and my five-year-old niece, Stella, clings to his hip, her eyes reddened from crying.

"Are you alright?" I ask, before he can speak.

"Rainy's asleep with the baby."

"That's fine." I brush past him and enter the kitchen where a mountain of dirty dishes dominates the sink. I turn on the tap and find the dishwashing liquid.

"Tea?" Steven asks, bewildered.

"Sit down. I'll make us one once I'm done here."

But Steven remains standing, uncertain how to behave. I continue pottering around the kitchen. I know I have a *lot* of making up to do, but this seems an appropriate starting point. I silently vow to offer help more often. To be a better sister.

I'm done focusing on people who do not deserve my respect. My entire relationship with Caleb was a farce. A collection of lies and deceit.

I don't know what my future holds with my sisters, but we're *family* – it's worth at least finding out.

I pour water into a teapot and fetch three mugs. While the tea is brewing, I fill the children's water bottles and distribute packets of crisps among them all.

Just as everyone settles in front of the television and Steven sits in the kitchen, clutching his tea and looking profoundly less harassed, Rainy appears with a tiny, rosy-cheeked infant in her arms. Rainy looks exhausted, as though she hasn't slept in weeks.

"Oh, Rains, she's gorgeous," I exclaim, rushing toward her.

Rainy steps back, bewildered, keeping Blue out of my reach. "What are you doing here?"

"I wanted to help," I explain.

Rainy's brows furrow as she glances at Steven.

He shrugs. "She ... tidied the kitchen," he states, as if trying to make sense of it himself.

Her eyes widen as she takes in the clear countertops and empty bin. "Thank you," she says, though she still sounds unsure. "Did Mum make you come?"

"She mentioned you were poorly. I wanted to do something nice."

But my words seem to bounce right off her. She shifts her weight onto one hip and looks at me suspiciously before sitting at the table and bringing Blue to her breast.

"Rainy, I came to say I'm sorry," I admit. "I'm sorry I haven't been here for you. Sorry for being distant and rude. But just so you know, I care about you, and I'd like to put it right."

She slowly sips her tea, mulling over my words. "I heard about what you did. About the attack," she finally says. Steven looks away, embarrassed. "Why did you do that, Mais?"

"I wish I knew," I whisper. "The truth is, I don't know anything anymore."

Her expression softens as she meets my gaze, but her words are harsh. "I don't think I'll ever be able to trust you."

Her words are like a stab to my heart, but I can't blame her. Not only have I lied about the attack, I feel as if I have been hiding behind my lies for so long, no one truly knows who I am. Damn, I'm not even sure I know who I am anymore.

But now I have the time and inclination to discover myself. Start afresh. I have a little money saved. So if Mum is happy for me to stay with her for a while, I'm going to start from scratch, get qualified in something that interests me, find a new job, and move on with my life. I'm determined to become the best daughter and sister to my family.

"I understand," I tell Rainy. "But I want to at least try to make it up to you. If you'll let me."

She studies me over her mug until Blue lets out a tiny whimper as she finishes her feed, capturing Rainy's attention.

"May I hold her?" I ask. I've never asked to hold her children before, and I'm as shocked as she is.

Rainy hesitates.

"Go on, love. Maisie can hold the baby," Steven encourages.

Reluctantly, Rainy transfers Blue to my arms, and I cradle her gently. Blue's eyes are enormous, her hands impossibly tiny. She's precious. Utterly perfect. Something within me shifts, and warmth spreads through my veins.

"She's so beautiful," I gasp. "Oh, Rainy, you're the luckiest woman in the world."

"All my kids are beautiful," she states.

I look at her and nod. "Perhaps I could babysit sometimes?"

She laughs then, a joyous, barking laugh that makes Blue jump. "You're getting a bit ahead of yourself, aren't you?" She wipes a tear from the corner of her eye and exhales sharply, shaking her head. "Jesus, Maisie. You're being really weird. You've shut us out your entire life, and now you're here playing house. Why now?"

I widen my eyes at her, imploring her to understand. "Just gained some perspective lately." Blue strokes her hand down my cheek, her expression stern and grumpy as if she's trying to figure me out, too.

"She's about to shit," Steven announces.

And sure enough, Blue's bottom releases wet bubbles, and I thrust her into Steven's arms.

Rainy's laughter erupts anew, louder and more vivacious than before. "Let's postpone the babysitting idea for now, yeah?"

"That's probably for the best," I laugh. "I can visit more often and help out though, if you're up for it?"

"Let's just take it slow, yeah?" Rainy suggests, though she touches my hand, a gesture of reconciliation that I accept with a sigh of relief.

"I'd like that," I smile.

***

Imarah doesn't even let me into her apartment. She answered the intercom cheerfully, but upon hearing my voice, she hung up.

I try again. And again.

"What do you want, Maisie?" she finally answers.

"Can we talk?"

"About what?"

"About everything!"

"No." And she hangs up again.

Imarah is my best friend; she's stood by me through everything. It's her withdrawal that hurts the most. I'd fight to the death for her.

I press the button with my thumb and don't let go.

"What?!" she eventually yells into the speaker.

"I know you hate me. As you should. But if you're going to shut me out forever, at least tell me face-to-face."

She sighs, and just as I think she's about to hang up again, the buzzer sounds and the lock clicks open.

When I enter her apartment, she's standing in the living room, arms folded and her face livid. "Say what you must and then leave," she instructs through gritted teeth.

"Fine. It won't take long." I dip my head at her, ensuring she's listening to every word. "Imarah, I've been through so much lately. The public humiliation, Caleb breaking up with me, being attacked with what I thought was acid, finding out that Caleb was cheating on me. But nothing – absolutely nothing – hurts more than knowing I've caused you pain. If you want nothing more to do with me, I understand, but please, you must know how sorry I am."

She just presses her lips together and continues to stare at me. A tear traces down her cheek. "Why did you lie like that?" she finally asks. "What made you do it?"

The million-dollar question, it seems. I've admitted to everyone that I did it for attention, to control my relationship with Caleb. But Imarah knows me intimately; she already knows this. So I opt for the raw, painful truth. "Because I'm selfish. Because I couldn't see beyond my own upset to appreciate the pain I was inflicting. Because I'm fundamentally horrible." The last words are barely more than a whisper.

Still Imarah doesn't move, but her expression has changed from defiance to one of agony. I wish I had words to wipe away that look. Knowing I've hurt her will eternally scar me.

Finally, she speaks. "My therapist says I have a rescuer complex." She laughs humourlessly. "Apparently I'm drawn to people I believe need saving."

"Is that why you've put up with me all these years?" The question pains me.

"Maybe at first." She looks me in the eyes. "But that's not why I stayed. You were there for me when my mum died, Maisie. When everyone else didn't know what to say to me, you just sat with me. For days. You didn't try to fix it. You just … existed with me, in that terrible space."

I remember those dark days, how small and broken Imarah had seemed. "I know there's nothing I can do to make this up to you. But I am genuinely sorry, Imarah." I move closer to her. "And please know, you've been the bestest friend. I never deserved you. Thank you."

She doesn't say anything.

I hesitate, gripping the door frame as though it might hold me together. "So where does that leave us?" I ask.

"I don't know. Not fixed. But not broken beyond repair, either. But it's time you left."

So I leave.

Chapter 29

Walking down Mum's front path, I notice something unusual stuck to the side of the door.

"Mum, that black thing next to the door? Is that a doorbell camera?" I ask once I'm inside.

She cocks her head and continues past me into the kitchen, clutching a basket full of laundry. "Honestly, Maisie, do you ever listen? Yes, it is! I told you weeks ago. Best purchase I've ever made. I saw Mr. Henson from down the road take a tumble a few days ago. Funniest thing I've seen in ages."

How could I have missed that? I really have been too focused on myself.

This sounds almost too good to be true. Surely not. "Mum, how long do you keep the recordings?"

She presses buttons on the washing machine, tongue sticking out in concentration. I watch with rising blood pressure.

"I don't know, darling," she says, finally granting me her attention. "I just check the app when notifications pop up on my phone. I don't fully understand how it works."

"Do you mind if I have a look?"

"Help yourself. You'll need to find my phone first. I've put it down somewhere. I can never keep up with that thing."

I discover it wedged between sofa cushions. There are no security measures on her lock screen, and the app is easy to find. There are literally hundreds of video snippets showing people walking by, and I head straight to footage from three hours ago. My heart pounds as I scroll through the recordings. A man walks a chihuahua. A courier delivers a package across the street.

Then – there. A flicker of movement. My breath catches in my throat. And ... *bingo*. I watch the video over and over.

"Impressive, isn't it?" Mum asks, creeping up behind me.

Imarah was definitely right – my stalker is female. I can tell by the skinny jeans and shapely legs. She's tall, taller than me, and slim, wearing a plain black hoodie with the hood raised and a maroon scarf pulled up over her mouth. She moves quickly, face turned from the camera, the dark scarf obscuring her profile. There's something about her posture, the purposeful way she moves, that triggers a memory. But I can't quite place it.

"It could be anyone," I sigh.

Watching for the tenth time, I spot a gold watch glinting on her wrist. One of those smart devices, but with a fancier strap. It looks so familiar.

At least I now know definitively that it's a woman. So that eliminates half the population.

Brilliant.

I watch as the figure hurries towards the house, hands thrust deep in pockets. She pulls out the note and pushes it through the letterbox before rushing off to the left. She practically runs away. I continue to replay the video.

"It's great for watching the neighbours," Mum says.

"It's amazing," I agree. I forward the clip to myself and hand the phone back to her. "Thanks, Mum."

She shrugs indifferently. "Any time. Shall I go to the chippy for dinner? I'm not in the mood to cook tonight."

"I'll go," I offer. "Fish and chips, lots of salt and vinegar?"

"You know me so well," she giggles. "Thanks, love."

The fish and chip shop is only at the end of the street, so I decide to walk. The sun is starting to dip below the horizon, and dusk provides a layer of protection from being recognised. For an added sense of security, I take a leaf out of my stalker's book and raise my hood, guarding against anyone else who might want to throw anything at me.

I'm sick of this woman calling the shots. I hate that she has power over me. But does she really? Everything is out in the open now. What more could she possibly do to inflict pain? What else have I got to be scared of? There's nothing left to reveal.

Although I know, deep down, that my secrets are no longer the target – my safety is. I have no idea what this woman is capable of. She is clearly unhinged, and after today's frightening encounter, I'm terrified of what desperation might make someone do.

I type a message on my phone. Then common sense takes over and I delete it.

No, screw it. I type it again and press send: *Next time, wave for the camera. I've got you now.*

No more playing games. If she wants to scare me, fine. But I won't make it easy for her. If I must engage in her game, I want to at least dictate some of the rules. Because I like to win.

I order our food with a sly smile. Gaining some of the power back offers catharsis. I still feel vulnerable, make no mistake, but fighting back feels so good. It's time I gave her a taste of her own medicine.

My phone beeps as I'm walking home: *You didn't actually see me though, did you? Silly Maisie. Always three steps behind.*

I type back furiously: *I'll find you. And I'll end you.*

Then I turn off my phone.

It's not until after dinner that I dare turn it back on. I've been forcing food down my neck, nausea making it hard to eat. My thoughts constantly return to the stalker, to the war I have chosen to engage in. I'm frightened, yes. I want to run, but I also know that isn't an option. I need to fight back.

Or lose.

Mum is washing dishes in the kitchen, so I seize the opportunity to check my messages alone. I take a deep breath, steadying my nerves. If I'm going to fight this nasty piece of work, I need to toughen up. No more cowering in fear of her next move.

There's nothing from the stalker, but four missed calls from Imarah. I run straight upstairs and return her call, my heart hammering in my chest.

"Maisie," Imarah says, her tone urgent. It feels so good to hear her voice.

"Are you okay?" I enquire anxiously. Why is she calling me so soon after severing ties?

She stutters before pausing, as if to compose herself. "I think so," she finally responds. "I thought I heard someone here. But maybe I'm just being paranoid."

My racing heart stops and plummets into my stomach. "I'm on my way. Did you call the police?"

"No. I wasn't sure and didn't want to bother them for nothing, you know?"

"Lock your door. I'll be there in ten."

I find her on the sofa clutching a glass of wine. She appears more relaxed now than she sounded on the phone.

"What happened?" I ask immediately.

"Oh, a whole lot of nothing, it turns out. I think I was just on edge after seeing you, and it made me paranoid. I was being silly."

She has every right to be worried. The stalker has already been in here and seems hell-bent on frightening me – and now, my friends too. There's every possibility she might return here to terrify us further. Or worse, inflict punishment.

"Imarah, I know you hate me, and I can't blame you for that," I implore. "But we need to sort this out. I need to know you're safe. And you need to let me in so I can do just that. Afterwards, you can go back to hating me."

She exhales slowly, gripping the stem of her wine glass and staring into the golden liquid. "I don't know, Maisie. I don't trust you." She swirls the wine gently. "But ... I don't trust this stalker, either. And just for the record, I don't hate you. I just don't think I know who you truly are anymore."

I approach and kneel before her. "I completely understand. But I swear, from this moment forward, you'll only see me – the *real* me. I'll never lie to you again."

She taps the side of her glass, her eyes boring into mine. "I can't forgive you. Not yet."

"I don't want your forgiveness. I don't need anything from you. But just a chance to make things right would be the best thing ever. Please, Imarah."

"Let's just find this stalker and go from there, yeah?"

I nod. "Yes. Yes, great idea." I sit beside her on the sofa.

"So what do we do?" Imarah asks before draining her glass in one swig. She gestures for me to fetch the remainder of the bottle, which I do, along with a glass for myself.

"I think we should go back to the police," I suggest. I don't know what else to do. There must be *something* they can do to help.

"Good. I'm pleased you've said that. I don't think vigilantism would look good on me."

"No? I think you'd rock a Batman costume."

She laughs softly. "You'd rock a bin bag."

We both sit quietly, immersed in our thoughts and drinking wine. We finish the bottle, and Imarah opens another. Evidently, we won't be visiting the police station tonight.

"So, what information do you have about this person? Let's lay it all out."

I share everything I know about the stalker, which isn't substantial. But I can confirm her gender.

Imarah scoffs. "Crazy bitch," she says. I laugh in acknowledgement. She reaches for her laptop. "Have you checked the online posts about yourself lately? Perhaps she's actively participating in the 'Hate Maisie' campaign."

That's a good idea. With the barrage of insults directed at me, I've deleted my accounts, but Imarah's right – perhaps a pattern will emerge that exposes the perpetrator.

I move closer to her as she signs in and opens multiple browser tabs. Within minutes she's accessed various sites, all discussing me. I was aware my story was popular, but I never fully realised the extent of the venom directed at me. I read one vicious statement after another. A lot of them are lies, ironically. But everyone seems determined to hate me.

One woman has composed an extensive post detailing the damage I've supposedly inflicted upon victims of sexual crimes. She claims I deserved to have acid thrown in my face; that it would be nothing compared to the suffering I've caused.

Post after post. Comment after comment, we read through it all. My hands shake as we scroll. The words blur together. My breath catches and my stomach twists as though I might throw up. This isn't just hate; it's a lynch mob.

I know I did wrong. I readily hold my hands up and admit that. But what specific harm did I inflict upon each of these people? It's as if I've personally wounded every one of them. To receive this level of vitriol? This should be criminal in itself.

"Does anyone particularly stand out to you?" Imarah asks, glancing at me for the first time. "Oh, Maisie! Are you alright?"

I quickly wipe away my tears. I don't get to feel upset. This is all my fault. "I'm fine," I say.

She places a comforting hand on my leg. "Look, what you did was ... abhorrent. But that doesn't mean these people speak the truth. They're deliberately malicious, Maisie. Don't listen to them. They don't know anything about you."

I simply nod. They might not know me, but they know what I did. I deserve this backlash. People are bound to despise me; it's just having it all concentrated in one forum that devastates me. The shame is intense.

"No one is jumping out at me," I confirm. "Can we stop now?"

Imarah throws me a sympathetic glance and closes her laptop. "Stay at mine tonight," she suggests. "You can't drive back after drinking all that, anyway."

"Thank you," I murmur, allowing her to refill my glass. I know I have a long way to go to make it up to Imarah, but having her by my side strengthens my resolve and I finally feel my icy core beginning to melt.

CHAPTER 30

I jolt awake to frantic hammering at the door. My mind scrambles, disoriented, but Imarah is already moving beside me, a shadow slicing through the dark. That's when I remember I'm at Imarah's. And something is very, very wrong.

We rush downstairs. Imarah slides a knife out of the block in the kitchen while I approach the door, my pulse racing so violently I'm certain Imarah can hear it.

"What if it's her?" Imarah's voice is barely louder than a whisper, but I can still detect the edge of fear beneath it.

"No. This isn't her style." I press my ear against the wood. "She's a coward who lurks behind a screen. She wouldn't knock."

Imarah joins me in pressing her ear to the door, both of us ludicrously attempting to identify our visitor through sound alone.

"Maisie, get your arse out here!" Faith shouts through the thick wood.

I breathe a sigh of relief. Not my stalker. However, Faith sounds furious, and an angry Faith is never good news, especially in the middle of the night.

I yank the door open, and Faith storms inside like a hurricane. Her oversized T-shirt is twisted with perspiration, her hair a wild tangle, but it's her eyes that cause my stomach to sink – feral, bloodshot, fixed on me as though I'm prey. She doesn't even acknowledge Imarah standing beside me, clutching a knife to her chest.

"Fai— Faith," I stammer. "Why are you here? What's happened?"

"Don't give me that shit. You damn well know why I'm here. Do you have any idea of what you've done?"

I'm confused. What have I supposedly done now? I made amends with her and Rainy. Mum and I are in a really good place. How have I upset her?

Faith jabs a finger into my chest. "Don't look at me like that," she snarls, spittle flying from her mouth. "Don't you dare pretend you don't know. You know exactly what you've done, playing your games as always. But why? Maisie, why is it that every time we get close to being a real family, you have to ruin it? What the fuck is that about? Rainy is heartbroken."

I take a step back. "Faith. Wait. I honestly don't know what you're talking about. I haven't done anything. The last time I saw Rainy, we were on good terms. Better than good, actually!"

"I just—" Faith chokes on her words, shaking her head as though she can't process the situation. "Maisie, this isn't a joke. That message? It wasn't just cruel, it was fucking vile. What is wrong with you?"

Imarah appears beside me and hands me my phone so I can try to make sense of all this. But there are no messages on my phone. "I haven't sent anything to Rainy. See?"

Faith groans and takes her own phone out of her bag. "Here," she says, thrusting it at me, slamming it into my chest with enough force it winds me slightly.

On the screen is a screenshot of a message supposedly sent from me to Rainy two hours ago while I was asleep: *It's time we put things straight. I want nothing to do with you or that ugly baby. Come near me again and I'll slit that baby's throat.*

The words sear into my brain like a branding iron. My lungs seize. I can't breathe, I can't think. The phone slips from my fingers, clattering onto the kitchen counter, but I barely register the sound over the rush of blood in my ears. This can't be real. But the words are there in black and white, my name beside them.

What is happening? I don't understand. I did not send that message, but I can't articulate this to Faith. The words are trapped inside me. I don't know how to respond. I'm panicking.

Imarah reaches for my shoulder, and I look at her with pleading eyes. *Help me.*

She understands. She knows me. Pulling me close, she embraces me tightly. Her arms brace me, making me feel secure and protected. As seconds slip by, my breathing gradually returns to normal, and I no longer feel as though I'm knocking on death's door.

Imarah shifts, preparing to speak, but before she can, Faith wrenches her away with a sharp tug. The sudden movement knocks me off balance. "That's enough," she hisses, stepping between us like a shield. "You might have her fooled, but she'll get to know you, too. The hard way. Don't you dare act all innocent. That message came from your account. Clear as day. You're sick, and you can fucking stay away from all of us."

"Wait, has Mum seen this?" I finally manage to ask.

I was finally reconnecting with them all. I was opening up, and we were starting to understand each other. My heart cracks. How can everything deteriorate so badly in such a short amount of time? In getting my family back, I was starting to get myself back in the process. And now I'm completely gone.

"No, she hasn't, and she isn't going to. It would break her heart." Faith's voice softens, but her expression hardens. "But Maisie, you need to stay far away. I'll talk to Mum. I'll make up some excuse, but you must stay away. You're poison to this family."

"No," I protest. "I didn't send this, Faith. You must believe me. Why would I do something like this?"

"Why do you do any of the shit you've put us through?" She grabs her phone back and pushes past me, her shoulder colliding with mine.

"Wait! I was with her!" Imarah shouts at Faith's departing figure. "She didn't send that message, I swear!"

"You're a bigger fool than I thought. I always found your friendship with her a bit weird. Let her go, Imarah, before she drags you down to her level."

I watch her go then, stunned into silence as Imarah hurries to lock the door behind her. For the first time, I see how frightened she is. Her panicked action at locking the door is frantic, like the stalker is about to burst through.

Imarah turns to face me, her mouth agape. "This is getting out of hand," she finally says.

"I didn't do it," I gasp. "I didn't send that message." It feels as though a million insects are crawling across my skin, digging in with their feet and claws, making me itch. It burns. "Imarah – I didn't do it!"

"Hey, I know. I know." She wraps her arms around me and gently guides me to the sofa, encouraging me to sit down. "Police tomorrow, yeah?" she asks softly, brushing hair from my face as I sob.

I nod, but deep down, I know the truth: no one is coming to save me. The police won't believe me. Faith won't believe me. And if I don't find out who's doing this, I might lose everything.

Chapter 31

The police station reeks of industrial bleach, sharp and artificial. It sticks to the inside of my nose despite barely masking the acrid scent of stale sweat and vomit. Whatever nightmares they had to scrub from these floors last night.

"Hello," the desk officer mumbles without bothering to look away from his screen.

"I have a stalker," I blurt out, the words hanging in the air between us. Imarah gives a small, encouraging nod beside me.

The officer slides a clipboard across the desk with two fingers, like he's passing over something contaminated. "Fill this out."

I go through the motions yet again, but differently this time. I fill in my details with conviction instead of that tremor of doubt I felt last time. I'm here because I have every right to be here. Even liars deserve safety. At least that's what I tell myself. But my hand trembles as the pen hovers over the paper, because what if they've been right all along? What if I don't deserve any help?

"Maisie? Everything okay?" I look up to see Evelyn approaching, clutching a wad of papers. "Hang on."

She places the papers on the front desk and exchanges hushed words with the desk officer, who finally deigns to look at me. They're talking about me.

"Stefan says you have a stalker?" Evelyn asks, dark circles shadowing her eyes. "Want to come and talk it through?" She looks as exhausted as I feel. Maybe she's been working all night.

We follow her into a small office that looks like it's been hit by a paper tornado. "Sorry it's a mess. We've had a busy night. A bunch of idiots tried to rob the local KFC and met their match in the manager who beat the shit out of them." She cracks a tired smile. "It was … interesting."

I study Evelyn as she settles behind her desk. She's impressive. The kind of strength that doesn't crumble when tested. Maybe I can borrow some of that.

"So, this stalker?" Evelyn prompts, leaning forward. "Still bothering you, then?"

I place my phone on her desk and open the message thread, stomach clenching as I display them all in sequence. Seeing them laid out like this sends ice through my veins. The hate pouring from the screen makes me feel physically sick.

Evelyn scrolls through, her expression unreadable until she stops, eyebrow raised. "'I'll end you,'" she reads, pointing at my last response to the stalker. "That's a little threatening, isn't it?"

That's what she focuses on? You've got to be kidding me. I feel heat rising to my face, but before I can defend myself, she holds up her hands.

"Look, I'm on your side here. Just want to address the elephant in the room. Get it over with."

I guess that makes sense. "Well, yes, I was tired of it all."

"I bet! Jesus, Maisie, why didn't you come to us sooner?"

My cheeks burn as I glance toward Imarah for support, but she's suddenly fascinated by the clock on the wall. "With everything that happened with the attack …"

Evelyn sighs, running a hand through her hair. "I had to pull a lot of strings to stop my boss bringing you in for questioning. I'm not asking if what happened was true or not. I'd rather not know. And honestly, I think you've already paid the price."

The shame blazes hotter now. "Will you help me?"

She leans back in her chair, weighing me up. The silence stretches between us. Unbearably long.

"Look, Maisie, I'll pass your phone to our IT guy, but I need to be straight with you. These cases are tough – stalkers cover their tracks well, and they're rarely caught. But I *will* push for this to be taken seriously, but …" She lowers her voice. "I'm saying this as a friend, not in my official capacity – I wouldn't hold your breath."

"So you won't even try?" The words come out sharper than intended.

"Of course I'll try! It's my job. I just want you to have realistic expectations about how far we might get."

Imarah leans forward suddenly, her finger jabbing the desk for emphasis. "Can you at least see who hacked her Facebook account and sent that message to Rainy?"

Evelyn shrugs. "You'll need to speak to someone at Facebook. If you've been hacked on their platform, they're the ones who can trace it."

If. One tiny word that tells me everything I need to know. She doesn't believe me.

"I've already tried that," I say, frustration tightening my voice. "You can't get through to an actual human, and when you flag it as a security issue, nothing happens. Absolutely nothing."

Evelyn bites the inside of her cheek, thinking. "Then your best option is to delete the account completely. Make yourself harder to target. They'll eventually get bored and move on."

"Or they'll take more drastic measures," I counter.

"*Then* we'll have a case."

"So you're telling me you'll do nothing until I'm actually harmed?"

"I never said that," she replies. "I'll take your statement so we have it on file, and I'll see what evidence we can take from your phone. These investigations are about *building* a case. Consider this the foundation."

I scoff. "Thanks for nothing."

Evelyn raises her hands in surrender. "I'm doing what I can. I appreciate you're frightened, but with your history …" She doesn't finish the sentence. She doesn't need to. "It'll be an uphill battle to get the department fully on board. But I'll push for it."

I cringe at the reference to my past. "Fine," I mutter, admitting defeat.

"No, hang on a minute," Imarah says, leaning forward so suddenly that Evelyn startles slightly. "There must be *something* you can do. This isn't just harmless online trolling. She's a genuine threat – she's been inside my home! She's destroyed Maisie's family!"

"That's the problem, though," Evelyn says. "There are no explicit threats we can act on. Disturbing, yes. Invasive, absolutely. But not technically threatening. And we can't prove she sent that message to Maisie's sister without Facebook's cooperation. Get me something concrete to work with."

"So you're asking victims to do police work now?" Imarah's voice rises dangerously.

Evelyn's expression hardens. "We simply don't have the resources for digital forensics on cases without clear and present danger. Now, shall we get on with taking your statement?"

***

"Still nothing from Facebook," Imarah huffs, slamming her laptop shut. "How does the world's biggest social media platform not have actual customer service? It's beyond ridiculous."

I just shrug, downing more wine. "Maybe that's why they're so profitable – they've eliminated the pesky expense of actually helping their users."

"Yeah, well, it's disgusting."

I nod absent-mindedly, eyes fixed on my screen. Getting mad about Facebook's failings is a pointless dead end that won't get us anywhere. Something tells me the answers are hidden right here in plain sight, buried in the comments and messages. This person radiates hatred for me, and this level of hatred surely makes people careless. She must be here somewhere.

"Something's bugging me," I say, more to myself than Imarah. "The night of the break-in – how did she know I was here? How did she know where to find me?" I look up sharply. "Did you tell anyone I was staying with you?"

Imarah's eyes widen, clearly affronted. "No! I didn't breathe a word to anyone."

"I'm not accusing you," I backtrack quickly. "I'm just trying to understand what we're dealing with here. This person knows things about me that aren't public: where I'm hiding, who I'm with, my family connections, even my sister's personal details."

"When you put it like that, it's creepy as fuck."

"So either they're some kind of digital detective genius, combing through every trace of my existence online ..." I pause, the alternative forming a cold knot in my stomach. "Or they already know me."

Imarah presses her lips into a thin line, eyebrows furrowed. "Right, we're not leaving this sofa until we find something." She pulls her laptop back open and hunkers down beside me, the glow of the screen illuminating her face as she concentrates.

We work in silence for nearly an hour; the only sounds are the soft click of keys and occasional sips of wine. Then suddenly, Imarah lets out a gasp so loud that I physically jump, sloshing pinot grigio down my shirt.

"Jesus Christ, Ims! What the hell?"

"Nothing," she says too quickly, eyes darting away from her screen.

"Show me," I demand, reaching for the laptop.

She watches me carefully as she surrenders the computer to me. I know what's coming before I even see it. Caleb's profile.

Caleb Rush is in a relationship with Stephanie Poleni.

So, it's official then. The pain cuts through me with surgical precision, and I have to physically fight the tears threatening to spill. I can't break down in front of Imarah right now. We've got enough to deal with without adding a mental breakdown to the mix.

"I'm so sorry," she whispers, watching me carefully. "Are you okay?"

"I'm fine," I lie with forced joy. "I knew this was coming. It's hardly a shock. Besides, after what I did to Caleb …"

"You're allowed to feel hurt, you know," she says. "What happened was complicated, and yes, you made mistakes. But that doesn't mean you have to pretend you don't feel anything."

"Please, Imarah. I'm okay." I hand the laptop back and refocus on the tablet, though the words swim meaninglessly before my eyes as I mindlessly scroll to create the illusion of concentration.

That happened fast. Too fast. And to announce it so publicly, like some kind of achievement. I couldn't help but notice the flood of likes and congratulatory comments, everyone celebrating that Caleb finally shed the toxic baggage that is Maisie Tallow.

"Well, she's not even close to being as pretty as you," Imarah declares, scrolling through Steph's photos. "Seriously, she's got nothing on you."

I manage a grateful laugh, even as we both know she's blatantly lying.

Imarah cocks her head to the side and looks up at me. "Hey, you don't think it could be her, do you?"

"Her what?"

"The stalker ... Could it be the new girlfriend?" She sits up straighter. "You said they were together before you broke up, right? Maybe she orchestrated all this to drive you out of the picture."

The idea hits like a punch to the gut. It makes a terrible kind of sense. Sort of. My stalker knows things about me, intimate details that Caleb could have shared. They have a hatred for me that would make sense coming from a jealous new girlfriend.

My stomach lurches violently.

Is it her? Stephanie?

But no. My shoulders drop. "No, if it was her, why continue all this? She's got everything she wanted. She won. She got the guy."

"People who do this kind of stuff are clearly unhinged, Maisie. I think she deserves the top spot on our suspect list."

I watch Imarah from the corner of my eye as she mutters to herself, pressing her tongue against her cheek the way she always does when deep in thought. A sudden wave of gratitude nearly overwhelms me. What would have happened if she hadn't been in my life? Taking me in probably saved more than just my sanity – it might have saved my life.

The emotion catches me off guard. "Thanks, Imarah," I whisper.

She looks up, genuinely surprised. "Eh?"

"Thank you," I repeat, more firmly this time. "For all of this. For everything."

She frowns at me. "Where's this coming from?"

"I'm just ... I'm so grateful to have you in my corner. I don't deserve you."

"Come here, you soppy idiot." She wraps a protective arm around me and pulls me close. I rest my head against her shoulder, finally letting myself feel safe, if only for a moment. "The past is in the past, right? We're moving forward."

"Definitely."

"And we're going to take down this psycho bitch."

"Damn right we are."

For just a fleeting second, I allow hope to worm its way through the cracks in my defences. But the feeling dies as quickly as it came – what if my stalker really is Caleb's new girlfriend? What if this is just the beginning of her plan to punish me for what I did? What kind of crazy has Caleb got involved with?

CHAPTER 32

The smell of old coffee and Jan's perfume smacks me in the face the second I step inside the office. The buzzing fluorescent lights flicker overhead, casting shadows over the lockers that never shut properly and the half-dead plants no one remembers to water. I let out a slow breath. This place is still a dump.

My desk is exactly how I left it. Keyboard pushed back to encourage the cleaners to wipe my desk. They haven't. A pink nail file stands sentinel in the mug where I keep my pens. The unicorn sticker Alec gave me for actually remembering to turn my monitor off peels at the corner of my keyboard.

I sink into my chair and press the PC's power button, watching as it starts its slow on-routine.

"Nice of you to join us, at long last." Alec appears at my shoulder, panting slightly, his tone carrying that particular blend of sarcasm and forced cheerfulness that management adopts, probably learnt at some pointless management course.

"Sorry, Alec. I've been really poorly. You wouldn't have wanted me to bring it into the office."

We both know it's a lie. I don't want to lie, but the truth feels like a luxury I can't afford right now. I need to keep this job until I find another. I turn away, hoping he'll take the hint and leave me to sift through the hundreds of junk emails I've missed. But he clears his throat pointedly. I pretend not to hear.

"Maisie, can you step into my office please?"

I follow him up the stairs, my gaze drawn to his round physique. He looks like an apple in his red shirt and green chinos. His thick neck, the stalk that tops the fruit.

We sit down, and I feel my mood turning solemn to match his sombre expression.

"Maisie, I don't like doing this, but we need to talk about your absences." His hands hover over a sheet of paper on his desk, fingers twitching as though he's afraid to touch it.

"Yes, annual leave and sick leave. I'm entitled to both." I inject confidence into my voice, but we both know I've burned through my allowance weeks ago.

"You certainly are, but we can't ignore the fact that you weren't indeed sick."

I bristle. "I was. Sickness and diarrhea."

He runs his tongue over his top teeth, a nervous habit I've noticed whenever he's about to deliver bad news. He looks somehow more uncomfortable than I feel, which is quite an achievement. "We have seen the furore that has been following you online, Maisie."

My attention snaps to the window where people hurry across the car park, hunched to escape the wind that's whipping through town. My eye catches movement – a woman standing among the trees at the edge of the property, half hidden in shadows. Is she watching me? My pulse quickens.

"HR have been undertaking an assessment of the quality of work across the team."

HR? But we don't even have a dedicated HR department. That's just him. He means himself. My stomach lurches. Did they check my search history? The two weeks I spent obsessively planning a Bali trip I was never going to take? The weightlifting programme I bookmarked but never started? The printer logs ... Oh God, the printer logs. I force myself to breathe, to maintain some semblance of composure. In short, my quality of work has been shocking.

"Everyone received an email about it ..."

"But I haven't been here!" My voice rises, panicked.

"I sent it to your personal email address, too. I felt it only fair considering your extended absence."

"Has everyone been assessed? Because Jan spends more time filing her nails than making sales calls." The accusation sounds petty, even to my own ears.

"All staff's work has been assessed and addressed accordingly," he replies stiffly.

An awkward silence fills the room, pressing down on me until I physically slump forward. The irony doesn't escape me – I don't even like this job, but it's the only thing holding me together at this point. I can't lose my boyfriend, my home, my family, and now my income.

I can't lose this. Not now. Not after everything else. If I lose my job, I lose rent money. I lose the last shred of routine holding me together. I lose another excuse I can use to pretend everything is fine.

Imarah cannot prop me up forever.

Alec continues his corporate sermon about ethics and the company's reputation, words washing over me. Then he turns over the document he's been fidgeting with and slides it across the desk towards me. The movement pulls my attention back from my internal panic.

"This is a letter of termination."

"Excuse me?" The words come out as a squeak.

"Maisie, we're terminating your employment contract. We will pay you another month, but we'd like you to pack your bag and leave this morning. Without making a fuss."

"You can't do this." My voice betrays me completely now, high-pitched and childlike.

"I can assure you everything is above board. I have had our solicitor look over everything. You're welcome to appoint your own if you'd like to double-check."

I shake my head, defeat washing over me in a cold wave. "No. No, it's okay." Because we both know I cannot afford one, and even if I could, what would be the point?

"I have included a letter of reference."

I scoff before I can stop myself. That should make for an interesting read.

"You produced some good work, Maisie. I have focused on that."

I nod. Every last drop of energy has been sapped from my body, and all I want is for this uncomfortable chair to fall through the floor and take me with it.

"I wish you all the best, Maisie."

Dismissed. Just like that.

As I step out of the office for the last time, the wind cuts through my coat, making me shiver violently.

Across the car park, near the trees, that same figure stands motionless. Watching. The hairs on the back of my neck rise. I blink, and she turns away.

"Hey!" I call out, my voice carried off by the wind.

She moves immediately, stalking away with impressive speed. I take off after her, chest already burning with the effort. If this is my stalker – and I have no doubt in my mind that it must be – she's incredibly fit and practiced at quick getaways.

She pulls away from me and fury rises in me, hot and sudden. To have her so close yet still unidentifiable is infuriating. I skid to a halt, bending to snatch a smooth stone from the ground. Without thinking, I hurl it with all the force my arm can muster. It arcs through the air but falls pathetically short, landing a good twenty metres from its target.

And just like that, she's vanished.

***

I somehow make it back to Imarah's, though I can't remember the drive. The apartment greets me with silence, Imarah still at her work. I pour wine into a glass that's definitely too large for midday drinking and take a generous gulp, hoping it will ease my nerves. But then, a gentle knock at the door startles me.

"Who is it?" I call out shakily.

"Mum."

Mum? What on earth is she doing here?

I open the door to find her bundled in that ancient wool coat she's had since I was in primary school. It looks even scratchier and more worn than I remember, like something even charity shops would reject. "Come in!" I usher her inside, out of the biting cold.

"I didn't know if you'd be in," she says, unwinding her scarf. "But I thought I'd try." Her eyes fix pointedly on the glass of wine clutched in my hand.

I shrug, defiant. When you're unemployed, every hour is drinking hour. "Tea?" I offer halfheartedly, sliding my glass out of sight.

"No, thank you." She turns to face me fully and sighs. "Maisie, what's going on between you and your sisters?" She raises her hand preemptively, cutting off my response. "And don't give me the rubbish your sisters keep trying to feed me. I'm your mother. I know when something bad is happening to my girls."

Screw this. I reach once more for my wine and take a rebellious gulp. "What exactly have they said?"

"Just that things aren't going to work between you and that we should give you some space. But Maisie, I don't understand why. Someone needs to tell me what's going on. We were all starting to get along."

"Take a seat," I gesture toward the sofa, but she remains planted in the kitchen, eyes not leaving my face.

"Mum, please. Just listen. Just for once. I didn't send that message." My knuckles whiten as I grip the counter edge. My breath comes too quickly, too shallow. "You always believe Rainy, you always believe Faith, but never me?"

I hear the petulant edge in my voice, the childish plea, but something is snapping inside of me. I step toward her, hands extended in desperation. "Someone hacked my Facebook account. They sent an awful message to Rainy. It was horrible, vicious even. But it wasn't me."

Confusion clouds her features, but her gaze remains steady. "What exactly did it say?"

I pull up the screenshot and hand her my phone. Her eyes widen as she takes in the words, reading and re-reading like she's hoping the letters might rearrange themselves into something less horrible.

"Why would you send this, Maisie? I thought you were making amends?"

"Mum, I didn't send it. You need to believe me."

"It says your name at the top?"

"Yeah, I know, but that's what I mean – I was hacked, Mum."

She sighs. "I don't really understand what these words mean. Hacked. Phished. Hooked. Whatever."

Hooked? Despite everything, I almost laugh.

"It means someone broke into my account, pretended to be me, and sent that message. But it wasn't me." I emphasise the last words, desperate for her to understand.

"But why would someone do that? It seems unnecessarily complicated."

"That's what I'm trying to figure out!" I say, frustration mounting.

"Okay, so say someone did do this 'hacking' thing to you. Who would do that? Who would go to such efforts?"

The million-dollar question. How I wish I had an answer to that. Instead, I lift my glass and take another long sip. The room is starting to spin.

She watches me with a mixture of disappointment and pity. "Oh, Maisie. Look at you."

I glance down at myself. I'm still in my work clothes. I don't think I look that bad, considering.

"You're here, drinking in the middle of the day. I hardly recognise you anymore. And so many lies."

"But I'm not lying about this!"

"How can we be sure, though? I just don't buy this hacking business. Those things happen to banks and government people, not ordinary people like you and me."

"No, Mum, I—"

"Maisie, I'm just so tired of all this upset. Your sisters were right."

"Mum!"

She's already moving towards the door, her mind made up.

She pauses with her hand on the doorknob. "For the record, Blue isn't ugly, Maisie. She's beautiful. Unlike your heart. I don't know where I went so wrong with you."

I watch her go, unable to move, unable to call her back. Tears blur my vision. The wine glass slips from my suddenly numb fingers and shatters on the floor.

CHAPTER 33

By the time Imarah arrives home, I am spectacularly drunk.

"Do you really think it's her?" I blurt out the second she walks through the door.

She takes one look at me – disheveled hair, glassy eyes, empty wine bottles lining up on the coffee table – and sighs, her shoulders visibly sagging. "Who? What?"

"Caleb's new girlfriend. Do you think she's destroying my life? Because she is, you know, destroying my life. Doing a real good job of it, too."

"How much have you had to drink?" She glances around and notices the wine glass still lying shattered on the floor. "Wait, how long have you been home?" She checks her watch as if it holds all the answers.

"Since this morning," I say. "I texted you."

"No, no you didn't."

I giggle. "I must have forgotten to press send."

"Oh, Maisie," she says, exasperated. "I'll cook you some food and you should get to bed. And weren't you supposed to be back at work today?"

"I got fired today!" I announce, swaying dangerously close to her as she attempts to take off her shoes. "Can you believe it? At first I was devastated, but you know, I think this might actually be a good thing. This is my chance to start anew. All I have to do is stop Caleb's girlfriend from wrecking my life and I can work on re-building it. I can have a brand new start!"

The sober part of my brain knows that I'm speaking too quickly. I can hear the slur in my voice, but can't seem to rein in the drunken chatter. Words spill out of me, messy and unstoppable.

Imarah makes frustrated grunting noises as she moves to the kitchen and gets to work tidying up the broken glass. She hasn't even had time to sit down and I feel awful for her. But when I lurch forward to help, my arm sweeps across the counter and knocks over the spice rack. Bottles roll in every direction. Imarah doesn't shout – she just gently guides me to a chair and places a glass of water in front of me.

"How you feeling now?" Imarah asks, watching me with wary eyes.

"Better." The slur still clings to my words, but my frantic energy is gone. In its place is just shame. "Sorry, Ims." To my absolute horror, I feel my face crumple. The tears come hot and fast – big, ugly, childish sobs.

Imarah rubs her temples. "Maisie, you're making it really hard to be on your side right now." She sighs, long and slow. "I know you're struggling, but you can't just keep … God, Maisie. You can't just keep doing this."

"I know," I manage between blubbering sobs. "But Ims, it's been the shittest day."

I pour it all out: the humiliating meeting with Alec, Mum's visit and her crushing disbelief, the way she walked out on me. I can't handle any more.

I have nothing left. No job, no boyfriend, no home. My entire identity has been stripped away in a matter of weeks. Who am I now? The disgraced liar? The unemployed ex-admin assistant? The homeless person crashing in my overly-generous friend's apartment?

Panic tightens around my chest. My savings will soon run out. How will I support myself? What employer will touch me now that my name is plastered across the local news?

I press my face into my hands.

"Where's the energy you thrust at me when I walked through the door?" Imarah offers a small smile, though it's edged with sharp annoyance. I'm losing her patience.

I shrug helplessly. "It comes and goes." I look at her with hope. "I do think it'll be good to get a new job. It's just a shame I had to be pushed."

"Would you have been motivated to get a better job if you hadn't been pushed, though?"

She has a point. I was comfortable before. With work, with Caleb. Comfortable but far from thriving. In fact, my life was boring. Perhaps that's why I resorted to lying.

Imarah's phone buzzes. "Crap, I left something at work. Will you be okay until I get back?"

I nod. "Of course. What else could possibly go wrong?" I jest, but there's a bitter truth beneath the words. I have nothing left to lose. Except Imarah. "Go careful, yeah?"

She waves away my concern as she grabs her keys. "Wash the dishes while I'm gone! And have some coffee!"

I get to work tidying up, slowly, cautiously, trying really hard not to let my drunken state break something else.

My phone chimes and I pivot too quickly, my hands dripping water everywhere as I lunge for it.

I can see you.

Cold dread slithers down my spine despite the alcohol warming my blood. I scowl and stalk to the window. The sun has slipped beneath the horizon and my eyes scan the darkening street with desperate intensity. *Where are you?* I think, forcing down my fear.

I can't see anyone out there. In a gesture of defiance, I thrust my middle finger toward the empty street and yank the curtains closed with my free hand. "Fuck you!" I spit, turning back to the dishes, determined to keep my hands busy.

But then, impulse takes over.

Want to come in for a cuppa? It's worth a shot. Better than cowering here, jumping at shadows.

Mine's a coffee.

I freeze. Is this for real? Is this nightmare actually going to end over a hot drink?

My thumbs hover over the keyboard, trembling slightly. This is beyond stupid. This is insanity. But if I don't do this, I'll spend the entire night waiting and wondering, drowning in fear.

Door's unlocked.

Okay. I'm coming. It's time we talk.

The wait is excruciating. I stand in the kitchen, a knife clutched in my sweating hand. In my mind, it's Caleb's girlfriend about to walk through the door, but I don't know for sure and the suspense is killing me.

Footsteps approach outside, then halt in front of the door. I'm simultaneously frozen to the spot and desperate to run away. But where to? The front door is the only exit, and the living room window is barely large enough for a child to wriggle through.

There's no knock. The door opens, inch by agonising inch. A hand appears, fingers curled around the edge.

Blind panic swarms me. I lunge forward, bringing the knife down with all the force my terror can muster.

The scream that follows slices through the room, high-pitched and raw. It makes my ears ring and my stomach heave. Blood is everywhere, bright crimson, sickeningly vivid. It drips from her hand and forms a growing pool on the floor. My breath catches in my throat. No. No, no, no.

"Maisie! What have you done?"

"Imarah?"

She is standing in the doorway, clutching her wounded hand to her chest, blood seeping through her fingers and staining her shirt. "Maisie?" Her voice breaks, tears streaming down her face. "You hurt me."

"I'm so sorry," I sob, rushing to grab a kitchen towel to wrap around her hand. The amount of blood is horrendous. "Oh my God, I'm so sorry." I repeat the words over and over.

Imarah backs away from me, as if retreating from a predator. Her face has gone chalk-white, her eyes wide with shock and something worse – fear. Fear of *me*. "You— You stabbed me." She stares down at her bloodied hand as though it belongs to someone else. "Jesus, Maisie. I should call someone."

But she doesn't. Instead, she collapses onto the sofa, her complexion ashen. She holds her tightly wrapped hand against her chest, her jaw clenched and eyes squeezed shut. All I can do is look on, paralysed by the horror of my own actions. In a desperate attempt to help, to do something, I slam the door shut, checking the lock repeatedly as if that might somehow protect us from the true danger – me.

"Imarah, please ..." I stumble towards her, the alcohol still coursing through my veins.

"Don't talk to me, Maisie. Call a taxi. I need to get to the hospital."

My phone blinks up at me from the kitchen counter where I abandoned it. I grab it with trembling fingers.

Oopsie daisy. Silly you. Do you think she needs a plaster?

Every hair on my body stands on end. The curtains are drawn tight. There is no other window facing the street from this angle.

I turn back to Imarah, her pain-filled eyes watching me with a new wariness I've never seen before. I've lost her trust. And somewhere, someone is watching; someone is laughing at the destruction they've created.

Someone who knows exactly how to break me, piece by piece.

Chapter 34

Imarah disappears in the taxi, having rejected my desperate pleas to accompany her. "Haven't you done enough damage?" she spat, her final words before the driver slid the door closed from inside, sealing her away from me.

The weight of what I've done presses down on me. I stabbed her. My best friend. The only person who's stood by me through everything. I keep replaying the way she looked at me – the pain, the betrayal. How do I even begin to fix this? How do I ever make her trust me again? The thought squeezes the air from my lungs.

But then, like poison seeping into my body, something shifts inside me. This isn't really my fault. This is *her* fault. *Steph*. She's the real reason everything is falling apart. I cannot let her do this anymore.

I have to end this before someone else gets hurt. Or killed.

I grab my coat.

I drive slowly, painfully aware of the alcohol still in my system. The incident with Imarah has sobered me up a little, but I know I'm still well over the legal limit.

The road seems to tilt beneath me, a sickening sway. Streetlights smear at the edges of my vision. Oncoming headlights slice through the darkness, too bright, too sharp, carving painful paths across my retinas. My hands clutch the steering wheel, but it feels strange in my grip, as though I'm not the one in control of it.

I take a deep breath in, trying to focus. The road feels too narrow, the car moving too fast even though I'm barely pressing the pedal. One wrong move could end everything. But in this moment, I find I don't care. I have to do this. I have to confront her.

Caleb's van sits in the driveway of what was once our home. I'm not sure if that's a good thing or not. Do I want him to witness this? Probably not. He'll no doubt believe every word that comes out of her mouth. There's no denying she's clever. I bet she has him wrapped around her little finger.

Hammering on the door offers cathartic release, so I keep doing it, channeling all my rage and frustration into each slam against the glass panel.

"Whoa, hang on a minute," Caleb calls from the other side, his voice muffled. When he pulls the door open and sees it's me, the expression on his face goes instantly from anger to disgust.

"Oh, Maisie, not now."

"No, now is good." I push past him. "Is she here?"

"Who?"

"What do you mean *who*? That nasty little bitch you call a girlfriend."

"Don't you dare come in here and insult Steph. I thought we'd moved on. I thought *I* had finally moved on. Please, Maisie …"

He looks tired, fed up. His arm is in a cast from his crash, and he's wearing nothing but baggy jogging bottoms slung low on his hips. Despite everything, he looks good.

"I don't care about you being in a relationship, Caleb." Not true. "But I do care about you being in a relationship with *her*. Do you have any idea who she really is? What she's capable of?"

"I know her a damn sight better than you do. Are you drunk?!"

I groan. What does that matter? "No, Caleb, you don't. Look." I thrust my phone toward him, showing him all the abuse Steph has sent me.

"Who needs a plaster?" he asks, his focus immediately drawn to the most recent message. "Did someone get hurt?"

"Imarah," I admit, the name catching slightly in my throat. "She had an accident."

His eyes widen with concern. "Is she okay?"

I nod. "She's at the hospital now."

"Hospital? Jesus, Maisie, tell me what's going on."

I take a seat on the sofa, determined to get every detail across to Caleb as calmly and precisely as I can manage. I need him to understand. I need him to see the nightmare I've been living. And I need him to recognise what kind of dangerous woman he's welcomed into his bed.

I talk. He listens, expression carefully neutral, body unnaturally still. I go through every torment his girlfriend has inflicted upon me, every violation, every threat. I need him to see the truth. And, if I'm honest, a small part of me hopes he realises how lucky he was with me. The grass was never greener with Steph.

When I finally finish, he huffs and leans back, one hand pressed against his forehead. His eyes meet mine, and despite everything, electricity crackles between us. Does he feel it, too?

He exhales sharply, running his fingers through his hair. "Maisie, listen to yourself." His tone is careful, almost rehearsed, as though he's had this conversation with me in his head a thousand times already. "You're drunk, you just admitted to hurting Imarah, and now you're blaming Steph for something she couldn't possibly have done. You're out of control."

"Did you hear a single word I just said?"

"It wasn't Steph," he says simply.

"You can't know that."

"You said she was watching you while everything was kicking off earlier. It couldn't have been her."

"How would you know? She's not even here."

"No, but she has been here all day. She left about a minute before you turned up, to get some things from her house."

"No, you're wrong," I say. "She was at Imarah's. She was watching us."

"Maisie, I'm so sorry all this is happening to you. For what it's worth, if any of this is real, I don't think you deserve any of it. And I really hope the police get to the bottom of it. But— Are you listening to me?"

I force myself to meet his eyes.

"I'm categorically telling you that it wasn't Steph. She hasn't left my side since you left. I'd know if she was stalking you."

Since I was kicked out, he means. The correction burns even though it remains unspoken.

"If this was her, I'd know about it."

Would he, though? Caleb has never been the sharpest tool in the box. But then how else can I explain that the stalker was somehow watching me at Imarah's while Steph was allegedly here with Caleb? How could she possibly have been in two places at once?

Unless.

No. No, this isn't possible. My thoughts scramble for another explanation, but they keep circling back to the same horrifying conclusion. Steph wasn't watching from outside. She was watching from inside.

She must have planted cameras in Imarah's apartment.

"I've got to go," I tell Caleb abruptly, already moving towards the door.

"Does that mean you're going to drop this now?" he calls after me. "Because I really can't be bothered with any more of your crazy."

"I'll show you who's crazy," I throw back over my shoulder. "I'll get you proof."

He sighs as I hurry out, leaving the door hanging wide open behind me.

***

Two hours later, I have turned Imarah's apartment upside down.

I've searched everywhere. I have yanked drawers open, knocked over picture frames, strewn sofa cushions across the floor, and now the apartment resembles a war zone. Every time I think I've found something, it proves to be nothing – just another screw, another dust-covered trinket, another ordinary piece of Imarah's life. My heartbeat slams against my ribcage, aggravating the pain in my side from the effort. There has to be something. There has to be. But where? I shove the last picture off the wall, my fingers trembling violently. Silence. Nothing.

And then: *Did you find it?*

"Fuck off!" I yell at my phone, my fingers working furiously to tap out a reply: *I know you're watching me. I'll find it.*

Frantic energy surges through me then, and I'm screaming, crying, thrashing around the apartment like a wild animal. This bitch isn't going to win. I won't let her.

I return to the bookshelf, where books now lie scattered across the floor in disarray. Standing on a chair, I stretch to reach across the top shelf, my fingers exploring every inch of dusty wood. Then my fingertips brush against something small and round, stuck to the underside of the top shelf where it would remain invisible to anyone not specifically looking for it.

My heart thunders as I carefully pry it loose – a tiny black disc no larger than a watch battery, with what appears to be a pinprick lens on one side. A camera. I'd been right all along! I knew it!

Caleb is adamant this wasn't Steph. But if it wasn't her, then who? I mentally run through everyone who's been in the apartment recently. Has Imarah had any maintenance guys over? Has the landlord been around? What about friends or colleagues? I need to speak to her.

I drop the device into a glass of water, and watch it spark and die.

Nice work finding a camera. You look so pleased with yourself. Cute.

There's more than one.

My eyes sweep the room, suddenly seeing potential hiding spots everywhere.

Overwhelmed and exhausted, my knees give way, and I collapse in a heap amid the chaos I've created. I sob, my cries echoing loudly in the silent apartment. I allow myself to slump forward onto the cushions, curling onto my side and drawing my knees up to my chest, hugging them tight.

And there, surrounded by the wreckage of my desperate search, I break down completely, until exhaustion finally pulls me into deep sleep.

My phone beeps persistently somewhere nearby, cutting through the edges of my awareness. But I'm too far gone to care. I'm done.

I can't do this anymore.

***

I wake to a sharp nudge in my stomach. Instinctively, I curl into a tighter ball, my hangover kicking in with immediate intensity.

"Maisie, get up."

I force my eyelids open, only to squeeze them shut again instantly. The overhead light seems determined to burn through my retinas. My head aches. A pathetic groan escapes my lips.

"Maisie, what have you done?!" It's Imarah, returned from the hospital. The fury in her voice is palpable.

I force myself upright, my eyes still closed. My lower back throbs with dull pain, and my left arm feels completely numb. Where am I?

My hand knocks against something hard, and I finally manage to prise my eyes open enough to focus. It's a framed photograph of Imarah and her mother. Her mother has a colourful scarf wrapped around her head, her eyes sunken deep into a face too thin for its bone structure. The background shows a hospital bed, surrounded by monitoring equipment. They're clinging to each other, their smiles so big yet tinged with heartbreak.

Their last hug before her mum died.

A crack now spiders across the glass, fracturing their faces.

Imarah reaches down and snatches the frame from my hands. She stares at the damaged picture, her eyes welling with tears. I notice her hand is professionally bandaged where I sliced it open.

"Your hand ..." I begin, but she silences me with a glacial stare that makes me physically recoil.

"You need to leave." She says it so calmly, so devoid of emotion, that I don't believe her.

"I can explain," I say, pulling myself onto the sofa with effort.

"GET OUT!" Her scream shatters the artificial calm, sending shockwaves through my dehydrated brain.

"Imarah, please. I need to tell you something." She needs to know about the cameras. They're here somewhere, monitoring us, and if anyone has any idea of who placed them, it's Imarah.

"No." She drops the picture frame, glass shards spraying across the floor, before grabbing my upper arm with her uninjured hand and yanking me upright with surprising strength. "You're not doing this. You're toxic, Maisie." She drags me toward the door, her grip painfully tight.

I stumble over debris littering the floor but somehow maintain my balance. "It was her!" I shout desperately. "She did this!"

"So your stalker person trashed my apartment? Broke my things?"

"Well, no, that was me. But Imarah, I was looking for the cameras. I was—"

"There are no cameras!" she roars. "There's just you, Maisie. You and your endless need for drama."

Her words hit me like physical blows. Is she right? Have I imagined this entire nightmare?

"Get out," she says, her voice suddenly, terrifyingly calm. "I can't do this anymore. I can't keep setting myself on fire to keep you warm."

As she pushes me towards the door, I catch a glimpse of her face. She's not just angry; she's heartbroken. Like she's finally accepting a truth she's denied for far too long.

"Imarah, wait—"

"No, Maisie. You twist everything until I can't tell what's real anymore. Until I start doubting myself." She sounds like someone breaking free from a spell, and it terrifies me more than her anger ever could.

She shoves me out onto the street with such force that I stumble backwards, my heel catching painfully on the doorstep. "You don't get it, do you?" Her voice cracks, but there's not a hint of hesitation. "You ruin everything, Maisie. I don't care what excuses you have. I don't care if there's some grand conspiracy. I'm done." She tosses my phone and keys at my feet.

Chapter 35

Once again, I drive.

Tears burn trails down my cheeks, mixing with the thick, viscous snot dripping from my nose. I gasp desperately for air between ragged sobs, my entire body convulsing with each cry. The car shrinks around me, suffocating, the world beyond pressing in with crushing weight.

I don't know where to go now. I officially have nothing left.

No friends, no family, no home. I have nowhere to go. So I drive.

At a red light, I make the mistake of checking my phone. Another dozen notifications flood my screen, each one a fresh wound. Someone's created a TikTok video 'explaining' my case – a complete stranger who's never met me, speaking with the authoritative confidence of an expert about my motives, my mental state, my 'history of attention-seeking behaviour.'

It has fifty thousand views already. I guess bad news lingers when distractions are scarce.

I scroll through post after post, a masochist with nothing else to live for. There are screenshots being passed around of private messages I never sent. Stories from 'anonymous sources' claiming to have known me for years. Elaborate theories about my 'disturbed childhood' and 'desperate need for validation.'

A total stranger is constructing an entire narrative about my life, and thousands of people are consuming it as indisputable fact. Believing it. Sharing it. Adding their own embellishments to the fiction.

The light turns green, but I can barely see the road through my tears.

Rain lashes down in sheets, reducing visibility to almost nothing. My windshield wipers battle frantically, their efforts futile.

I drive slowly, but I don't know if I'm moving forward or just circling back into the mess I've made. The houses blur past – too large, too perfect, belonging to lives I'll never fit into. Maybe I should stop. Maybe I should just disappear into the storm.

A cat darts into the road. My hands jerk the wheel instinctively, and the tyres shriek in protest as I slam the brakes. The car jolts over the kerb before bouncing back onto the slick road, hydroplaning for a moment before the tyres regain their grip. My breath comes in shallow, painful bursts.

Then I see them. Blue lights flashing in my rearview mirror.

Shit.

I have two options: pull over and face the drunk driving charge, or accelerate and try to lose them. The latter option is obviously fueled by the remaining booze in my system, and I force my rational mind to take control. I press my foot on the brake.

I don't know where to look as I wait for the police officer to approach. What's the right thing to say in this situation? I vaguely remember Faith getting away with a drunk driving charge once, but can't remember the details.

She probably batted her eyelashes at some flattered male officer and walked away with a warning. Given the state of me right now, this officer will have to be really desperate to fall for my 'charms'.

A sharp rap on my window startles me. I lower it, rain immediately spattering my face. It's a woman. Damnit. She bends down to look inside the car.

Recognition dawns on me. Evelyn.

Oh, thank God. Relief and terror wage war inside me.

"Maisie?" Her eyes widen as she leans in further, disbelief written across her face. "Jesus Christ. What the hell are you doing? You were driving like a lunatic!"

"I swerved to avoid a cat!" I say. "Didn't you see it?"

She frowns and shakes her head. "No, no cat. Though I did see you swerving all over the road. You drunk?"

I press my lips together, suddenly conscious of my alcohol-infused breath. "No."

"Oh, Maisie. I'm going to have to do a breathalyser. Can you step out of your car, please?"

"Evelyn, please."

"Step out, Maisie." She sounds tired. Tired and impatient. It's probably best if I don't challenge her.

We walk through the rain to her car where she takes something out of the glove box and begins connecting a thin tube to a small device.

"Take a deep breath in and blow into the mouthpiece until it beeps."

She offers me the device, and I stare at it as though it's a loaded weapon.

"Come on, Maisie. Let's get this done. I want to go home."

"You're on your way home?" I ask.

"Right after I've dropped the car off at the station. Now, breathe."

I inhale deeply and exhale into the tube until the device emits a satisfied beep. I hand it back to Evelyn, watching her face as she reads the result.

She sighs, her shoulders slumping. "Lock your car and leave it there. Get in the back of the police car."

"I failed?" I know the question is ridiculous even as it leaves my lips.

Evelyn laughs, but it's sad and defeatist. "Just a bit. You been to a party?"

I shake my head. "I wish."

She laughs again, but this time it carries a hint of genuine amusement. "Oh, wouldn't that be nice. I can't remember the last time I let my hair down."

We get into her car, rain drumming on the roof. "Everything okay at home?" I ask, not entirely sure why. Perhaps I want to keep her talking, to soften her resolve in the vague hope she might let me go.

I see her jaw tighten in the rearview mirror. "We broke up," she says flatly. "For good this time."

I feel sad for her, though I know it's probably for the best. She deserves better than someone who cheats on her.

"Let me guess. You think it's for the best." Her voice has turned brittle, like she's about to crack.

I hesitate, weighing my words carefully. "I think … only you get to decide that."

She releases a shaky breath. "That's the thing. I didn't get to decide anything. He broke up with me."

"What?!" I'm genuinely surprised. "Oh, Evelyn, Troy is a prick. I always knew it."

"Yeah, he said he wanted to be one hundred percent honest with me. So he told me about all the affairs he's had over the years. Then when I forgave him, he told me he'd lost all respect for me and broke it off."

It's only now that I realise we're not heading towards town. The streetlights have become increasingly sparse, and we appear to be traveling down a country road.

"Wow, he's got a nerve," I say, trying to get my bearings. "He was never good enough for you."

"Maybe." Her voice sounds different somehow, a new edge creeping in. "But don't you think I should get to decide that, too?"

Our eyes meet briefly in the rearview mirror. There's an iciness to her gaze that sends a shiver down my spine.

Something's wrong. My gut knows it before my brain does. The streetlights have vanished completely. Dense trees crowd the narrow road, their branches forming a claustrophobic canopy.

"Where are we going?" My voice wavers.

After everything that's happened, I can't fight the crawling paranoia that something terrible is about to unfold. I've been living with that sensation for weeks, but now it peaks, adrenaline flooding my system, making me jittery and my thoughts race.

"Where it all began."

I sit in stunned silence, trying to process everything. Evelyn has driven in completely the opposite direction from the police station. We've left town completely, surrounded now by a wall of trees.

My sense of unease crescendos as she turns onto a track.

Recognition dawns. I've been here before. It's where I called Caleb that night, pretending to be attacked.

"Why are you bringing me here?" I ask, panic strangling my voice. Why would Evelyn come here? To go over everything again? Have they found evidence I somehow overlooked? Evidence that proves I lied? Is she going to arrest me?

I want to scream at her to turn around, but fear has frozen my vocal cords. I don't know what to do.

"It's time we met face to face," Evelyn says, pulling to a stop in a small clearing among the trees. She shuts off the engine, plunging us into darkness. I can just make out the whites of her eyes in the mirror. "I must admit, teasing you has been incredibly fun. But games get boring after a while."

Chapter 36

She spins to face me through the metal grid separating the front and back seats.

"What's going on?" I ask stupidly. But deep down, I already know. My mind just refuses to admit it to myself.

"You didn't check your phone," she says. "I messaged you. I thought that was why you were driving like a crazy bitch. Turns out you're just a crazy bitch."

She's right. I haven't looked at it since I fell asleep at Imarah's. Everything else got in my way – Imarah kicking me out, my despair, then Evelyn's sudden appearance.

I shift my weight, but freeze mid-movement, suddenly unsure what the right thing to do is here.

"Go on. You can check it now," Evelyn says with sickening sweetness.

I reach for my phone and open the message. A wave of nausea hits me. The image on the screen blurs before I can fully register it, and when comprehension finally sets in, a lead weight drops in my stomach. My throat tightens, acid rising fast. *No. No, no, no.* The world tilts around me. I squeeze my eyes shut, desperately willing it all to be some terrible mistake.

Evelyn giggles.

"What did you do?" I whisper.

"You're not the only one to have upset me lately. It only seemed fair that I punished you both."

My hands shake with such violence I can barely turn my phone over, unable to bear looking at the horrific image on my screen. "You're her? You're the stalker?"

She grins, her teeth glinting in the moonlight. She looks feral. "I have to admit, you're really fun to wind up."

"But why?"

"Why?!" Her voice cracks with something that sounds almost like desperation. "Do you even know what you did to me? I had it all under control, I was fixing things, until you stepped in and tore it apart. You didn't just ruin my relationship – you humiliated me."

She leans closer to the metal divider, her face contorted with fury. "If you hadn't told me about Troy's infidelity we could've carried on living our lives. We could've all been happy. But thanks to you, it all had to end. Troy meant *everything* to me. You hear me? Everything! Then you came along and ruined everything."

"I didn't do this," I sob. "I didn't do *that*." I motion at my phone, still turned face-down on my lap.

"Of course you did." The certainty in her voice is terrifying.

"I need to call him an ambulance." I turn my phone over with desperate, clumsy movements. I manage to tap 999 before Evelyn launches herself from the front seat with shocking speed, wrenching open the rear door and hauling me into the mud outside.

I cling desperately to my phone, but she brings her boot down with crushing force onto my wrist. Pain explodes up my arm as I cry out, my fingers involuntarily releasing their grip. She snatches the phone from the mud and hurls it into the back of the police car.

"You can't do this!" I cry, cradling my throbbing wrist against my chest.

"I can do whatever I want. Have you not realised that yet?"

"But can't you see? You're risking everything for a man? Evelyn, you can't get away with this. You're better than this."

She laughs, the sound devoid of humour. "I'm not stupid, Maisie. I can most certainly get away with this."

I scream then, hoping against hope that someone, anyone, might be within earshot in these desolate woods.

Her response is quick and brutal – a savage kick to my face. My nose explodes, blood spattering across my cold, wet skin in a warm, sticky spray.

The image from my phone burns into my thoughts. "What did Caleb do to deserve that?" I ask, unable to erase the sight of his bulging eyes staring at the camera, blood trickling down from his battered skull. There's no way to know if he's dead or alive, and for my own sanity, I force myself not to think about it. If I'm to survive this, if I'm to help Caleb, I need to stay focused.

But if Caleb is dead … The thought threatens to unravel me completely. I push it down. I can't afford to break. Not now.

Evelyn steps back, seemingly taken aback by the audacity of my question. "He encouraged Troy to break up with me! Apparently dropping you was the best decision he'd ever made. And Troy follows suit like his little lap dog."

"Caleb has a new girlfriend!" I say, my voice high-pitched. I need to keep her talking while I look for an opening. My fingers splay in the mud beside me, feeling for something – anything – I can use as a weapon. A rock, a stick, anything solid. If I don't act soon, I might not get another chance.

Or maybe if I can get her to open up, to connect, she'll soften. Just enough. It's a dubious plan at best, but a crappy plan is better than no plan at all. Especially when my situation is so dire.

"Surely he showed Troy that being in a relationship is a good thing."

Evelyn shakes her head, rainwater flinging from her hair. "Too little, too late. The damage had been done. Troy had made up his mind."

Blaming me and Caleb for her break-up is a far stretch. But Evelyn is clearly unhinged; blaming us for her toxic relationship hardly seems the most irrational part of this nightmare.

Despite every instinct warning me against it, I ask the question plaguing my mind. "Is Caleb dead?"

I look away, afraid to hear the answer.

"Oh, he was easy to take out. He was weak." The casual cruelty in her voice is unbearable.

"He's dead?" My voice trembles violently. "Caleb is dead."

"Just as he deserves. You can't go around ruining lives and not expect repercussions. Think of it this way – now he can't hurt anyone else. I've done the world a favour."

She might as well have stabbed me in the stomach. The pain is so intense, that I double over and vomit down my front. How could she? And for what? Because she was *dumped?* She's a monster.

"How is this any better than what I did? Jesus Christ, Evelyn, you're a police officer. It's your job to protect people!"

She regards me with contemptuous pity, as though I'm too stupid to grasp a simple concept. "Which is exactly what I'm doing. Funny thing is, if you hadn't done the whole 'I've been attacked!' thing, I might have just left it. I felt sorry for you! I defended you, pushed your case in front of my superiors. But you made me look like an idiot in front of the entire team!"

She paces in a circle around me, her boots squelching in the mud. "I thought I was helping you. And do you want to know how many people we questioned?" She doesn't wait for a response. "We were truly clutching at straws, but I was so determined. I didn't want to let you down. I wanted to help. Despite what you did to me and Troy." Her voice breaks. For a fleeting moment, I almost feel sympathy for what I did – until I remember what she's done to Caleb. What she's about to do to me.

I hear my phone ringing from inside the car, the sound cutting through the rain and darkness. The urge to lunge for the vehicle is so intense, my body jerks forward before I can stop myself.

Evelyn notices and leers at me. "Just try it," she hisses. "And I'll show you what I'm truly capable of."

I slump back into the mud, defeated. The air around us is thick with the metallic scent of my blood mingling with the acrid stench of vomit. Cold mud seeps through my clothes, pressing against me like a second skin. I have never felt so utterly pathetic.

"So, walk me through it," Evelyn says, her tone suddenly conversational, as though we're colleagues discussing a case. "How did you imagine that night went?"

I stare at her, confused.

"I mean, where did you see yourself when you were attacked? Was it here?" She gestures to the ground by her feet. "Or over here? You said he dragged you to a tree. Was it this one?" She points to a massive oak looming nearby. "Or this one?"

"Please stop," I say, timidly.

"What did you say?"

"Stop. Please!" I cry, rising to my knees in the mud. "Whatever it is you're planning on doing, just do it."

Because the truth is, I don't care anymore. There's nothing else Evelyn can take from me. She might as well take my life.

I always imagined my survival instinct was stronger than this. I assumed I would fight with every fibre of my being. But when push comes to shove, I find there's no fight left in me. I suppose that's what happens when you've been picked apart for weeks.

"But we've still got so much to discuss."

"Please!"

"NO!" She kicks me in my side, sending me flying back into the ground. I cough up thick phlegm. "We're talking," she says, once again calm. "So talk."

"How did you do it? How did you overpower Caleb?" I splutter, spitting blood.

She smirks, enjoying my morbid curiosity. "Flashing your badge gets you in the door; flashing your eyelashes makes them weak at the knees. Having a pretty face weakens their resolve." She giggles, the sound girlish. "And Caleb was such a gent, didn't put up much of a fight. I'm stronger than I look." She grins at me as if I'm supposed to share in her twisted pride.

Evelyn's smirk deepens. "Oh, and speaking of weak men, you should have seen how eager Peters was to run with the story when I called his station. Men have such simple desires, they're so ... *pliable*."

"That was you?" The pieces are clicking into place, despite my pain. "You were the one who tipped him off about my statement being false?"

"I just mentioned that the police were looking into validating your story. He's such a dear friend, he ran with it." She laughs, the sound echoing among the trees. "He practically salivated at the potential controversy. Some people will do anything for ratings."

I realise, Peters and Evelyn aren't so different, both willing to destroy lives in pursuit of their own twisted agendas.

"So, what's the plan now?" I ask through a wince of pain. Do I really want to know? Surely the way I die would be better as a surprise.

She smiles, clearly relishing my fear. "I haven't yet decided. But I *do* know that it'll either involve this ..." She holds up a switch knife that was hidden in her gloved hand. "Or the shovel I have in the boot of my car."

My eyes flit towards her car. Surely it has some sort of tracker, some GPS system that would lead police right to this spot. Even if I don't survive the night, they'll eventually connect my death to Evelyn. The realisation offers a cold comfort. I might die, but at least she won't get away with it.

Headlights appear in the distance, filtering through the trees, and we both freeze, holding our breath. I silently pray they'll turn down this track. Evelyn no doubt is praying they continue down the road.

Evelyn's wishes are granted. The lights fade.

The pause seems to bolster my resolve. With a sudden surge of energy, I lunge at Evelyn's legs, catching her off guard. She falls forward with a surprised grunt, collapsing on top of me, her elbow driving into my lower back with excruciating force. I cry out, but the pain only fuels my determination.

We crash onto the wet earth, my fingers clawing frantically at the mud as we struggle for control. Evelyn's fist connects with my jaw, sending pain shooting through my skull. A low moan escapes my lips, but I use the momentum of her attack, throwing my shoulder into her stomach with all the force I can muster. She gasps – a sharp, startled sound as the air explodes from her lungs – and I seize the brief advantage to push her backwards. We're locked in a desperate struggle, the mud making every surface too slick to grasp, the smell of earth and blood overwhelming my senses.

With incredible strength, Evelyn forces me onto my back, pinning me down with her weight. "You stupid bitch. You never know when to just *stop*, do you?"

I spit in her face. She roars.

My eyes dart frantically around, searching for anything that might save me.

The knife lies in the mud by my knee, just out of reach. If Evelyn makes a move for it, I might be able to knock her off balance. It's the faintest glimmer of hope, but it's all I have left.

I struggle beneath her, but she bears down harder, using her full weight to trap me. She's panting, struggling to catch her breath.

"Now what?" I ask, surprising myself with the challenge in my voice. "This is the part where you kill me, right?"

She bends down until her face hovers mere centimetres from mine, her breath hot against my skin. "No, this is the point I knock you unconscious. When you come to, I'll have dug your grave. I want to bury you alive."

I renew my struggle, thrashing desperately beneath her, but Evelyn has recovered her breath and with it, her full strength. She has me completely at her mercy.

She raises her fist, her lips peeling back in a feral snarl.

I close my eyes and wait.

Chapter 37

The knife is cold and unfamiliar in my grip, satisfyingly weighty. Her blood is warm against my sodden skin.

The smile freezes on Evelyn's face as her eyes lock onto mine, disbelief replacing the triumph that had been there just moments before. She falls sideways, her weight suddenly releasing me from its crushing constraint.

I stand up and step away, chest heaving with laboured breaths. Every nerve ending in my body seems to crackle with electric awareness, my senses impossibly heightened by adrenaline.

I won.

I'm alive.

But my hands won't stop shaking as I scramble backwards, still clutching the knife. Evelyn makes a blood-curdling wet groan. She's pressing her hands against her side, and when she pulls them away to inspect the damage, her gloves are stained red, saturated with blood. Her eyes find mine again, panic now written across her face.

"What did you do?"

But the words don't come from Evelyn's lips. They come from behind me.

I spin around, to find Imarah standing at the edge of the clearing. She's holding her bandaged hand protectively in front of her body, her car keys dangling from her finger. Her hair is dripping wet and plastered to her face. She's staring at me, her expression pure horror.

My mouth opens and closes, but no sound emerges.

"Maisie ..." Imarah's voice is barely audible over the patter of rain, her fingers tightening reflexively around her keys. "Tell me you didn't—"

I didn't mean to! I long to plead innocence. But I *did* stab Evelyn. How can I possibly deny it when I'm standing here covered in blood? How do I even begin to explain all that has happened tonight?

I glance back at Evelyn's crumpled form, then down at the knife still clutched in my hand, before meeting Imarah's horrified gaze once more. "It's not what it looks like," I say weakly, finally releasing the knife. It lands with a soft thud in the mud.

"She stabbed me," comes Evelyn's voice from the ground.

"In self defence!" I cry, incredulous that I should even need to explain. "Imarah, Evelyn is the stalker. She was going to kill me!"

Imarah doesn't hesitate. She plunges her good hand into her coat pocket and retrieves her phone. Within seconds, she's kneeling beside Evelyn, fingers flying across the screen as she requests police and an ambulance.

This isn't real. It can't be. I fought so hard to survive, and now they're going to lock me away like a monster.

I cannot go through all this only to end up in prison.

Imarah turns towards me while speaking into the phone, checking that I haven't bolted.

It's a slim chance, but I have to try to win Imarah over. She's my only hope. "Imarah. Evelyn killed Caleb. She kidnapped me." I struggle to keep my voice steady, but it cracks despite my best efforts. I sound frantic, unhinged.

I sound guilty.

She shakes her head, a gesture of dismissal so final it steals my breath. "Just stop it, Maisie. Stop lying."

What proof do I have to offer? It's my word against Evelyn's – the upstanding police officer versus the compulsive liar.

Imarah looks at the knife on the ground before looking back at me with absolute terror in her eyes. It breaks my heart. Does she really think I could hurt her?

I nudge the knife toward her with my foot, a desperate gesture meant to prove I'm harmless. She eyes me warily as she reaches out to pull it closer to herself, keeping it safely out of my reach.

Eventually, she stops speaking into the phone. Evelyn appears unconscious. I seize the opportunity, raising my hands. "Imarah. You've got to believe me, I didn't do this. You know me, I'm not a violent person."

"How many times have you lied to me, Maisie?" Her voice is raw with emotion. "The attack, the messages, hurting Caleb – how am I supposed to believe you now?"

Hurt?

The word catches in my mind.

He's not dead?

"What do you know about Caleb? Is he okay?" Hope surges through me, so powerful it's almost painful.

"He was taken to hospital. If he's lucky, he'll live. No thanks to you." A sob catches in her throat, quickly suppressed. "Why did you do it? Because he didn't want to be with you anymore? Fucking hell, Maisie."

I glance back towards the distant road where headlights are visible, accompanied by the faint thrum of music drifting across the countryside.

Imarah continues. "I went round to Caleb's to try to find you. I was worried you were sleeping rough. When I got there I found Steph, distraught and waiting for an ambulance."

"How did you know I was here?"

"Caleb's tracking app."

"That's how you found me?" I gasp, grateful that Caleb never thought to delete the app I'd insisted he download so long ago.

She nods. "I drove past the track at first. It's pretty well hidden. So I came on foot."

She'd come looking for me, despite everything. Had driven into these woods in the dead of night, risking her own safety, all for someone she had every reason to abandon.

"Why?" I whisper. "After what I did to your apartment ... Why would you still care?"

Her laugh is bitter, devoid of any genuine humour. "That's the thing about toxic relationships, Maisie. Even when you know you should walk away, you can't help worrying. Can't help thinking, 'What if this is the one time they really need me?'" She looks utterly exhausted. "Twenty years of friendship," she says softly. "I couldn't let it end with you alone in the woods."

Tears glisten in her eyes. "I keep telling myself, 'This is the last time.' But it never is." She holds back a sob. "I was scared you'd be doing something stupid. Something you regret, you know?"

She turns her attention back to Evelyn and offers her soothing words, pressing her hands firmly against the wound to stem the bleeding.

The wind picks up suddenly, sweeping through the clearing and tearing away the clouds that have obscured the moon. In the flood of silver light, I see Evelyn properly for the first time since Imarah's arrival. Her eyes are open and locked on mine.

She's smiling.

Realisation crashes over me, alarm surging through every cell in my body. I run forward, desperate to reach Imarah, to pull her away from the predator disguised as a victim.

The knife flashes, a silver streak in the moonlight, as Evelyn brings it to Imarah's exposed throat and slices in one brutal movement.

Blood erupts from the wound, soaking both Imarah and Evelyn in crimson. I'm so close now that warm droplets spray across my face, a horrific baptism.

But I'm too late.

There's nothing I can do now.

Imarah slumps forward, somehow still clinging to life. She makes wet, gargling sounds as she fights desperately for breath that will never come. The struggle is brief; she quickly loses strength, her body surrendering to the inevitable. Her eyes find mine one final time, desperately seeking answers, or perhaps offering forgiveness. Answers I cannot provide. Forgiveness I don't deserve.

"Imarah," I murmur, her name a prayer, a plea, an apology all at once.

And then she's gone, the light fading from her eyes.

I stand paralysed, time seeming to stop around me. The clearing is silent except for the soft patter of rain and Evelyn's laboured breathing as she moves away from the body. The world has narrowed to this single, terrible moment: Imarah's body collapsed in the mud, her blood mingling with the rain in grotesque rivulets. My best friend, the one constant in my chaotic life, extinguished in seconds.

Evelyn's smile widens as she watches me, a predator savouring the final, exquisite moment of the hunt. She has taken everything from me now. There is nothing left.

The distant sirens begin to wail, cutting through the night, but they're coming far too late. For Imarah. For me. For any hope of justice in this twisted nightmare.

CHAPTER 38

My cell smells exactly like I thought it would. Bodily fluids and sickly cleaning products mix to form a noxious fume that sticks to the back of my throat and clings to my skin.

I've been on remand for three weeks now. Three endless weeks since the magistrates' court sent my case to the Crown Court. My plea hearing is still another week away, and according to Mary, my solicitor with her perpetually tired eyes and carefully neutral expressions, the actual trial could be months away.

"The CPS is still building their case," Mary explained during her last visit, her voice clinically detached as though discussing some other stranger's life entirely. "They're waiting on more forensic reports and witness statements from the scene." She didn't need to spell it out – they want a watertight case against me.

Murder convictions come with life sentences in this country. My future measured not in days or months, but decades. Months of my life, spent in this grey limbo. All while Evelyn walks free, breathing clean air, feeling sunlight on her skin.

Imarah's face haunts me. Not the pretty features I knew for so many years: the dimple when she smiled, the way her eyes crinkled at the corners when she laughed. No, what haunts me is her final expression, stamped with horror as the realisation of her own death dawns in her eyes. In my dreams, I hear her voice, crying out to me, begging me for help that never comes. I wake up screaming, sweat pouring over my skin.

The pain of Imarah's death is so intense, I know it will never leave me. It has become part of me. I talk to her like she's here, a desperate pretense that might take the edge off what I am going through.

And for those few seconds, she's in the room with me, and I experience a sense of bliss. I'm back in her apartment, laughing with her, cooking together in her tiny kitchen. She looks more beautiful than ever, and I have never known such perfect happiness.

She seems so real in these moments that I'm convinced if I reach out, I would feel her warmth. I can hear her joyful laugh with perfect clarity, as though she's standing right beside me.

But I keep my hands firmly to myself, because there's always that cruel part of me that lives in the truth. The side I probably should have listened to throughout this entire nightmare.

Murderer.

That's what they believe I am. A murderer. While Evelyn is out there somewhere, I am in here bearing the crushing weight of my best friend's death and facing the consequences of a crime I didn't commit.

I have cried until I was empty, yelled until my voice gave out, fought until there was nothing left to fight with. I don't even know who I am anymore. The woman who stares back at me from the small metal mirror above the sink is a stranger – hollow-eyed, gaunt, haunted. How did I get mixed up in all of this?

And it all started with one lie ...

I regret everything immensely now: the harmless fibs that seemed inconsequential at the time; the twisted truths I justified to myself; the moments I convinced myself I was the victim. I see it clearly now. I built this trap with my own words, and now I cannot escape. And Imarah paid the ultimate price.

My thoughts inevitably stray back to Evelyn. Apparently, she's still in the hospital, her wound serious but not life threatening. She's given a statement, revealing me as the person who took Imarah's life. According to the police, it was that cut and dry.

Evelyn is undeniably clever. A police officer who knows exactly how to spin the truth. And I handed her the perfect story.

I feel utterly powerless. Devoid of hope.

And now I sit here, exhausted beyond measure and profoundly alone. Was this my destiny all along?

I curl up on the thin mattress, pulling the rough blanket tightly around my shoulders, and let sleep find me, praying the nightmares grant me mercy tonight.

CHAPTER 39

"How are you doing?" Mary asks for the millionth time. She's wearing a green suit with a pale yellow shirt underneath. She looks like someone out of a Roald Dahl book.

I don't bother to respond. How does she expect me to feel after six weeks on remand?

We're sitting in a consultation room at the Crown Court. My barrister, Ms. Okonkwo, is reviewing papers beside us, her expression utterly inscrutable behind gold-rimmed glasses. Today is my bail application hearing – a last-ditch attempt to get me out of prison while we await trial.

"The judge is unlikely to grant bail given the severity of the charges," Ms. Okonkwo warns in her precise, measured voice. "But we have compelling arguments about your lack of previous convictions, and community ties."

The court is imposing, all dark wood paneling and echoing corridors. I've seen places like this in crime dramas, but nothing prepared me for its oppressive reality, the way it seems designed to make you feel small and inconsequential. Already guilty.

"The Crown is opposing bail," Mary explains quietly, leaning toward me. "They're citing the seriousness of the offence and arguing you present a flight risk due to your—" She hesitates, clearly uncomfortable. "History of fabrication."

My lie about being attacked has become Exhibit A in their case that I'm fundamentally dishonest and dangerous. The irony is almost too much to bear. One lie, meant to garner attention, has spiraled into this nightmare.

"If bail is denied, how long until trial?" I ask, dreading the answer.

Ms. Okonkwo doesn't sugarcoat it. "Months. The system is severely backlogged. I would estimate nine months. Give or take."

The weight of it crushes me. Nine more months in that cell. Nine more months of my life suspended in limbo.

I've seen the papers. I've seen how they have presented me as the delusional psychopath on a rampage of hate. I murdered my best friend out of jealousy. I injured a police officer who was onto me. I attempted to kill my ex who dumped me for someone else.

Caleb survived his attack, but only just. The blow to his head was so severe, he experienced a bleed on the brain that led to seizures, and he had to be put into an induced coma. Last I heard, he'd never fully recover – if at all.

Resigned to my silence, Mary huffs. "Well, hopefully we won't be waiting too much longer until we're called in."

Ms. Okonkwo responds with a noncommittal sound, still not looking up from her notes.

I was supposed to be called in over an hour and a half ago. I was told to expect delays; court proceedings are generally messy and there's a lot going on behind the scenes. But with each minute that passes, my anxiety increases until I feel like I'm fit to burst.

Mary taps her pen against the table, a rhythmic clicking that cuts through me like a serrated blade. I have to resist the overwhelming urge to rip the pen from her hand and throw it against the wall.

The last few weeks have been a rollercoaster of emotion. My grief for Imarah still overwhelms me, a pain so vast and consuming I feel like I can't draw a full breath.

My worry about the court case feels strangely muted in comparison. Almost as if in respect of my grief. How can I feel bad for myself when Imarah is dead?

Dead.

None of this feels real. But the truth of it all keeps knocking. A cruel joke that won't leave me alone.

Mary suddenly coughs, as if choking on her own breath. Her face immediately flushes crimson and she takes a hasty sip of water. I watch as the liquid catches in her throat and she erupts into coughs so violent she can barely breathe.

Ms. Okonkwo watches her with undisguised disdain, shaking her head.

"Calm," I say, instinctively reaching towards her. She recoils from my outstretched hand as though I've threatened her with a blade.

So much for her having faith in me. Is she really scared of me? Does she think I'm guilty? This doesn't bode well for my case.

I pull back and wait for her to steady herself. When she finally regains composure, she looks at me with barely concealed horror behind her eyes. "Sorry about that, went down the wrong hole."

"Right," I say flatly. What little faith I had in this woman is gone.

I slump back in my chair and let my thoughts drift. When I go to court I will have to face Evelyn. She'll be on the witness stand, giving evidence of how I slit Imarah's throat. They'll explain that only my fingerprints were found on the knife that did the deed.

She'll tell them how I trapped her that night, persuaded her to come to my aid in the woods so that I could hurt her. How I wanted to punish her for revealing to the press that my attack wasn't real.

A psychologist will analyse all the messages I allegedly sent from a burner phone, pretending I had a stalker to trick my friend into sympathising with me.

Caleb's new girlfriend, Steph, will recount how I was sending him disgusting messages from the same burner phone, the one found amongst my belongings, further proof of how disturbed I am.

The police will provide evidence, the weapon I allegedly used against Caleb, a rock taken from outside – the same rock I threw at Evelyn outside of my office – the one that I had touched with bare fingers, leaving irrefutable evidence.

I have nothing to cling to.

I'm done for.

Of course the phone wasn't mine, it was Evelyn's. I never sent those messages. I never physically hurt anyone. I did lie about the attack and apparently that proves my nature as cruel and wicked. Selfish and broken. Violent? I don't think so, but the public disagree.

Prison has been an interesting experience. It's not how it's presented on TV. I try to keep to myself as much as possible, and for a long time, I desperately fought to stay awake, terrified of the noises that haunt the nights, the whispers and sobs and occasional screams.

My cellmate made it very clear from day one that she had no desire to be my friend. Thankfully she's kept herself to herself, refusing to engage, not even looking me in the eye. For that, I am grateful – I don't want to engage with criminals. Real ones. But that doesn't mean I haven't felt unbearably lonely. The thought of returning to that greyscale hell brings me out in hives.

The door suddenly opens, distracting me from my thoughts while simultaneously filling me with a sense of dread.

"Miss Tallow?" someone in an expensive suit asks. He looks shifty, like he's about to announce something important. I wonder what role he plays in my undoing today. There's a police officer by his side.

"Yes," Mary answers for me, as though I'm incapable of identifying myself. "Who's asking?"

"I'm Derek Driessen from the CPS. Can we have a quick word?" He directs the question at Ms. Okonkwo who, ever professional, visibly bristles at the interruption.

"Can you just spit it out? We're eager to get started and go home."

Home. I almost laugh.

I nod, curiosity temporarily overpowering my dread. If Imarah were here, she'd be laughing at his badly placed toupee, whispering jokes in my ear about small animals taking residence on his scalp.

"Further evidence has come to light," he tells my legal team, his tone carefully neutral. "It seems a few days ago, Caleb Rush awoke from his coma."

I gasp , drawing the attention of everyone in the room. "Is he okay?"

Last I heard, the doctors on his case suspected his brain damage would be so severe he'd never again be the Caleb we all knew, just a shell of his former self.

"His cognitive function has been appropriately assessed," the man says. He pauses to lick his lips, the gesture stretching the moment unbearably as I wait desperately for more information. "It seems Mr. Rush has come through mostly unscathed. He's experiencing pain, which is to be expected after surgery, but his brain is functioning well.”

Oh, thank God. Relief floods through me, so powerful it makes me lightheaded.

“Which means he's able to provide evidence,” says Mary.

I swear my heart stops beating entirely. Ms. Okonkwo leans forward in her seat, suddenly intensely alert, absorbing every word.

“Mr. Rush has given a statement, claiming Evelyn Campbell as the perpetrator of his attack. The police have undertaken a search of Evelyn's possessions.”

I sit in stunned silence, letting his words of hope wash over me. It's as though I've been drowning for weeks and suddenly found myself breaking the surface, gulping sweet air.

Thank you, Caleb.

“So, they're investigating the stalking claims?” I ask, trying desperately to keep my voice level, to not sound too eager or hopeful.

Derek nods, glancing through sugh his notes. “The search warrant turned up some interesting items. Surveillance equipment. Technology for accessing phones remotely. Evidence of social media account hacking. A smart watch that reveals her whereabouts. The evidence has revealed that Evelyn has abused her position to access police tracking software, using it to monitor Tallow's movements while appearing to be at work."

"So ... they believe me?" My voice catches. After weeks of doubt, suspicion, and accusation, the validation feels almost unreal, like I'm dreaming.

"Miss Tallow, the judge has adjourned your trial until the evidence has been appropriately investigated."

I force myself to look at Mary, desperately seeking clarity, but she offers nothing. She's staring at Derek with her mouth hanging open in shock, a wisp of hair stuck to her lipstick.

"What does this mean?" I finally ask her, my heart pounding. "Mary?"

It's Ms. Okonkwo who answers, her professional mask finally cracking to reveal a brilliant smile that transforms her entire face. "It means, dear girl, you're free."

Chapter 40

"She's smiling at you," Rainy says, watching me bounce Blue on my lap with careful attention.

Blue is indeed smiling at me. She's giving me that look that makes your heart swell – a baby's superpower.

"You sure you've got this?"

I roll my eyes at my sister. Rainy looks incredible in a mid-length dress that shows just the right amount of cleavage. She's lined her eyes with a perfect flick, and that shade of red lipstick looks stunning against her olive skin.

Apparently date nights don't come along that often, and my sister really makes an effort when they do. I silently vow to babysit more often; Rainy deserves a break every now and again.

"Just go, Rainy, we'll be fine. And Mum will be here soon." Because trusting me to babysit alone for the entire movie is a tad too far for Rainy.

I understand.

The old me would have been bitter about it, would have taken it as a personal slight and nursed that grudge for weeks. But I know now that trust isn't given, it's earned. And I'm willing to build it, brick by brick, however long it takes.

Ever since the judge announced all charges against me would be dropped, my family closed in around me. Despite everything, they believed in me when no one would.

When I was fighting against the hate spilling out at me from every direction, they backed me. When the press were debating my innocence, they spoke up in support of me. When I hid at Mum's house, never wanting to face the world again, they gently lifted me up.

They knew I could never have murdered my best friend.

We're a unit through and through – we just didn't see it before. It's amazing how a cataclysmic event can change everything.

Then I had to face Evelyn's trial. Where *I* was on the witness stand. I had to testify, go over and over what I'd been through, reliving each moment of terror.

The press had a field day, of course. Who was lying, me or Evelyn? How had I so successfully swung this around in my favour? Could Evelyn be the face of evil I was accused of being for so long? It was a long and tiring debate, one I tried so hard to avoid.

When it came down to it, Evelyn wasn't as clever as she thought she was. Once the loose thread was pulled, everything came tumbling down. CCTV footage showed her following me. Her laptop revealed how she'd scour the internet, searching for me, planting seeds of hate. Her accomplice in police surveillance, who she was sleeping with for information about me, folded before the investigation even began.

It's amazing how easy it is to find something if you just bother to look.

Troy stood on the stand and told the jury about months of abuse he'd endured at the hands of that woman. Physical, mental, financial. It seems I wasn't the only one Evelyn set out to destroy.

Everyone who's ever crossed her has experienced her wrath, and she always got away with it. But she got cocky and arrogant, and that apparently spilled over when she met me, the woman who brought on her downfall.

To Mary's credit, she fought tooth and nail to get what she thought I deserved: an apology. If the police had the balls to investigate one of their own, to do their jobs properly, none of this would have happened.

A formal apology was issued. Compensation was paid.

Even Peters was suspended from Shine FM after texts were found between him and Evelyn, colluding to take me down.

Blue gurgles, giggles, then burps, making me break out in fits of laughter. I must tell Faith what just happened – she loves a joke about wind.

Faith took me out for a drink a few days ago. She confided in me that she's going to try for a baby; and she doesn't need Mum's approval. But she did need to tell someone. And that someone was me.

I'm honoured. And excited. Faith will make a great mum. She doesn't need a man to move forward in life, and I respect that.

Steven coughs quietly, capturing my attention. "Time to go or we'll miss the start of the film."

With the rest of the kids at friends' houses, offering to take care of Blue so they can get some alone time seemed like a great idea. With a lot of thought and trepidation (and persuasion from Steven), Rainy accepted my offer. On one condition: Mum join me.

And Mum's late.

I spoon orange gloop into Blue's open mouth, babbling at her in that stupid baby-language I used to scorn. "Rainy, if you want to wait for Mum, I understand. But I promise you, we'll be okay."

She looks at me, then turns to Steven with exasperation.

He gives her hand a gentle squeeze. "Come on, let's go."

Rainy kisses Blue on the head. "See you later," she whispers.

They leave, Rainy looking worried, and I continue feeding Blue. "Imarah would love you," I tell her.

Imarah had a way with babies that always made me jealous. She had a way with everyone that made me jealous.

And I hate that about me.

I often wonder if she knew just how horrible I was. Or was she blissfully unaware, too pure, too kind to notice the river of jealousy that ran through her best friend?

I loved her; I still do. And we had some amazing times: times we laughed until we cried; times we held each other up; times we'd hold one another when we were down.

Ultimately, we were strong, and our relationship was built on love. I can't think about that night she died – I crumble. I'll never forget the look on her face, the second it dawned on her that I was telling the truth. She was heartbroken; not for me, but for not believing me.

I often think it should've been me that died.

But I didn't. I'm here, and I know sure as shit Imarah would be fuming at me for thinking like that. So I hold my head high and soldier on.

For her.

Mum walks straight into the house and comes to find me in the kitchen. "They've gone?" She has a twinkle in her eye. I *knew* she'd done this on purpose, forever trying to fix the gap between me and my sisters.

"Mmm hmm," I confirm. I open my mouth to encourage Blue to do the same, but she's clearly had enough and presses her lips together, her eyes looking longingly at her nana. "I think she wants a cuddle," I tell Mum.

With the skill of a well-practiced mother, Mum wipes Blue down, pulls off her bib, and scoops her into her arms in about half a second. No mess, no fuss.

"Everything okay today?" Mum asks me, hooking Blue onto a hip and pulling her close for a cuddle.

I can't answer. Mum has a knack for making me cry without meaning to, and I'm too tired to cry. It's all I seem to do these days. Instead, I take Blue's dish to the sink and begin washing it.

"Maisie. Open and honest, remember?"

"Open and honest," I mumble back. Our new family motto.

"Rough day?"

"I guess. They're all pretty rough, though, to be honest."

Mum nods and presses a hand on my back. "Come and sit down," she says gently. Blue garbles an agreement.

"I saw the news," Mum says when we take a seat. "Is that what's getting to you?"

I nod. Six months after Evelyn was arrested, she still haunts me, and today was probably the worst of it.

According to the national news, Evelyn tried to take her own life today. She was found this morning by a guard who administered sufficient enough first aid to save her life. She's now receiving urgent care in the hospital where she's detained.

Truth is, I don't know how I feel about that, and it's the confusion that's getting me down.

The court deemed Evelyn mentally unstable, meaning her ability to make rational decisions was impaired by her compromised mental health. Although detained indefinitely, she's imprisoned in the psychiatric unit just forty miles from my home. I feel her proximity like a blade pressed to my throat. We have complained, but were met with excuses and patronisation.

"I made a call today," Mum tells me.

I don't look at her; I'm not really interested in her calls to her bingo buddies right now.

"To that nice man at the courts. Right after I saw the news."

My eyes snap up to meet hers.

"He tells me they're moving Evelyn. They're not equipped to handle a case like hers at Hollowbell. They're arranging the transfer as soon as she's recovered. Scotland, apparently."

Tears spill over then. I don't know why, but knowing that woman is going far away has lifted something in me. I feel a small breath of life re-enter my soul. Evelyn will always be a blight on my life; I know that. But the fight is so much easier knowing the opponent is out of arm's reach.

"Good news, isn't it?" Mum passes Blue to me and moves to put the kettle on. "Now, for the bad news." She throws me a wary look.

"Go on," I urge, eager to face the grenade and get it over with.

"I saw Caleb today, with that new girl of his."

"Steph?"

When I was released from prison, Steph came to see me. She was deeply apologetic. Sorry for their affair. She explained how Caleb had desperately tried, after my 'attack', to make things work, and Steph had stood back and let him. She said no one should persuade a good man to do the wrong thing.

Steph asked me to stay away from Caleb. I agreed and I fully respect that request. I wouldn't want me near him, either. But her request was made with sympathy and respect, and the conversation ended with a hug and well wishes.

The truth is, I liked her. I liked how she handled the situation. I like how she loves Caleb. The right way; not the desperate, pathetic way I did.

For so long, I convinced myself we were perfect, that I just had to try harder, be better. But love isn't supposed to feel like chasing someone who doesn't want to be caught. I see it now – the way he looked at me, like I was a burden instead of a partner. I held on, not because we were right for each other, but because I was too scared to let go. To be alone.

Yet being alone was exactly what I needed. Being alone has forced me to heal, whereas being with Caleb was akin to constantly picking at a scab, over and over.

"That's the one," Mum says. "Well, Steph was a little plump around the middle, if you know what I mean."

I crease my brow. I have no idea what she means. So what if Steph's gotten a little bigger? Who am I to judge?

But Mum throws me a look, that kind of look someone gives you when they're trying to get you to reach their point without them having to say it.

"She's pregnant?" I ask.

"If she isn't, the poor girl has eaten a bowling ball."

I'm stunned into silence. Even Blue presses her lips together as if to acknowledge the tension in the room. Well, that was … *fast*.

I don't know what to say, and the silence presses against my temples, pressuring me to say something, anything. Thankfully, I don't have to think of something as Blue lets out the biggest fart known to man. We burst out laughing, Blue joining in, clapping her hands.

And just like that, the tension is gone. Any negative feelings I had for Caleb's new family disappear, and a rush of genuine pleasure runs through me. I'm pleased for him. He'll make a fantastic daddy. And a loving partner to Steph. I just hope she knows how lucky she is to have him.

Mum looks at me with kindness in her eyes. "He called, you know. When he woke up. Wanted to make sure we were alright, if we needed anything. Said he felt responsible for not seeing the signs earlier. That boy carries the weight of the world on his shoulders, always has."

Tears burn the backs of my eyes, and I turn away, busying myself with nothing in particular.

"How are you feeling about tomorrow?" Mum asks me now, apparently eager to change the subject. She's let the cat out of the bag and is now pulling it close in case it loses control.

"Excited, but nervous."

"Perfectly normal," Mum says, nodding knowingly. "Starting a new job is supposed to be one of life's most stressful experiences."

I catch her eye and press my lips together. We burst out laughing. Mum can't really think a new job can stress me out more than a stalker, the murder of my best friend, and being falsely accused of that same murder. Her comment is so ridiculous it makes me laugh louder.

We laugh so uproariously that Blue starts to cry, and I have to force myself to stop.

"I'm so sorry, sweetie," I tell her, holding her close. She looks tired. "Nana is just a massive silly billy."

"That I am," Mum agrees, though she's smiling. "That I am."

I am still rebuilding, and I start my new job tomorrow at the community centre. The compensation from the police misconduct claim gave me a financial cushion, but I knew it wouldn't last forever. This new job is nothing glamorous, just administrative work, but they knew my story and hired me anyway. A fresh start.

The media coverage of Evelyn's trial had done what months of my denials couldn't – shifted public perception. Not completely, not universally, but enough to make walks through town bearable again. The Facebook groups built out of hate for me have mostly disbanded, their members moving on to the next outrage, the next target.

There are still whispers, still occasional messages from strangers who haven't heard the full story, or who don't want to accept the truth. The internet never truly forgets. But the hurricane has passed, leaving me to rebuild in its wake.

I settle Blue into her cot, the soft lullaby from her mobile filling the room with gentle notes. Mum's in the kitchen brewing yet another pot of tea, and I take a moment to myself, gazing out at the darkening sky. There's something peaceful about these ordinary moments that I've come to treasure.

My phone buzzes in my pocket. Probably Faith checking in about my first day at work tomorrow. I pull it out absent-mindedly, still watching the sunset paint the clouds in brilliant orange and pink.

Unknown number.

Missing me?

My fingers hang frozen above the screen. The peace of the moment shatters like glass. I stand paralysed, unable to breathe, unable to move. The mobile plays its lullaby. Mum clatters cups in the kitchen. The world continues its ordinary rhythms while mine tilts on its axis once more.

Evelyn's in the psychiatric unit. I'm sure no phones are allowed – are they?

I stare at the message again, my hands trembling.

Who sent this?

Like this book? Want Killing for Innocence for FREE? See BookHip.com/ZRJFVTW to join the mailing list and receive your copy today.

www.ingramcontent.com/pod-product-compliance
Lightning Source LLC
Chambersburg PA
CBHW020641120726
47906CB00001B/70